The

Anorexic

Assassin

In Memory

Of

Mary Hager Smith

January 8, 1923 to June 13, 2013

Library of Congress Cataloging-in-publication Data

T. Michael Smith 2015

The Anorexic Assassin/T. Michael Smith

Control Number: 1-2172375731

ISBN: 978-0-692-40966-4

BRUSH FORK PRESS LLC

Printed by CreateSpace, an Amazon.com Company

ISBN: 978-0-692-40966-4

THE
ANOREXIC
ASSASSIN

By T. Michael Smith

Brush Fork Press LLC

Sex

Wealth

Love

Lies

Alcohol

Prologue

I have been a perpetual liar for most of my life. I seemed to revel in the chaos that lying precipitated. Only once did I experience serious consequences from my lies.

I am waiting for my sponsor in Centennial Park. We have our special spot at a picnic table near the band shell. Centennial Park is a large urban park located approximately two miles west of downtown Nashville, across West End Avenue from the campus of Vanderbilt University and near the headquarters campus of the Hospital Corporation of America.

I am staring at the Parthenon or at least a replica of the Athenian Parthenon. Ours was built in the 1920s as part of some fair or exposition that dubbed Nashville the "Athens of the South." To some folks in Nashville, this is more suitable than the "Country Music Capital of the World." The preservation of the Parthenon is one of my mother's many causes.

I was born in Nashville, a true Belle Meade baby boy. My parents, Trip and Mary Lynn Jeter, live about a mile from the scene of their respective childhoods in Belle Meade. This enclave was absorbed into the government of Nashville-Davidson County in 1963, but retains its independent city status, and its residents pay taxes both to the Metro government and to the City of Belle Meade. The streets have distinct signage; the city has its own police force, its own mayor and its own city hall. It is considered the most fashionable place to live in the entire world, particularly by the incestuous crowd that has lived there all their lives.

I am not about to blame Belle Meade or my parents for all my troubles. But I was probably born a few kilos short because of the belief that those born to a Belle Meade family should stick with their own. My Dad thinks I am an over educated, ungrateful, brainless piece of shit and my Mom is mortally embarrassed by my status as a convicted felon. I agree with them both, but I'm trying to put things back together.

I'm a sick guy who is trying with all his fiber to get well. That's why I'm here in this park waiting for Rex R. I met Rex seven months ago on the first day of my new sober life at the Aphesis House. My life has gotten measurably better since I met him. I am beginning to find out with clarity who and what I really am. I have been sober for seven months and I clear every decision I make with Rex. In my earlier life I was often wrong, but never in doubt. Most of my decisions were not good.. I often took the easier softer way.

Rex was a lawyer before he got busted for conspiracy to distribute drugs. He was an outstanding defense attorney in Miami, made lots of money defending drug dealers, but eventually got greedy. He joined the other side. His life became filled with adventure: trips to Columbia, meetings in the Arizona desert and clandestine meetings in LA and Atlanta. He lived large for a while. But when you are dealing with people like Lissette Guerra and Elwood Garmin, the risks rise exponentially.

Rex was convicted on five counts of conspiracy to import and distribute controlled substances, conspiracy to harbor a fugitive, and conspiracy to violate the RICO continuing criminal enterprise statute. The charges arose from the activities of a large drug organization that operated across much of the southern United States. The organization was led by Rex, Elwood Garmin, and several other co-defendants, who were the "top managers" in the organization. He spent sixteen years in jail, got sober, joined AA and began a better way of life. When he got out, he moved to Nashville to avoid all of the temptations of Miami.

My life was not as exciting, but I had just spent six years in the Charles B. Bass Correctional Complex. I went to AA in prison for something to do with my time. They say if you stay around long enough you might get it. I drank a lot, but that was normal for my family and friends. It turns out I am an alcoholic and my life was unmanageable. I am a felon because of unmanageability.

Finally, here comes Rex. Plaid shirt, khaki pants and Nike tennis shoes were part of the package every day of the week. Rex was a slow walker because of emphysema.

"Hey Jimmy Joe, how ya' doin' sport?"

"Good Rex."

"Ready for a fifth step?'

"I think so. I'm as ready as I'm going to be."

And here it is.

Chapter 1

Mary Lynn Jeter controlled every aspect of my life from birth to eighteen years of age. It seemed to come with the territory. Every kid in Belle Meade had some sort of parental control issue.

My mother never wanted for anything, except maybe to be a man. In the eyes of John L Bradford, her father, being a girl meant that she was not fit to be a part of JL Bradford & Company, a Nashville-based regional brokerage firm. Big Jack was a man that loved to bird and duck hunt, drink Tennessee sipping whiskey and make money. He was good at all three. He loved his wife Jeannette and his daughter, but he didn't want either of them near his business. And, of course, that was exactly what Mary Lynn wanted most in life: to be in charge of the business.

So she married James Josiah Jeter III, a man she thought she could control. I think it was reasonable to expect that a guy named Trip would not be particularly tough. But Trip had grown-up under the tutelage of his father and, for a time, his grandfather. Both men believed that women had three basic functions: keep a good home, produce and care for the children, and entertain friends, family and business associates in a well-kept home.

Trip learned his lessons well. He did listen to his wife since she was as smart as a whip and could be as mean as a snake. However, he did insist that she adhere to the Jeter principles of womanhood. Mary Lynn kept a wonderful house with some assistance, produced two children, but it was in the entertainment side that she excelled and truly helped my father.

When Trip (Mary Lynn's substitute) went to work for Big Jack, he convinced Mary Lynn that they were a team. Her role was to be the best hostess in Nashville and to gather information from others when they attended parties together. At these events, my parents were never together. They were on a clandestine mission to find who was in and who was out. Trip's role was to become indispensable to Big Jack. They both exceeded expectations. It seemed more like a business deal than a marriage.

I was born in March of 1964. Big Jack was delighted that Trip had it in him to father a boy—"This firm will go on forever," he said to Trip. Big Jack had three girls.

Shortly after my birth, Big Jack convinced Trip to use "Jim" as his name going forward. "Jim is a solid name. It sounds more mature and professional," he said. From then on, it was Jim. Even Mary Lynn started calling him Jim. I must admit that I can't seem to think of him as anything but Trip.

My sister, Allison Lynn, was born two years after me. She seemed cute enough as a baby, but by three it was clear that she was a clone of Mary Lynn and would be a thorn in my side.

In Nashville or maybe it's just Belle Meade, you begin to think about schools for your children at birth. Mary Lynn decided that THE school was not as important for me since it had been predetermined at age six that I would go in the business. I would go to Harding Academy for grades K-6.

Within a balanced program that combined rigorous academics and a nurturing atmosphere, Harding Academy provided a wealth of opportunities for student learning and growth, both in and out of the classroom. At Harding, I was not only successful in the classroom, but I excelled as an athlete and a leader. I grew at each grade level as these uniquely qualified teachers developed a relationship with me that extended beyond the classroom, particularly Ms. Cindy Dunham. These adults were mentors, advisers, and coaches in addition to being classroom teachers, particularly Ms. Cindy Dunham. I loved my time at Harding. As long as I did well, I didn't have to put up with Mary Lynn's bullshit.

Cindy Dunham was a math and science teacher at Harding. I had a massive crush on her and she knew it. My crush on Cindy Dunham started in the third grade. She was tall, had long legs, short brown hair, and deep blue eyes. Her shoulders were broad and she was thick through the body, but certainly not fat. She was funny and made science and math very interesting. I loved her and she truly liked me. We seemed to be horsing around a lot of the time, grabbing and touching, playing tricks on each other and laughing a lot. She came to the football and basketball games and I thought it was great.

When I was in the 6th grade, we were hanging out in her room, when I leaned over and kissed her. I was only twelve, but she kissed me back. It scared me a little. I steered clear of her for a few days, but ventured into her classroom one afternoon to see if things had changed. It seemed to me that we were still friends and I was relieved.

Then she shocked me by saying, "I liked kissing you Jimmy Joe. Did you like kissing me?"

Of course I answered yes.

She lowered the blind on her door, walked toward me, put her arms around me and kissed me passionately. I was clueless, but I was boiling over inside. The kiss seemed to last forever. About that time, there was a knock on the door. She moved away and I sat down. Mr. Fielding came in and saw me.

"Getting a little tutoring in math, Jimmy Joe?"

"No sir, science."

That was the first of my many misadventures in sexual matters. I left her room never to return. I had almost peed all over myself and I didn't want to be in that position again. My lust would have to be from a distance. I mean, I was only twelve. Ms. Dunham kept her distance as well.

Allison was sent to Ensworth. Mary Lynn felt she would get a more gentile education and would be introduced to the finer families of Nashville.

Ensworth School is a pre-first through twelfth grade coeducational independent school. The School promotes academic excellence and inspires students to be intellectually curious, to use their talents to the fullest, to be people of integrity, and to be contributors to society. My sister was pretty, smart and as mean as a snake, a clone. She went to Enswoth through the eighth grade.

Allison met Kathleen Morgan at Ensworth. They became fast friends. Of course Allison was from Belle Meade and Katie, as she was known, lived in Green Hills fairly near the school. This caused some concern for Mary Lynn, but Allison held her ground, something I couldn't seem to find the guts to do. She also changed her name to Allie so she could be like Katie.

Allie and Katie were together in school and on the weekends. They had frequent sleepovers and I had to put up with two girls. I was at some athletic practice or event most of the time; otherwise, I stayed in my room to avoid all the women in my life.

When I was about 15 years old, I was in my room as usual. My parents were at a neighbor's house and I was nominally in charge of the house. I told Allie and Katie that I would be in my room. They both were typical 13 year olds, but Katie had become a little flirtatious with me.

Anyway, I was looking at a Playboy that Billy Corbett had given me. I had a boner and decided to jack the beanstalk. I must have been breathing hard or groaning, because both girls burst into my room without knocking.

"Jimmy Joe! What are you doing?" Allie screamed.

"What the hell—get out of here," I screamed back.

I was on the floor in a fetal position trying to cover up my nakedness and my stiffy.

"Jimmy Joe, it's so big." Katie was moving across the room for a closer look.

"Can I see it a little closer?"

"Get out of here." I scooted back to the bed, found my gym shorts and tried to put them on. I stood up despite being embarrassed and my hard on stuck up like a flag pole. I sat on the bed.

"Get out!!"

"I'm telling Mom." Allie said in that snooty tone she had learned to use.

Katie shook her head and lead Allie out of the room for some discussion of the events.

From then on Katie treated me like she had me by the balls and I would have to do her bidding. I ignored her for the most part, but knew she could get Allie and my Mother on my case at any time. As I moved on to high school, the little witch began to torment me even more, rubbing up against me with those big brown eyes boring a hole through me.

"Come on Jimmy Joe, you know you want me!"

I warned myself repeatedly, "Don't even think about it or she really will have you".

When I went to Montgomery Bell Academy in the seventh grade, I needed a distraction. Athletics were no longer enough. I needed a girlfriend. I didn't want anything to do with Katie and I no longer had Ms. Dunham as an advisor. And I was in an all-male school.

Montgomery Bell Academy enjoys a 146-year history as a college preparatory school for young men in grades 7-12, offering a progressive approach to traditional education. MBA folks like to believe that students pursue academics, the arts and athletics equally. Truly we were immersed in an environment where trust and support were paramount. Because of this support, we saw the benefits of taking the initiative and using our resourcefulness as a means to pursue self-discovery, develop leadership skills, and claim a sense of self-worth.

I was a good student, but for my age and size, I was an even better athlete. As a younger kid, I played football, basketball, and baseball. In the fifth grade I found lacrosse and gave up baseball, much to my father's chagrin. He had a good high school career at MBA as a pitcher and gained some interest from the Tigers and Dodgers. But making money was more important, so he went to college at Dartmouth and got an MBA at Harvard. He solidified his ambition by marrying Mary Lynn.

I had four goals at MBA: play football, play lacrosse, make grades and find a girl. The first three were easy compared with the fourth.

On the freshman football team, Billy Corbett was the quarterback and I was a running back. We were playing Oakland High's jayvee team and the score was tied 22-22 with about 2 minutes to go in the game. Billy dropped back to pass and was immediately under siege. I was out in the flat to his right and somehow he threw a wobbly pass that I caught at the 45 and took in for the winning score.

After the game, everyone was giving high fives and thumps on the helmet. I was dirty, smelled bad and needed a shower, but this very pretty, small girl came up and gave me a big hug.

"Awesome game, Jimmy Joe! You were really fab out there."

"Thanks."

"You remember me from Ensworth?" she asked.

"Yeah, you're Lanie, uh, Lanie Miller".

"Good boy. Why don't you call me some time?"

"I don't have your number".

She pulled out a pen, grabbed my arm and wrote her phone number on it. I am in love. And she was an older woman—an eighth grader at Harpeth Hall. She came to me—she must really like me—but why—don't ask.

"Hey Man, what's wrong?" Billy was looking at me with this strange expression.

"I gotta' get this number in a notebook!"

"It's on your arm?"

"Yeah!"

"Who wrote it there?"

"None of your business—fuck off man."

"Some girl. Come on man—who?"

"Lanie Miller."

"Holy shit!"

For several days I stared at the phone number, wondering what to say. I finally called and asked her if she would like to go to a movie. She said yes. I said OK and hung up. Lanie called me back and said we should set a time and place. We agreed to meet at Green Hills Mall and see TAXI DRIVER. I don't remember much about the movie, but I do remember kissing Lanie more than once. It was thrilling.

Rex interrupted me. "Jimmy Joe, get on with it. This will take a month. I need a piss break."

Rex trundled off to the restroom, which was about 20 yards from our table.

I resumed my fifth step when he returned.

Lanie and I were a steady couple for the rest of my seventh grade year and most of my eighth grade year. She dumped me for a junior at MBA in the spring of that year.

Katie really enjoyed giving me a hard time about being dumped. She and Allie were still tight.

I cringed every time I saw her. "Poooor Jimmy Joe, Lanie doesn't love him anymore."

For the rest of my high school career, I found several girls to like and enjoy. I was a football star after all. I made the varsity team as a ninth grader and actually played some as the season wore on. By my senior year, I was over six feet, weighed about 175 and was fast with quick feet. I was a rising star. So I dated Sarah Caraway, Suzanne Francis,

Emily Atkins, but my absolute favorite was Cora Jane Davis. She was a Harpeth Hall girl and a year behind me.

Cora Jane and I met in the summer before my senior year at the swimming pool at Richfield Country Club. I was there with Billy and a couple of other guys. We were talking about college choices. Billy was going to get a scholarship offer from Rhodes College in Memphis and maybe from Western Kentucky. I had already let it be known that this would be my last year in football. I wanted to play lacrosse at the next level.

I looked across the pool and saw her sitting on a chaise with several girls. She had blonde hair, freckles and a great tan. She caught me staring.

"Billy, who's the girl across the pool? The blonde."

"They're all blond you dope!"

"The one in the red bikini."

"You mean Cora Jane—the ice queen--don't bother man—she's frigid?"

"How do you know?"

"Trust me, I know!"

I walked over to the girls. I sat down next to Cora Jane and introduced myself. She knew who I was—interesting. We sat and talked for two hours. I was enchanted. The next day I told Emily I wouldn't be calling her anymore.

Cora Jane Davis was destined to be the love of my life—at least for a year or so.

I had a great senior year at MBA. In football, we were 9-1; I scored 12 touchdowns and ran for 1086 yards. My SAT scores came in a combined 1295. I was accepted at Dartmouth and UVA. Cora Jane and I had great fun together. The lacrosse team went 12-2 and I was named to the all-Metro team as a midfielder. Cora Jane and I had great fun together.

I had a black 1979 Camaro Z28, which my father considered a redneck car.

"Why can't you be a normal Belle Meade kid and get a used Beemer?"

I wanted to be different. I had followed the model for so long, I was bored with it. Cora Jane loved it when I roared up the drive at Harpeth Hall to pick her up in the afternoons. We also loved to cuddle and kiss in this terrific car.

One evening in the spring we drove out to Percy Warner Park. It was getting dark and we pulled off the road into one of the hidden picnic areas. It was very difficult to see my black car in the dark. We were kissing, cuddling and sort of fooling around—you know, touching and feeling. I decided to take off my shirt since it was getting hot.

Cora smiled, "I can do that." She unbuttoned her blouse and took it off.

"You still have something on."

Slowly, she reached around and took off her bra.

My mouth flew open and I gasped, "Wow they are beautiful." Indeed they were—round, firm, and aroused brown nipples.

"Can I touch them?"

"I hope you will."

I did—softly-they were lovely to the sight and the touch. I pulled her to me and kissed her with a passion unknown to me.

I undid the top button on her jeans and she slipped out them. I did the same. We stared at each for the longest time, sitting in the Z28 with only our underwear on.

"You are popping out there. Can I touch it?"

"Yes."

She did. Then she slid her hand all the way in. "Wow, Jimmy Joe, you think it will fit?"

"Where?" What a dope.

"You know—in me."

"I don't know—yeah, I think it will. We can always try." I learned at that moment when a girl or woman has your Johnson in her hand, the answer is always yes.

She slid down into the seat with me. We both slid somehow out of our bikinis and boxers.

It fit.

I will never forget that evening or Cora Jane for the rest of my life.

My sister was a sophomore at Harpeth Hall. I have to admit that she was turning into a beautiful girl, a clone of Mary Lynn. She was about 5'10", slim not skinny with blonde hair. Billy was really smitten with her, but I forbid him to do anything about it. I didn't want to lose my friend to my sister. He cooled off when I told him he would have to take Katie if he asked Allie out.

Katie and my sister were still inseparable. Even though Allie was a natural athlete and Katie was not, they were still so close they seem to be stuck together. Katie was about 5'4, weighed about 95 pounds and had dark hair and eyes with black eyebrows.

Mary Lynn believed in single gender schools, particularly for girls. She wanted Allie to be in an academic and social environment where she could discuss issues pertinent to young women her age and develop a positive self-awareness. The academics at HH were rigorous and the girls learned to be tough through their athletic program. Allie played basketball and was a swimmer. She had her friend Katie to help her with the academics.

When I came home after spending a little time at Cora Jane's house on the evening of "THE" event (we both lost our virginity), these two witches were up watching TV. I was elated and hungry. They must have heard me rattling in the refrigerator and came running to the kitchen.

From Allie, "Late, aren't you?"

"No, I'm not late."

Roast beef sandwich with cheese and pickles. Mustard or mayo? Mayo I think.

Standing right behind me, almost touching me, Katie whispered, "you were making out with Cora Jane—I can smell the sex on you—she's got a strong scent."

Aw shit, she has a way of making everything seem dirty.

"Why don't you try a real woman?"

"God, you look like you're twelve. Get away from me. Allie do you have to have this little bitch over here all the time?"

I made my sandwich and went to my room hoping I really didn't smell like sex. Mary Lynn would be all over that.

Chapter 2

I decided to go to college at the University of Virginia. After visiting Dartmouth and Virginia, the latter just seemed to suit me better. I liked the campus and the students I met. Plus I received a small lacrosse scholarship and a small academic scholarship for mathematics.

"Jimmy Joe you don't understand the significance of an Ivy League education," my father ranted. "UVA is an OK school, but you'll be a legacy at Dartmouth. That counts for something."

"My guidance counselor, Mr. Cleary, thinks UVA will be a great fit for me. I really liked the guys I met up there. And a couple of my friends from MBA are going there. So it just makes sense for me. I love having the same name as you and grandpa, but isn't that legacy enough. I want to be somewhere that I can do it myself."

"Huh, Ok. It'll be cheaper. I guess that's something."

My old man isn't a total prick. I may even like him some day. Mary Lynn is an altogether different situation.

I checked in to my dorm on August 20. 1982. My father and I drove up from Nashville in a huge rental van. His plan was to drop the van in Charlottesville and get a plane back to Nashville on Sunday. My dorm was Hancock in the McCormack Road Residence Area.

McCormick Road Residence Area houses almost 1300 students in ten buildings which accommodate approximately 125 students each. All of the bedrooms are doubles, with the exception of 30 small single rooms, located between the hallways of each floor. The buildings are co-ed, although the floors are single sex.

It took about an hour to get all of my stuff in the room. We took the van to parking area and then went off to hear the President's address in Old Cabot Hall Auditorium. My father then took off to check in his hotel and get some rest. I went to find the dining hall and then on to the Resident Advisory meetings. I had been accepted into the McIntire School of Commerce and my first courses were set, with a heavy emphasis on math and accounting.

On the third day, I met Robert Marshall Gibbs who lived on my floor. I liked Bobby from the start. He was from Chevy Chase, Maryland and was a graduate of St. Albans. He knew a lot of people at UVA and that was a positive for me since I knew only one other person from MBA, Ronnie Begley.

Bobby and I have been friends since the first day we met. We roomed together our 2nd and 3rd years at the University. We lived in Faulkner, a cluster of three apartment buildings near the John Paul Jones Arena (basketball).

Each apartment contained four bedrooms (three standard singles and one large single), a bathroom, living and dining room, and full kitchen with stove, refrigerator and sink. All apartments were air-conditioned and furnished with a sofa, two arm chairs, coffee table, two end tables with lamps, and dining table with chairs.

There is a convenient study lounge within the complex, as well as laundry facilities, vending machines and a public picnic area.

Late in the fall semester Bobby and I began the rush process. Inter-Fraternity Council Rush is the series of events during which a male student can decide to become a part of a fraternity. "Dorm Talks" are held late in the fall semester and are an informational session for men who are interested in joining a fraternity.

There are several parts to IFC Rush. "Open House" is a series of evening hours during which every IFC fraternity welcomes all rushes. After the Open House round, each fraternity makes a decision on who they would like to invite to the next round of Rush. There are three rounds of "Invites," "first," "second," and "third." Typically rushes attend fewer chapter houses during second invites than first, and even fewer for the third invites. We participated in laser tag, bowling, crab leg dinners, and talent shows, all pretty lame. The last round of Rush is "Final Hours." This round resembles Open House in appearance, except this time, the rushed will know most of the brothers of the fraternities he likes. Final Hours lasts for three hours; a rush has the option of going to up to three different chapters that night. The last fraternity a rush goes to is his first choice, the second to the last fraternity, his second choice and so on. Bobby and I went to Sigma Chi, SAE and KA. "Bid Day" is when every fraternity delivers bids to the rushes they want to join their brotherhood. Booby and I became part of the Sigma Chi pledge class.

One of the largest chapters in the Inter-Fraternity Council, the Psi chapter of Sigma Chi has continuously had a strong presence around grounds. The chapter boasts a brotherhood diverse in both interests and geographic backgrounds, and it has one of the highest average fraternity GPA's. Sigma Chi has brothers active in the Inter-Fraternity Council, Student Council, Pancakes' for Parkinson's, Madison House, and more. Every year the chapter hosts the week-long Philanthropy, Derby Days, which brings the Greek community together in order to raise money for UVA Children's Hospital and the Children's Miracle Network. The chapter puts on several social events each semester, including its signature 60's Party in the fall and Bahamas Party in the spring.

My first Thanksgiving home was eventful. Cora Jane and I sent letters and talked on the phone a couple times a month. I sent one letter a week and she usually sent me two. But for the last two weeks before Thanksgiving, I did not receive a single letter. I was flying home on Tuesday, so I called Cora Jane on Monday night to set up some things for the long weekend to come.

"Hi, it's me," I said softly.

"Oh, hi," she responded in the perky manner she reserved for mere acquaintances.

"I haven't heard from you in a while." I said

"No, I've been very busy."

"Everything Ok?"

"NO, no, it's not."

"What's wrong?"

She went into a whisper. "My mom found my diary. It had stuff in it; she didn't like it and got really pissed?"

"What stuff?"

"You know, stuff about you and me, sex and all. It was so great and all and I wrote about it. She won't let me see you anymore and if my dad finds out, no telling what he will do."

Oh shit. I'm in trouble now.

I heard Cora Jane's mom in the background. "Cora are you talking to that boy? Give me that telephone."

"Jimmy Joe Jeter don't you ever see, touch or call my daughter ever again. I am going to call your mother. Don't you come near our house."

I could climb up to Cora Jane's room in a heartbeat. Actually, I was a little relieved. I mean, I was a university man, a Sigma Chi pledge (pin to prove it) and didn't need to be dating a high school girl. But I liked Cora Jane.

Dad picked me up at the airport. I wouldn't take the Z28 back until after Christmas.

"Expect a lot of grief from your mom."

"Mrs. Davis?"

"Yeah, Mrs. Davis."

"What about you?"

"Boys will be boys, I told her. Girls are more aggressive than in our day. She was worried about what others will say. The women will be aghast, the men will say 'atta' boy and me, and I say are you using rubbers?"

"Well?"

"Yeah I'm using rubbers?"

"Glad to have you home son. You take some of the heat off me."

We arrived home.

"Jimmy Joe what on earth were you thinking. None of our friends will want you anywhere near their daughters again. I'm worried that people will cancel for our party Saturday night. Well what do you have to say for yourself?"

"Hi Mary Lynn, it's great to see you. Happy Thanksgiving."

"Don't talk to me like that. I am your mother. Trip, make him show respect."

"Jimmy Joe, show some respect for your mother."

"Mom, we just got carried away. We liked it, so we kept doing it. It seemed kind of natural. I mean Cora Jane is pretty and sexy. We both like sex and so we did it. It's not really anyone's business."

Mary Lynn turned beet red and was so angry she began to tremble. "This is not a conversation a mother should be having with her son."

"OK."

"Don't move an inch." She was right in my face and had the collar of my jacket in her hands. "Don't go near Cora Jane Davis. Got it!! We are still responsible for you. She's underage you know!"

"Got it!"

"Make sure you do, mister!"

I looked at my dad. He had that look on his face—"I'm glad it's you not me she's after." He gave me a little half smile. "Listen to your mother Jimmy Joe!"

My holiday was off to a great start. I threw my bag on the floor, reached for my headset and decided to chill for a few hours. I wanted to think about things. I had been thinking recently about Cora Jane—about how she was going to fit in my life going forward. I had decided to break it off with her because there were some women back at school that I wanted to date. There are probably guys here for Cora Jane. But now, I was being forced to break it off—that didn't feel right.

How was I going to get together with Cora Jane?

Follow her when she left her house? Meet her at Harpeth Hall? Was school on for tomorrow? I really wanted to climb up to her window and see her. What was I supposed to do?

About 9 that evening I went to my sister's room and knocked.

"Yeah!!"

"It's me—Jim!"

"Whatta' you want?" She opened the door. "It's all over school you know."

"You and Cora Jane are all anyone's talking about. It's so embarrassing."

"You have school tomorrow?"

"We get out at noon! Please don't show up there. Her mom has been picking her up every day. She's not allowed out of the house. You really screwed up Jimmy Joe!"

"How about I pick you up?'

"Just so you can see Cora Jane?"

"Yes. You're my sister! Help me out. I just want to see her. I won't try to talk to her or anything like that—OK?"

"Ok! OK I'll get a ride with Dad to school. And you have to take Katie and me to lunch at Dalts!"

"Deal!"

The next morning I had the Z28 parked in the Harpeth Hall drive at 11:40 am so that I would be in position to see most of the girls as they headed to the parking lot. Most of the seniors new me at least by reputation, a few waved and a few others looked my way and giggled.

Cora Jane started down the steps, saw me and headed straight toward me.

"Jimmy Joe, I'm sorry. I can't talk to you. I can't see you again! This is so hard. Don't try to see me--promise?"

"I am so sorry Cora Jane. I don't want to hurt you. I promise! You won't see me again. I'm sorry!"

About that time a silver Mercedes screeched to a halt.

"Cora Jane—get away from that asshole!" Cora Jane's mother screamed. She was getting out of her car.

Luckily, my sister and Katie arrived at the Z28 about the same time. Although only a sophomore, Allie rose to the occasion. She shouted at Cora Jane as loud as she could, "Get away from my brother. You're trying to ruin his life and our reputation you bitch!!" Cora Jane fled and her mother got back into the car. Allie, Katie and I got into the Z28. The perfect cover.

I hung out with Billy Corbett some and stayed in my room for the rest of my time in Nashville. Mary Lynn fixed a pretty good Thanksgiving meal.

Mary Lynn and Trip had a little party on Saturday night. Mary Lynn's fear that the party would be shunned was wrong. Everyone showed up, even a few that were not invited. I overheard Trip saying that people came just to see the "Infamous Jimmy Joe Jeter." I kept to myself in my room with the exception of a trip to the buffet table.

A few minutes after I was back in my room, there was a soft knock on my door.

The Anorexic Assassin

I opened the door. There stood Jeannette Watson, wife of Ben Watson, a banker friend of my parents. She was in real estate. She brushed past me into the room.

"Close the door," she said and gave me this crazed look.

She came toward me and I backed up. She put her hand in my hair and started to rub up against me.

"I hear you're quite the lady's man Jimmy Joe. That true?"

"I guess," I stammered.

"Well how about showing me, Ok."

With that she moved to the bed, still holding on to me.

"We'll have to do it from the back. I don't want to wrinkle my dress."

She pulled her dress up and pulled down her pantyhose. She turned and bent over the bed. Her butt was up in the air and her private parts were staring at me.

"Come on Jimmy Joe, put it in." So I did. I was screwing Mrs. Watson. She had to be at least 45.

"Jimmy Joe, you are really a big boy. You fill me up and then some. Harder, harder."

I know I came, I'm not sure about her, but there was a lot of moaning and heavy breathing. Then she stood, pulled up her pantyhose with some difficulty and left the room. But not before giving me a sloppy, wet kiss, tongue and all.

I had listened to Mary Lynn preach to me for three days about morality and integrity. And yet, her friend came to my room, lowered her pantyhose and begged me to "fuck" her. I am through listening to Mary Lynn. I am free.

I needed to go back to Charlottesville!!

Final exams were given in the second week of December. The whole process was a little intimidating, but I was prepared and everything went well for me. I was not quite ready to go back to Nashville so I hung out at the frat house for a couple of days.

I developed a plan. I would hang out with Billy and Emily for the most part, but I would ask Janie Watson to go to a couple of parties with me. It seemed fitting since Mrs. Watson and I were so close. Janie and I were an item over the holidays. Janie said her mom seemed very anxious about our dating, but she assured her that I was a perfect gentleman. Unlike her mother, Janie kept her panties on.

My first semester grades were a little disappointing, all B's. A 3.0 GPA was not the norm for me. I needed to work harder and not worry so much about women. The spring semester was uneventful. I went through all of the pledge activities, played lacrosse, had decent game minutes and I finished with a 3.45 GPA. I considered everything a success. I went back to Nashville for the summer and worked as a gopher in THE firm. My main job was to pick Big Jack up every morning, get him to his lunch date and drive him home. In between, I delivered mail and got coffee for the guys on the trading desk.

Mrs. Watson and I got together four or five times. She was very horny and her husband wasn't too interested. Janie and I became closer as well. I was learning a lot about the joy of sex. Mrs. Watson was teaching me about how to truly satisfy a woman and I was trying it out on her daughter. Mary Lynn was thrilled that I was spending so much time with a wonderful family like the Watsons.

I was excited about returning to Charlottesville for my second year. Bobby and I had a good room location in Faulkner. His mom and Mary Lynn combined to get us some kitchen equipment, assuming that we might cook occasionally. I worked hard and ended with a 3.8 GPA. We spent time at the Psi house, went to the home football games and I was dating a girl from Randolph-Macon named Jackie Zimmer. My fraternity brother, Gil Cotton, introduced us. They were both from Roanoke, a small city in southwest Virginia. I liked her a lot. She was very smart, pretty, loved to talk and wasn't bashful about trying new things. I had the Z28 in town so we saw each other every two weeks or so. I played lacrosse in the spring. My sophomore year was uneventful.

I returned home for the summer. It seemed like déjà vu all over again. Jackie and I agreed that our two semester relationship had run its course. It seems that she and Gil had developed a "thing" for each other. Mary Lynn told me that the Watson women had inquired about my return and she told them that I was already home. I called Janie and we agreed to go out on Friday. Ten minutes later Mrs. Watson called. Janie was taking her kids to the pool and she wanted me to come over.

I told Mary Lynn I was going for a run and I jogged over to the Watson's house—I actually ran down the street by their house and ducked into the backyard. Mrs. Watson was standing at the back door waiting for me. She had on a very shear negligee leaving very little to the imagination. We made it to the sofa in the den. My shirt and shorts were off in a millisecond—it was like makeup sex—terrific!

Afterwards she said to me, "It makes me nervous that you're dating my daughter."

"I am a Virginia gentleman."

"You're way too advanced for her."

"Thanks mostly to you."

"She really likes you. Don't hurt her."

"Well, you understand that I can't take you to the movies or to a party or to dinner with my friends. You and I have a relationship that is clandestine. Mary Lynn would try to ruin you if she knew or maybe try to kill you since it would totally eclipse the first embarrassment I caused her. And Ben—well Ben would divorce you and try to kill me. And poor Janie—heaven knows what she would do."

"Just don't hurt her."

"We're cool. I like Janie, but you my dear Mrs. Watson are really hot!"

I was ready for action and so we went at it again. Is it possible? This time was better than the last? Maybe it was because we heard a car in the driveway.

She ran for the stairs and I headed to the back door trying desperately to get my shorts on. Luckily I never removed my shoes. I made it to the street and started jogging.

"Welcome home Jimmy Joe," Ben Watson shouted. "How was school?"

He walked over to the street. I hoped beyond belief that he could not smell his wife's scent on me.

I stopped running and said, "I ended up with a 3.8 for the year so I have a 3.4 overall and I had a decent lacrosse year."

"Great! Hope to see more of you over the summer. I think Janie likes you."

"Yeah, we're going to do something together on Friday."

"Good!"

He turned and walked away. I felt guilty and I felt sorry for this man. It made me think about marriage, relationships and love. I wanted someone to love. This was going to be a long hot summer.

I became entranced by the Watson women. Janie and I did the typical date stuff; hanging out with Billy and his girlfriend Trish, going to movies, hanging out at my house and there were a couple of over-the-top parties that were ever so cool.

Mrs. Watson and I continued our trysts including an overnighter at the Vanderbilt Plaza when Ben was out of town on a golf trip to Gulf Shores. I think her idea became to make sure my sexual appetites were fulfilled so I wouldn't pressure Janie. It was becoming less exciting and fulfilling.

The real excitement centered on Allie as she prepared to go to college. She would become a freshman at American University in the District of Columbia. The school has about 9000 students, counting both graduate and undergraduates. It is a private, coeducational, liberal arts university that has a Methodist affiliation. Academic programs focus on international service, public policy and public affairs, international law and human rights. The university has high rates of student participation in: study abroad, internships, community service, Peace Corps and political activism. Allie had turned into something of a radical so she would fit right in at American.

She and Katie decided to go to different schools to prove to everyone that they were not joined at the hip. But they had to be in the same city. Katie chose George Washington University. GW is the largest institution of higher education in the District of Columbia. The school has more than 15,000 students—from all 50 states, the District and more than 100 countries. It was perfect for Katie. And they were only 30 minutes apart by bicycle, which they both took with them.

Mary Lynn acted as if her own life was ending as the preparations for Allie's departure grew closer. She and Trip would take her to DC and help her settle in to college life. Since I would only be 90 minutes away in Charlottesville, Mary Lynn extracted a pledge from me to look in on her baby.

The Anorexic Assassin

I went back to school for my third year in the fall and Janie went back for her second year at Emory University in Atlanta. I invited her to Charlottesville for Sigma Chi's signature 60s party in late October. I went to Atlanta mid-November and Janie and I were intimate for the first time. Her dorm room was the venue and it was perfect, far better than my own room. Her roommate was away so we just spent Saturday night there after an evening of serious partying. It was very relaxed, very little angst and it happened as if it were meant to be.

Janie and I had a grand holiday season with each other and our families. I stayed away from Mrs. Watson. Janie and I rang in the New Year, 1985, at a party at Cheekwood.

In late January, I invited Allie and Katie to come down to Virginia for a week end. Bobby and I met them at the bus station as neither one of them had a car. We took them to Lottie Grahams' house, a weekend rooming place for University visitors. We were having a little function at the Psi house and the two girls began to relax after about an hour. One of my frat brothers was taken by Allie. I reminded Dickey Lynn that she was my sister. He was still smitten.

Interestingly, my great friend Bobby Gibbs was taken with the crazy Katie Morgan. I had a moment of terror grasp my heart, "what if he really liked that crazy bitch?" I decided that this was just a "port in the storm" kind of thing.

The weekend was a great success. Allie told me that she had a good time and I could report to Mary Lynn that she was doing great. Bobby and Katie showed up at Mrs. Graham's house and Bobby informed me that he was driving the girls back to DC. That was very worrisome, not because of Bobby's driving, but because of the way he was looking at Katie.

"Bobby, can I talk to you for a minute?"

I whispered, "Are you insane? Do not fall for this girl. She is nuts."

"She told me you would be jealous. Admit it Jimmy, you're jealous. She really likes me and I really like her."

"I'm not jealous and one day we will remember this and we will both be sorry."

"She's the one man!"

"She's just nineteen and you're just twenty-one."

"I'll get the girls back safely and talk to you when I get back."

Allie got in to the car and they drove off in to the sunset.

****

"Jimmy, weren't you supposed to protect your little sister?

"You don't think I was doing that?"

"I guess it was okay to trust Bobby. But his judgement wasn't very good."

"I take your point."

Chapter 3

Janie came to Charlottesville for a visit in April for the spring round of parties. I had spent a long weekend with her in March in Atlanta. Janie and I were becoming very close. I think I was falling ever so slowly in love with her.

My focus for the spring semester other than academics was my application to live on the Lawn in my senior year. The Lawn is used to refer either to the original grounds designed by Thomas Jefferson for the University of Virginia, or specifically to the grassy field around which the original university buildings are arrayed. The inner rank of colonnades, facing the central Lawn proper, contains ten Pavilions (which provide both classrooms and housing for the professors) and 54 student rooms, while the outer rank, facing outward, contain six Hotels (typically service buildings and dining establishments) and another 54 student rooms. At the head of the colonnades, facing south down the Lawn, is the Rotunda, a one-half scale copy of the Pantheon in brick with white columns, that originally held the University's library.

There are a total of 206 columns surrounding the Lawn: 16 on The Rotunda, 38 on the Pavilions, 152 on the walkways. The columns are of varying orders according to the formality and usage of the space, with Corinthian columns on the exterior of the Rotunda giving way to Doric, Ionic, and Composite orders inside; Doric, Ionic, or Corinthian on each of the pavilions; and a relatively humble Tuscan colonnade along the Lawn walkways.

Since my GPA had risen to 3.75 and I had a lot of activities on campus including lacrosse, Inter-Fraternity Council VP and a member of the Jefferson Literary and Debating Society. I was hopeful that my membership in the Society would turn the tide in my favor.

A student at the University who wishes to join the Jefferson Society must sit for an interview process and complete a semester as a Probationary Member. One of these requirements is that of a probationary presentation, an oral presentation that is delivered in front of The Hall and critiqued by a Regular Member. I successfully fulfilled all the requirements; I crossed into the Regular Membership of the society, which included current undergraduate and graduate students of the University. When Regular Members end their enrollment at the University, they become Associate Members of the Society, and may elect to become a Lifetime Member. The Jefferson Society grants Honorary Membership to distinguished individuals who have rendered exceptional service. Once a member, the society functions primarily as a social gathering. The main focus of the weekly meetings is the review of probationary presentations for the current probationary class. Most meetings also host a speaker on a certain topic, but the speaker generally delivers the address within the first half of the meeting. Meetings can last until the early hours of the morning; this rests generally on the whims of the Regular Members.

Being chosen for residence on the Lawn is one of the University's highest honors and is very prestigious. All undergraduate students who will graduate at the end of their year of residency are eligible to apply to live in one of the 47 rooms open to the general student body. Applications – which vary from year to year, but generally include a résumé, personal statement and responses to several questions – are reviewed by a reading committee and the top vote-getters are offered Lawn residency, with several alternates also given notice of potential residency. Five of the remaining seven rooms are "endowed" by organizations on Grounds: the Jefferson Literary and Debating Society(room 7; founded there on July 14, 1825), Trigon Engineering Society (room 17; founded on November 3, 1924), Residence Staff (room 26), the Honor Committee (room 37) and the Kappa Sigma fraternity (room 46; founded there on December 10, 1869). These groups have their own selection process for choosing who will live in their Lawn room although the Dean of Students renders final approval. The Gus Blagden "Good Guy" room (15) resident is chosen from a host of nominees and does not necessarily belong to any particular group. Residency in the John K..Chapell memorial pre-med room (1) is usually granted to an outstanding pre-med student from among the group of 47 offered regular Lawn residency.

Residence in the pavilions is also desirable. However, only nine of the pavilions have faculty residents, as Pavilion VII is the Colonnade Club. The University's Board of Visitors has final approval over which faculty members may live in a pavilion. Pavilion residency is typically offered as a three- or five-year contract with the option to renew. Pavilion residents are expected to interact with their younger "Lawnie" neighbors, as Jefferson intended.

I was chosen to live on the Lawn. I was never so excited by anything as this honor. Mary Lynn and Trip didn't quite get it, but Big Jack and Janie did and that was more than enough.

I went home with a full heart. My grades were good, I made it to the Lawn, and I was in love with Janie Watson.

Big Jack died in July. He hadn't been feeling good so he went to see his doctor. Three days later he got a terrible cough and major congestion. Two days later I took him to the hospital and seven days later he died of pneumonia. I felt lucky to be with him those last seven days. It was a revelation.

His last instructions to me were to graduate, join the firm, and watch over my father. "I want our blood—yours and mine-- in the firm. While you're doing that, get all the pussy you can and then find the woman of your dreams." I loved Big Jack with all my heart.

The funeral service was held at St George's Episcopal Church, a place where Big Jack and Jeannette went every Sunday of their lives. I went to mass with Jack on many Sundays. I know why I went now—I loved Big Jack a lot. So did everyone he touched. They're must have been 700 or more people who came to pay their respects. The Belle Meade police had to block off 2 lanes of Harding Road. I had cried enough at the hospital. I was ready to celebrate the life of a great man.

The priest was The Reverend Dr. George Kennedy, the rector of St. George's and a friend of Jack Bradford. He was wonderful and his homily was spot on. Mary Lynn gave a very good eulogy, surprising us all. George asked if anyone else wanted to speak and he looked straight at me.

I rose to speak. "I loved Big Jack. I'll miss him, but I have his blood coursing through my body. Five days ago he gave me the final instructions for my life. I intend to follow them. Good-bye granddad."

My father gave me a quizzical look. I winked at him and sat down.

Two days later we were in the offices of Caldwell, Bowles and Ritter, the most prestigious law firm in Nashville. Erskine Caldwell was my grandfather's longest living friend and trusted lawyer. Erskine walked with a cane, always wore a three-piece suit and had shoes that were polished to perfection. A watch chain and a pocket watch were his only affectation. My family plus my mother's two sisters, a son-in-law and two grandchildren were present... One of Mary Lynn's sisters, Caroline Bradford, was un-married and her life partner was not present.

Erskine began, "Outside his partnership interests, John L. Bradford left an estate of$11, 650, 500. There is a direction for distribution." Erskine took off his glasses and spent a long time cleaning them. You could hear a pin drop.

"Of this estate amount, 10% is to be used to establish the Big Jack Foundation."

"Alright," I shouted. Erskine looked at me with a little smile on his face. He knew I was excited because that was the name I suggested to my grandfather.

"The purpose of the foundation is to assist children from difficult life situations get an education or a trade. Jack has appointed his daughter's Mary Lynn, Caroline and Kathleen as trustees. Next, a grandchildren's trust has been established for Allison Jeter, Eloise McMahan and Cloe McMahan. The funds are to be used for each grandchild's education and the remainder will be divided among the three when the youngest reaches the age of 25. This trust will amount to 10% of the estate. The remainder of the estate will be divided equally among his three daughters, Mary Lynn, Caroline and Kathleen."

Everyone looked at me. Was I being left out? I didn't think so. There was more to come.

Erskine continued, "Now for the matter of the partnership points." Trip began to hyperventilate. "I leave 25% of my points to James J. Jeter III and 25% to Mary Lynn Bradford Jeter although she is never to work in the firm, but can vote at all partnership meetings. Of the remainder, 35% is to be held in trust for the benefit of James J. Jeter IV until he reaches the age of 25. The remaining 15% will be held in trust for Allison Jeter, Eloise McMahan and Cloe McMahon. Earnings from the points in each trust will accrue for the benefit of those named in each trust. Erskine L. Caldwell will serve as sole trustee of both trusts. Any questions?"

Trip was stunned; Mary Lynn was elated as was I. The two other sisters seemed surprised that they received anything. My sister and her cousins didn't know what to think.

I leaned over to Allie and whispered, "You won't have to depend on Trip for your dowry."

My dad came over to me and said very quietly, "I hope you will be reasonable in matters regarding the firm. What were the private instructions from your grandfather?"

"He's dead I think and they were private!"

"Don't be a prick!"

"He told me to have a lot of sex and find a good woman."

"Oh for God's sake! You'll be good at that."

Janie was waiting for me. She went to all the funeral stops with me for which I was very grateful. I was in pain. My Grandfather was my only advisor about life, women, education, loyalty, family, integrity and love. Janie was the only one who knew how much I missed him

We met at the Sportsman Grill on Harding Road. I was starving and wanted a barbecue on Cajun cornbread.

"How'd it go?" she asked.

"It went great. I got a nice piece of the firm. Actually I got a larger piece than my mom and dad did individually. Together they got more, but we could form an alliance and make it tough for dad. I don't want to do that, but anything's possible"

She leaned across the table and gave me a wet sloppy kiss.

"It's over."

"Yeah it is. I am hungry and thankful."

Harry came over to take our order. "What does she see in you? I can't figure it out."

"Me either Harry my man, but I'm glad she sees something! I'll have the barbecue; Janie wants the 'Big' salad."

I decided to not get together with Mrs. Watson anymore. It wasn't good for anyone. Besides I really loved Janie. I wanted to focus on my relationship with her. My thinking was that she was the one, but we would see.

My roommate, Bobby, called me about a week after my grandfather's death. He wanted to come to Nashville and he needed a place to stay. In my heart I knew this was wrong, but I loved the guy. He was going to get very involved with Katie. Hell, he was already very involved with Katie. I told him it would be fine and then I cleared it with Mary Lynn.

Bobby arrived two days later. He gave Mary Lynn a big hug which she seemed to enjoy a little too much. What is wrong with all these middle-aged women? I took him upstairs to the guest room.

Allie came down the hall and knocked on the door which was slightly ajar.

"Hey Bobby!" She came in and gave him a slight hug and an air kiss.

"Allie you look great! Listen you two; I'm really sorry about your grandfather."

"Thanks man. I miss him. He was…well you know…he had great advice for me on most things. I loved him."

Allie looked at me and then said, "Well, he didn't like girls all that much, so I don't miss him that much. But he did love Jimmy Joe."

"He treated you pretty good, little girl, and your cousins."

"Well, Aunt Kathleen said she was surprised she got anything."

"Listen Bobby, we eat around seven. You plan on seeing Katie tonight?"

"I don't know."

"He is. She'll be here in a little while and will probably stay for dinner like usual," said Allie.

"The little twit is always over here. I'm telling you Bobby, she's nuts, I mean like bat-shit crazy."

"She is not! And anyway she doesn't like you Jimmy Joe, Bobby's the guy she likes now."

Bobby stayed with us for three weeks. Katie tormented him for the entire time he was in Nashville. Some nights she was with him and others not. So many nights she was drunk or high or both. Some nights she treated him as if he were the love of her life. I never have believed that Bobby would ever be tortured by this little bitch, but I was seeing it with my own eyes.

"I told you, she's the one. I am in love with that girl."

"But she's treating you like shit," I said as I looked at him across the room.

"She's just playing a little hard to get. Allie says she really likes me."

"Well, she may be my sister, but you can't trust her. She and Katie have been devious little co-bitches since they were five. They are always together; they think alike, they act alike. Most guys in Nashville are afraid to date either one of them."

And so it went. I tried to stay out of it all, and focused on my own romance. Janie and I were becoming very close. Mrs. Watson called a few times to see if I wanted to frolic around. Finally I told her the truth.

"I am in love with Janie and it's just too awkward even for me."

"You can't be in love with her, she's just a baby."

"Well she's a baby with a future with me I hope."

"I wish you never met her."

"I'm sorry you feel that way."

I really felt good about doing that. I enjoyed being with Jeannette Watson, but enough was enough. Let someone else get shot.

Bobby came back to my house form Katie's house one night truly shaken.

"Man, you just won't believe what happened tonight?"

"What?" I responded.

"We were having dinner with Katie's parents and they were discussing some local political thing about some Congressman. It got really heated between Katie and her father. All of a sudden he jumped up and smacked Katie across the face. She immediately stood and with more fury that I have ever seen, she called him a bastard and told him to never touch her again."

"Slow down man. You're running out of breath."

"Yeah. I didn't know what to do. So I jumped up and held Katie in my arms. She pulled away and told me to get her out of there."

He was wide-eyed and a little pale.

"Let's go get a beer," I said. "It'll calm you down."

"But then her father said something that really got to me. He told her that she wouldn't get her boob job for graduation if he couldn't touch her."

"I have been trying to tell you they are all crazy."

Perry Morgan was one of Nashville's premier plastic surgeons. But he and Adelaide Morgan were considered to be eccentric by the in-crowd in Nashville.

"Where is Katie," I asked as I pulled two beers out of the fridge.

"She's upstairs with Allie." We went outside and sat on the patio nursing our beers.

"Did I not tell you that they are all crazy including her brother?"

"No as a matter of fact, you didn't. You just said Katie was."

"Well, at least you now see why you have to get out of this situation."

"No I don't see that. She needs me more than ever. I need to stay a little longer. She can go back to Bethesda with me."

Chapter 4

With all I had going on in my last year in Charlottesville, I decided that I needed a new car. The Z28 no longer spoke to the man I had become; no longer a redneck from Tennessee, I had turned into a Virginia gentleman for certain.

I got a 1984 BMW 325i. Trip helped me buy the car and made sure I got a fair trade on the Z28. Given all that had happened in that car, I began to wonder if I had done the right thing. I didn't want to give Mr. Emrick the keys, but I finally parted with them.

The positive was that Janie liked the Beemer; her memories of the Z28 were not as fond as mine.

The summer passed and it was time to return to school. I was really looking forward to living on the Lawn, going to a meeting of the Jefferson Society, football and party weekends.

Bobby, Billy Corbett and I decided to have a blow-out evening in Nashville a few days before we left for school. We were all leaving in early August. Billy had to get back for fall football activities. Bobby was actually going home to Bethesda and taking Katie with him. Allie would clearly go into withdrawal. As for me, I had talked Janie into a prolonged road trip along the redneck Riviera. We would stay in Panama City for a while and then drive on to Atlanta and then I would go back to Charlottesville.

So the party was on. The Bluebird Café was the venue. The Bluebird Café is one of the world's preeminent listening rooms and the place has gained worldwide recognition as a songwriter's performance space where the "heroes behind the hits" perform their own songs; songs that have been recorded by chart-topping artists in all genres of music. Located near Green Hills mall outside of downtown Nashville, the 100 seat venue is unassuming in appearance, but some of the most significant songwriters and artists have performed on this stage. Acoustic music is the signature style.

At The Bluebird, performers include up-and-coming songwriters along with those whose music is regularly on the charts, country music as well as pop, rock and Contemporary Christian hits. Kathy Mattea was the first star to be identified with The Bluebird and is still a regular guest performer; including the night we were there. Garth Brooks played on both Open Mic and Sunday Songwriter's Shows before he was discovered – at The Bluebird – and signed to Capitol Records.

On any given night, artists such as LeAnn Rimes, John Prine, Jojo Herman, (Widespread Panic) and Phil Vassar mingle with writers such as ; Billy Kirsch (Holes in the Floor of Heaven/Steve Wariner), Hilary Lindsey (Jesus Take the Wheel/Carrie Underwood) and Chris Tompkins and Josh Kear (Before He Cheats/Carrie Underwood). A typical nightly performance consists of three or four songwriters seated in the center of the room, taking turns playing their songs. It is an experience that few forget, and one that reflects why Nashville is known as Music City.

We got there around 8. There were four guys playing and singing. Kathy Mattea would be on about 10. We all ordered; I got a black bean burger with Havarti and a double order of the house made chips along with a Sierra Nevada.

Janie showed up around 9:30 saying she wanted to give us time to get all of the guy stuff out of the way. She ordered a Stella Artois and a vegetarian quesadilla.

We all sat around enjoying the music, only occasionally finding it necessary to talk. Even though the music was loud, our group seemed serene and peaceful.

That ended when Katie and Allie came through the door.

"I need alcohol quick," Katie shouted. "I have had the worst day of my life. I'm sure my father is going to kill me." She slumped into a chair and started to cry.

Appropriately, Kathy Mattea was singing "You Got a Soft Place to Fall."

I was visualizing how Janie would look in those brown leather pants that Kathy had on. My fantasy burst with the grand entrance and drama.

Poor Bobby. He immediately jumped up and began to hold Katie, telling her that everything was going to be alright. She continued to sob. People around us were getting pissed off. They didn't come here for high drama; just a little music and a few beers. In fact, that was why I was here.

I leaned over to Katie and said, "Could you turn it down a notch. Most of us here want to listen to the music."

Bobby looked as though he was going to punch me.

"Remember, I'm your friend. You're going to need me when she tries to kill you."

"Come on Katie, let's leave. These people don't understand."

He turned to me, "Don't talk to me again man until you come to grips with the fact that I love Katie. Try loving someone other than yourself. You might learn something, you asshole."

He turned his back to me and left with Katie. Janie gave me a hug.

Several days later Janie and I packed my Beemer with school stuff and headed for Panama City. The drive would take 9 hours or so, on I-65 south. The direct route takes you through Birmingham and Montgomery. It's not all that interesting, but we listened to music and talked. We had something to eat at a Denny's on the south side of Birmingham. Three eggs, three pancakes, some grits and the hash brown casserole put me in a great frame of mind.

"Janie, my love, I'm going to do something that will truly show you how much I care. I'm going to let you drive my car for an hour or so while I nap."

"Why Jimmy Joe, you really do care. I really wish you loved me, but caring is OK for now." She had a great southern drawl. I did love her. I just couldn't get the words to form in my mouth.

We pulled into the Beachcomber Inn around 10 pm. It was quiet, but the office was still being manned.

We were both a little tired, but I was really hungry. Janie was ready for some food, but she really wanted a beer. We drove over to Uncle Ernie's Grill for a shrimp sandwich and a few beers, which turned out to be five for me.

We spent four great days hanging at the beach, having late afternoon sex and drinking the night away. But finally, it was time to re-enter the world.

As we were leaving Panama City, I began to get excited about my fourth year at the University. This was going to be a great year. The summer had been traumatic with the loss of Big Jack, but his legacy would live on for me and I was committed to assuming my role in the firm he started. I needed to enjoy this year to the max.

Janie and I were both quiet as we crossed into Alabama on US-231 N. We passed through some interesting Alabama towns such as Dothan and Eufaula. We were truly taking the scenic route. We stopped for some barbecue in Eufaula and it was fabulous.

Finally, we found Interstate 85 just south of Columbus, Ga. From there, it was a straight shot into Atlanta. After some animated discussion, we decided that we should take Exit 86. After a few wrong turns, we made it to Emory.

It was about 5:30 in the afternoon. Janie convinced me that I should stay the night. I was anxious to get to Charlottesville, but it would be a while before we would see each other again.

There's something about sex in a dorm room. Janie was in a suite with four other girls, but each had a private room. So we climbed into her bed after bringing her stuff from the car and finding the cartons that had been delivered from Nashville. We had enjoyed a very large bed in Panama City, but now we were in a single bed that squeaked. The other part of the charm of a dorm room was that the suite mates were in the common room cooking, talking and listening at the door.

"You know they can hear every move we make."

"Sure. That's part of dorm sex. Everyone knows exactly what we're doing. They're jealous and want to make us uncomfortable."

Janie said in a very provocative voice, "Well let's give them a show."

And we did. Janie was something of an acrobat and we did things in positions I never thought possible. I certainly didn't have to fake any moans and groans. At one point Janie let out a shriek and there was a little knock on the door.

"Go away," Janie shouted breathlessly.

The next morning I was up early. Janie and her suitemates all were up to see me off. The suitemates tried to embarrass me, but I was determined to be super cool.

"Jimmy, what was all that noise last night?"

"I didn't hear a thing little darlin'."

The Anorexic Assassin

After a bagel and coffee, I was on to Charlottesville. Janie and I had a long embrace and a lovely kiss. It all felt a little stiff actually, but I ignored it. I wasn't about to let anything spoil the excitement I was feeling. It was 8 hours to Charlottesville via I-85 and US 29N and I was on the way.

After a pit stop in Anderson, South Carolina, I began to think about my relationship with Bobby. We hadn't spoken since that night at the Bluebird when he got so upset. I should have kept my damn mouth shut. I was certain that Katie was going to hurt Bobby in many ways. But it wasn't my choice for him to fall in love with her. I did introduce them, so I am somewhat at fault I guess, but he did the rest.

Bobby had been my best friend for the past three years. I couldn't let Katie spoil that for us both. This was a time when a car phone would be nice, but I would call Bobby when I got to Charlottesville.

I had something to eat at a McDonalds on the north side of Charlotte. A Big Mac fries and Dr. Pepper made me sleepy, so I took a half-hour nap in my car in the parking lot. I woke up wet from sweat: the temperature in the car must have been a hundred degrees. I turned on the car and the AC.

My thinking turned to Janie. I thought about last night and the great sex. My dick became instantly hard; moved through my jeans like a snake. Was my relationship with Janie just about sex or did I love her? Big question- no answer. And then there was her Mom. Since I had been seriously dating Janie, I had not seen her Mom for one of our romps. I wanted to congratulate myself for my success, but I did feel guilty. If Janie and I got married that would be a big burden of guilt to carry around.

I liked Janie a lot and she was really there for me when Big Jack passed away. We had a lot to talk about, a lot of things in common, and we were both from Nashville. Ultimately, my destiny was to be in Nashville and a part of the family firm. It would be nice for Janie and me to raise a family in the city of our birth. Was it my destiny to marry Janie?

I passed through Danville. Almost there.

My room on the lawn was number 15, the "GOOD GUY" room. At the meeting for the room lottery, it was announced that I had somehow been chosen to be the resident of the "GOOD GUY" room with no explanation. Another of those University secrets I suppose. I did do a fair amount of work at Derby Days as the Philanthropy Chair of the Psi chapter.

Every year the chapter hosts the week-long Philanthropy, Derby Days, which brings the Greek community together in order to raise money for UVA Children's Hospital and the Children's Miracle Network.

The week begins on Tuesday with a blood drive sponsored in association with the American Red Cross, which is open to the entire University community. This event is always very successful with a consistently high blood donation rate. Tuesday night's event is a scavenger hunt in which all the sororities are given a list of random items with various point values that need to be located in a period of one hour. The next event, on Wednesday night, is the Miss Derby Days competition in which each sorority gets to dress up one of their coaches for a walk off, in which a judge will determine which sorority did the best job of turning their coach into Miss Derby Days. Thursday night is a Bar Night in which cups are sold at two bar locations for points. The concluding event of the week is a skit competition where the sororities compete by performing some sort of skit, usually a dance. A panel of judges consisting of prominent University figures determines which sorority performed the best skit and thus will win the points for that event.

I also had a very good GPA, was captain of the lacrosse team and had a boatload of friends around the grounds. Hardly worth the accolade, but that was as close as I could get to an answer. I read about Gus and saw the requirements and was truly humbled. I didn't tell my family about it because they might have trouble understanding as well.

There is a University committee that selects an individual to live in the Augustus Silliman "Gus" Blagden, III, Room 15 West Lawn, based on nominations from the University community. The Committee looks for an undergraduate student in their fourth year of study at the University.

Gus was a student at the University in the early 1960's. During these years, he was beloved and admired throughout the University community. Gene Corrigan, past athletic director at Virginia, knew Gus very well. He wrote that "Gus was a very average student and a mediocre athlete, at best, but was so well respected by his teammates that they chose him to be co-captain of the 1963 Lacrosse Team. He was, above all, a kind, generous and gentle person." Gus died only a few years after graduation, but he had so affected the people with whom he had contact that this room was endowed and dedicated to his honor.

The room had a single bed, a desk and chair, a rocking chair, a small cabinet for clothes, a sink and no AC. I brought a fan with me, some rugs and a few other things including my lacrosse gear. The idea was to live simply but elegantly in the Jeffersonian tradition.

I stood in the middle of the room so I could soak up all the spirits inhabiting this place. I wanted to appreciate everything about this experience: the tradition, the wisdom, the integrity, and the life that was in here with me.

"Hey, good guy, are you in a trance? Can you come help me with something?"

Standing in my doorway was a young woman staring at me with an air of carefree confidence that was most noticeable in her serene blue eyes outlined with a dash of dark eyeliner. She had a soft face with rounded cheek bones, proportionally slim nose, high trimmed brows, soft pouty pink lips, and a rounded chin that was complimented by her easy, charming smile. Wondrous oceans of blue gazed out in playful curiosity as she smiled, though; there was a hint of a wild spirit lingering behind those lids.

"Ah, help you with what?"

"As much as I hate to admit it, there's a box out here that is too heavy for me to bring in alone. You're the "Good Guy", so help me out."

"OK, where is it?"

I came out of my room, turned left to follow her and found a big box sitting in front of the door to 16 west.

"What's in it?" I asked.

"A small compact fridge."

"Hmm, I thought the idea was to live simply."

"Maybe for you, but I'm going to be comfortable. Don't worry, I'll let you put stuff in it."

"I'll tilt it toward you, you grab it and I'll get the bottom."

We got the big box in the room and took the fridge out.

"Where do you want it?'

"In the corner over there. See the plug."

I moved it to the spot and made ready to leave. She stuck out her hand and said, "Hi, I'm Maggie Randolph."

"I'm Jimmy…………….."

"I know who you are, Jimmy Jeter or Jimmy Joe if you are a friend. We'll be friends Jimmy Joe."

"If you say so. I'll see ya'."

I really needed to talk to Bobby. This thing that just happened was really disconcerting. Yesterday I was thinking about marrying Janie and this girl pops into my life.

Maggie had blonde hair, groomed and shining brilliantly, which cropped her gentle face. Today she had it in two braids, but I was already imagining it glimmering down towards her shoulders where it ends, with perfectly cut tips. The uniform hair spills down between her shoulder blades in bladed formation, the rest of it cropping in circular fashion towards her shoulders where the shortest strands just barely tickle the skin of her collar bone. What was wrong with me? My imagination was running away. Maggie had a soft neck, but broad shoulders that formed into equally strong arms and large hands with particularly long fingers. Her midsection looked taut and trim. Overall her general shape was a toned, hourglass figure defining her chest and hips which are of moderate, if not winding, definition. Altogether her skin tone was a light and even tan. She was a solid woman, who owns many womanly curves and a confidence about her that belies her age.

I didn't know if Bobby was in Charlottesville yet, so I decided to go over to the Sigma Chi house.

"Hey there, Jimmy Joe. Where're you going?"

It was Maggie. She was standing in front of her door in a UVA sweatshirt, a pair of khaki shorts, and sneakers. How could she look so pretty in that garb?

"I'm heading over to the Sigma Chi house."

"Mind if I tag along?'

"I don't mind. You date someone over there?"

"No, I'm just a little bored and looking for something to do and someone to do it with and you'll do."

This year was going to be interesting. Nothing could be simple for Jimmy Joe Jeter.

"Hey Larry, have you seen Bobby Gibbs?" Maggie and I were standing in the foyer of the Sigma Chi house.

Larry and I shook hands and I introduced him to Maggie.

"Yeah, he's here. I think he's in the bar with Katie"

"How about you show Maggie around, while I go see Bobby. By the way, she lives next to me on the Lawn."

"No problem man. I'd be more than happy to show her around."

I went to the bar and found them sitting on a love seat in the middle of the room.

I heard Katie say, "Watch out Bobby here he comes."

"Hey Guys, Uh Bobby can I talk to you for a moment."

"I got nothing to say to you."

"I came to apologize to both of you. I was wrong that night at the Bluebird. Katie, I didn't know what you were going through. I was being selfish. I should have kept my mouth shut."

"My, my, the big Jimmy Joe Jeter admitting he was wrong. What a wonder!"

"Come on Katie, give me a break."

"OK I forgive you."

Bobby had a big smile on his face as he reached up to shake my hand. "Cool man, everything is cool."

About that time Larry Quigley came through the door with Maggie in tow.

"That was a quick tour."

"Yeah, I'm returning this witch to you."

"Next time don't try to cop a feel when you just meet someone."

Larry left the room quickly.

"Are all your brothers like that?"

"Pretty much. Hi, I'm Katie Morgan. Are you a friend of Jimmy Joe's?"

"I'm Maggie Randolph. I live next door to Jimmy Joe on the Lawn. He's my entertainment for the evening."

Katie's eyes narrowed and she cast a stony stare in my direction.

I was in trouble, I just didn't know how much. "Maggie and I just met." I'm sure I looked guilty, because I felt it for some reason.

I looked Bobby in the eye and said, "We're good man?"

"Yeah we're good."

"We're good too Jimmy Joe!" Katie said with a twinkle in her eye.

66

The Anorexic Assassin

My fourth year was off with a bang. I wanted it to be so simple and enjoyable; as with most things in my young life, chaos seemed to rule.

The next day I cornered Bobby. "Listen man, I need to talk to you. I think I have a real problem."

"You do have a problem pal and her name is Maggie."

"Look man, one day I'm thinking about asking Janie to marry me and the next day this girl pops into my life."

"Yeah and she seems to really like you!"

"And she's right next door and so good looking. I mean man she is a ten if there ever was one."

"Jimmy Joe you would be a lot happier if you would pick one girl and stick to it."

"You're right, you're right Bobby."

"Just look at me. Katie is the girl for me. And don't say she's going to kill me."

"Ok, Ok, I get it man. I get it. You are a great friend Bobby. Thanks for being there for me."

Chapter 5

The fall semester was good. The football team was 6 and 5 and they lost to rival Virginia Tech 28-10, but it was a fun season. Janie came up for a football weekend and we had a great time. We spent time with Katie and Bobby. Janie and Katie stayed at the same place, Lottie Graham's house. Allie was also in town and was staying there as well. She had another date with Dickey Lynn. This was getting to be a regular thing. I was feeling a little territorial. My sister was coming into her own as a beautiful and bright woman.

The three girls spent a lot of time huddled together talking, particularly on Friday night. The game, a little food and a great party on Saturday night made for a terrific week end. About midnight, Janie and I headed for my room on the Lawn.

"Hey, Good Guy is that you? Oh! Is this your date? You're bringing her to the "Good Guy" room? Isn't that some sort of blasphemy? I mean the committee would certainly be troubled by that."

Maggie Randolph was standing just outside her doorway giving us that steely stare. Then she walked over to us and held out her hand.

"Hi, I'm Maggie Randolph, Jimmy's conscience."

"I'm Janie Watson, Jimmy's girlfriend."

"Well don't let me interrupt."

Sugar wouldn't melt in her mouth. She was causing problems beyond belief.

"What's this about the "Good Guy" room?" Janie asked.

Maggie stepped forward, "Well it's quite an honor to be selected to live in room 15, Jimmy's room. It's given to the person who has served the University community and has high moral character. Apparently our boy here does a lot of philanthropic things though his frat, is a jock, has good grades and high moral character, or so we all thought."

She looked at Janie, who was glaring at me, and said, "Plus the single bed in there would really be uncomfortable."

"How do you know that?" Janie queried as her voice struggled to remain calm.

"I have one just like it in my room."

"I'm just going to show Janie what it looks like."

"Whatever! See ya' around."

I showed her the room. It didn't have the same charm and meaning for Janie that it did for me. She wasn't impressed.

"That girl lives right next to you."

"Yes, but look, she dates some guy who is in school at Yale. She has no interest in me or me in her."

"She's really pretty. And what's this "good guy" stuff all about."

"Because of things I've done around the grounds, a committee chose me to live in this room."

"Why didn't you tell me about it? If you love me, you should tell me everything."

"I didn't tell anybody. Not Trip and Mary Lynn. Not Allie. No one. Oh, Bobby new because he's part of what goes on here. I just didn't want to be a show-off and people in Nashville have a different opinion. But I've changed since I started dating you. I'm a better person because of you."

"But if you're supposed to love me, you should tell me everything and you haven't."

"Janie, I'm sorry."

"Take me back to Mrs. Graham's!"

"AH come on Janie, don't act like that."

"Take me back now Jimmy Joe."

All the way to Mrs. Graham's I was searching for the right words. I knew she wanted to hear the three words "I love you", but I just couldn't get 'em out of my mouth. I was screwed.

I walked her to the porch and as I bent to kiss her she turned her back.

"Janie, you don't have anything to be pissed about."

"Don't I Jimmy Joe?"

She gave me a little peck on my lips and went through the door. I went back to the Psi house. I needed a drink. Probably more than one.

I woke on a sofa at the Psi House about 9:30. Someone was shaking and shouting at me. It was Bobby.

"Hey man, what's up with you. You knew that Janie had an 8 am flight out of here. What's the matter?"

"Oh, shit! Janie got mad at me. That damn Maggie Randolph. Is Janie alright? Did someone take her to the airport?"

"Yeah, Katie and me. Katie called about seven and said you weren't around to take Janie and so I struggled out to get her. She made the flight."

"Who schedules an 8 am flight on a party weekend?"

"People with papers due on Monday. Anyway, you are in deep shit man."

"Maggie Randolph is a problem."

"Why?"

"Well I like her and Janie saw that. I took Janie over to my room and Maggie was there. Janie found out about the good guy stuff and came to the conclusion that I hid things from her. Then she wondered why Maggie was so interested in our being there. How do I get involved in this crap?"

"It's just life man."

"Maybe I should just give up on women."

Billy thought for a moment and then wisely said, "It would be good to find one and really stay with them no matter what, you know. Like me and Katie."

On that note I decided to stay quiet.

Later that night, I called Janie and profusely apologized. She was cold and non-committal. She gave me that old song—I need time to think—don't call me—I'll call you. Wow, I felt bad.

"What's wrong "good guy," lose your best friend?"

"Maggie you always know how to say the right thing."

"Want to talk about it?"

"NO! No I don't."

"Suit yourself. See you later. Oh, whatever it is, it's not the end of the world."

And it wasn't, at least not yet.

Absent the last 24 hours, I was having a really good semester. My grades were good. I was working on the planning group for Derby Days, was spending an hour or so in the weight room five days a week and was enjoying the speaker series for the Jefferson Literary and Debating Society.

For the next couple of weeks, I decided to concentrate on school work and the other activities I had been engaged in thus far. I wouldn't try to contact Janie and would try to straighten things out over Thanksgiving. And then there was Maggie Randolph.

I ran into her on a Wednesday and for some reason said, "Listen there's a speaker at the Jefferson Lit Society tomorrow night. It's a guy named Steven Seranovic, an international trade specialist from GWU, and he's talking about trade policy with China. Want to go with me?"

"Whoa, good guy are you asking me out on a date?"

"No! It's just a speaker. If you don't want to go, just say so."

"What time?"

"7:30 pm. Go over there around 7 or so."

"OK! I'll go, but remember it's not a date."

"Sure!"

My first social gathering with Maggie went fine. My friends all took note of the fact that I was with her and I dutifully ignored them.

I flew to Nashville for Thanksgiving break. Trip picked me up in the airport around 9:30 pm. I was tired and wasn't interested in conversation, but apparently Trip was.

"How was the semester?"

"Going great. I might have a shot at a 4.0, but no less than a 3.8."

"Terrific! Any thoughts about what you want to do after you graduate?

"I don't know. You have any ideas?"

"You can come to work for the firm or find something to do on the street, or you could get an MBA."

"I applied already to the Harvard MBA program."

"Really! That's fabulous."

"I applied to Wharton as well." I couldn't let him get too happy.

"I don't mean to pry, but is there something going on with you and Janie?"

"Well, we had a little fight, I guess, and we haven't spoken in the last few weeks. Why?"

"I saw Ben Watson earlier in the week and he was very curt with me. He told me to keep you away from his daughter. He didn't care about his wife, he said. I didn't know what to think and then Erskine's partner Roger Newton told me that Ben was staying with him for a few weeks. Roger's divorced and has a nice place so he says. You know anything about any of this?"

"Nope. This is news to me," I said, trying to stop hyperventilating at the same time.

We arrived at the Jeter hacienda around 10:30 pm. Mary Lynn was waiting for us at the side door.

"Jeannette Watson has called three times to see if you have gotten home yet. What is going on Jimmy Joe? Have you done something to Janie? Is she pregnant?

"Hello MOM, it's good to see you too."

"Well, I'm waiting."

"No I haven't done anything to Janie and she isn't pregnant. At least, she shouldn't be. She takes the pill and I use a condom."

"I don't want all the details."

"Seemed like it to me."

"Look Jimmy, what's going on? Something is going on and you're up to your neck in it," Trip said.

"It's not all that bad, if it's what I think it is."

Trip looked at me in an "aw shit" manner and said, "What"

"I think it's probably about Mrs. Watson and me. We had a sexual thing for a while. But I stopped it when Janie and I started dating."

Mary Lynn's hand was over her mouth as she began to wail. Trip rushed to her and looked back at me. He had a strange look on his face—a look of admiration.

Just then there was knock on the back door. I turned on the light and looked out. It was Janie and Mrs. Watson.

I slowly opened the door. "May we come in?" Janie said in a very stiff tone.

"Sure, come on in."

I led them into the living room. This appeared to be a very formal visit. I sat in a large cushioned chair. I needed a very comfortable seat for the execution. My heart was in my throat.

At that moment, Trip and Mary Lynn came in the room. "Mind if we join you?" Trip asked.

Jeannette Watson replied, "I think that would be good."

Janie looked at me with anger written all over her face. "Jimmy Joe you probably have guessed why we're here."

"I have no idea." She looked at me as if I were an alien. "Look, Janie, don't you think any problem we may have should be worked out between you and me?"

"Not this one. This one involves three people and your parents need to know what's been going on!"

"Aw shit!"

"Jimmy Joe, watch your mouth," Mary Lynn admonished.

About that time Allie popped into the room. "Hi everybody. What's going on? Everything OK? You guys are getting married! I knew it."

"Allie please, they are not getting married. Just go on upstairs"

"Well now I am interested. Think I'll stay!"

Trip stepped in, "Go upstairs please. Now!" She gave us all a funny look and left.

Jeannette cleared her throat, looked down at the floor and began to speak. "This is very hard for me and I am very embarrassed. And it has been costly to me, may even cost me my marriage and my daughter's love. As you know Jimmy Joe, you and I had a sexual relationship for a while a year ago or so."

"It was two years. Before Janie and I started dating."

"Don't interrupt please." She looked at Mary Lynn and Trip, "We got together every once in a while. We were very careful to not be obvious about it and no one knew about it but the two of us. Of course, while Janie was dating him, we didn't have any contact other than normal. But Janie has fallen in love with him and he was most likely going to ask her to marry him. I couldn't let that happen. She needed to know. I couldn't be a Mom who had slept with her daughter's husband."

Jeannette began to weep. Mary Lynn was frozen in position with her mouth agape.

Trip was stunned by this confession, but managed to say, "Here's a handkerchief Jeannette. Please try to compose yourself."

I looked at Jeannette and said, "You are a really selfish woman. No one knew, but you just had to let it out. Couldn't you just let well enough alone? Selfish in the extreme is what you are."

"Don't talk to my Mom like that."

"Janie I love you. I stopped with your Mom before we started dating because I thought I could care for you. And I was right. You can't let this stand in the way of what we have. We are great together. Please find it in your heart to forgive us."

"We don't have anything Jimmy Joe! I can't forgive you. My Mom and Dad are divorcing because of you. Our whole family is broken because of you. And Katie told me about you and that girl. You had a date with her."

"I did not!"

"You took her to that literary thing. Don't lie."

"I did go with her to that, but it wasn't a date. We both agreed on that."

"Well I don't want to see you again. Mr. and Mrs. Jeter, I am sorry we came over here so late, but no one is sleeping at our house and we didn't want to ruin your Thanksgiving Day."

"Come on Mother, let's go."

Jeannette stood and looked at Mary Lynn, "I am sorry."

Mary Lynn looked at her, "You seduced my son."

Jeannette started to say something, but turned and walked to the door with Janie.

I got up to go after Janie, but Trip blocked my way. "Leave it alone. It's bad enough. We don't need shouting in the streets. And stay away from the Watson house. And watch your back—old Ben might be lurking in the shadows."

"This is just awful. How embarrassing can things be—this just takes the cake," said Mary Lynn. "Keep that thing in your pants until you are ready to marry someone. Do you understand me young man."

Trip looked at me and said, "Are there any other of our friends that you have been diddling with?"

"Come on Trip. Look it started after the Cora Jane thing. I was home and you guys were having a party. She came up to my room, took her underwear off, told me she was ready and to have a go. That's how it started."

Mary Lynn put her hand over her mouth and let out a little squeak.

Trip looked at me in amazement, "You're kidding?"

"Nope! By the way, there is no one else, just her."

"Thank God."

"I'm going to bed." I headed up the stairs.

As I got to the top of the stairs, Allie was standing there looking at me with a smirk on her face.

"Mrs. Watson, that's the best you could do?"

"Well, she was available during a time that I wasn't thinking straight."

"Couldn't you see that it would never work with Janie lurking in the background?"

"No, I thought she would keep her mouth shut. That's what she said at least."

"I understand this new girl is really hot. Maggie is her name?"

"Jeez, Katie's got a fucking mouth as big as Texas."

"What about Maggie? You like her?"

"I'm afraid of her? Please don't tell Katie that."

On that note we turned to our respective rooms and settled in for a long sleep.

The holidays were pretty dull for me. I went out on Friday night and had a few beers with Billy Corbett and a few other guys. Other than that, I sat around the house with Trip, watched football and drank beer. Mary Lynn popped in every so often to ask a question about Jeannette Watson mostly to determine why I had been involved with her. She also displayed her anger with regard to Jeannette's seduction of poor Jimmy Joe. Trip said he was not surprised that I was taking the advice of "Big Jack" to heart.

Chapter 6

I was happy to be back in Charlottesville, even though final exams were the next week. I was more or less ready for finals, I just need to brush up on a few things and turn in one paper.

I had finished up the paper and was heading out to get something to eat, when I ran into Maggie Randolph.

"I'm heading for something to eat, want to come along."

"Sure, but that lovely girl of yours might find out."

"Not worried about that anymore. Plus Katie Morgan isn't around to be the snitch."

It was chilly so we walked pretty fast to get to the dining hall. Conversation was limited.

I was hungry so I put together a nice meal filled with comfort food and a large piece of apple pie. Maggie got a burger and fries.

Maggie looked at me in a quizzical way, "Are you OK Good Guy?"

"Yeah, sure I'm OK. I finished my last paper for the semester and I only have to take two exams. Things are OK. How about you?"

"I'm doing so so. The guy I was seeing from Yale decided to go visit his folks and didn't invite me along. And I haven't heard from him since before Thanksgiving. I really think he found someone more suitable. You know, more demure, less concerned about feminism and more concerned about her man."

"Are you a feminist?"

"Yep! I want more than the vote. I want an opportunity to do some things and get paid for it. I want kids and all those trimmings, but I want to feel satisfied that I have lived a complete life when I die."

"Work doesn't define you, you know."

"Easy for you to say. You have a career waiting for you."

"How do you know that?"

""Well Jimmy Joe, I've checked you out. You and your family own a big piece of a brokerage firm in Nashville. Very profitable, I'm told."

"I guess I should check you out."

"Not much to check. I'm just a part of the impoverished aristocracy of Virginia. We've lived off our capital too long and have not been all that good at preservation. So we live in a grand house, but my Father is too inept to have a top job. He has an adequate job that doesn't require great mental ability, but is barely satisfactory for the family to maintain a semblance of stature. It's all pretty sad. He sees the top dog of his company regularly at the Commonwealth Club, but never in the office. We can't afford the Country Club dues anymore, even though our family has been a member of CCV since its founding."

I gazed at her and said, "Sounds like a merger might be in order." I regretted it instantaneously.

"Are you proposing Jimmy Joe?"

"Sounds like it, doesn't it. I'm sorry, I'm sorry that was inappropriate."

"That's a first for me. I've been proposed to before the first date."

"Well, others are telling people we had a date to the Literary Society."

"We said it wasn't a date. Who said it was a date?"

"Katie Morgan, that witch, told Janie that we had a date. Bobby told her we went together."

"Did you and Janie breakup?"

"Yeah, we did. But not because of our supposed date. The whole thing is embarrassing."

"Want to talk about it?"

"May as well. Back when I was about 19, her Mother seduced me at a party at my own home in my own room. We had a secret relationship based totally on sex for about a year. I broke it off when I started dating Janie. Her Mother told Janie about it and she was furious."

"You certainly understand why, don't you? She was bound to find out."

"I do understand why she is angry and hurt and I suppose you're right, but I still don't quite understand why her Mother told her."

"Listen, Good Guy, don't ever sleep with my Mother. I'll cut your balls off with a dull knife. By the way, was she any good—the Mother that is?"

"Yes, she was!"

That was interesting I thought to myself. Does she think we're going to have a relationship?

I took my two exams and by my calculation did very well. I already had A's in my other three classes; one a graduate level statistics class. Exams were over for everyone on the 18th, but I decided not start the drive to Nashville until the 23rd which was a Monday. Christmas was on Wednesday this year. I planned to come back to Charlottesville on the 29th, unless something unexpected happened. I couldn't think of any looming disasters, but I was still apprehensive.

Bobby left for home and was picking up Katie in DC. He was truly mesmerized by that crazy witch. At least I wouldn't run into her in Nashville.

Interestingly, Maggie Randolph was staying until the next week as well. There were several others on the lawn who were staying over. Professors living in the pavilions were there to supervise us, although we were all honor bound to behave.

The Anorexic Assassin

I was doing some reading so I could get ahead of the curve in a directed study I was doing next semester, my last at the University.

On Thursday evening, Maggie knocked on my door and then opened it.

"Let's go eat. I'm starved! I haven't eaten all day!"

"Well, hello to you, Maggie my dear. I'd love to go eat. My mind is filled with this shit, I don't know if I'll be good company, but doing anything else would be a relief. How about Saigon café, the portions are big and it's cheap."

"How good is the food?"

"Acceptable!"

We both had pork and vermicelli rice. It wasn't bad. For the next three days we dined together, alternating between Saigon Café and Annie's Pizza.

"What are your plans when you leave here," I said to Maggie between bites of pizza.

"My brother and two sisters are already in Richmond. So I will be with my family for a few days and then I'm going up to my friend Joan's house in Chevy Chase. You should go to Bobby's house and we could all go out."

"Yeah, that's possible. Katie will be there. Maybe I can stand it. I really like Bobby's dad. "

Christmas at home was good. I enjoyed seeing Billy Corbett again. I ran into Cora Jane after Christmas and she was enjoying Rhodes College in Memphis. Trip and Mary Lynn were almost ready to forgive me. Allie was somewhat lost without Katie at her side, but I thought it was good for her and I sure didn't miss Katie.

So why was it I was going to Bobby's house? That's right; Maggie was going to be a few miles away. I called Bobby and he sounded like the sight of a friend would be more than welcome.

"Katie's been acting really weird. It's like she misses the craziness of her family."

I didn't take the bait.

I did hook-up with Maggie and her friend Joan. We met at Clyde's for a beer and a little food. Joan was attractive and was a senior at Bryn Mawr. I thoroughly enjoyed myself and so did they.

On New Year's Eve, Joan and her boyfriend, Marty, Bobby, Katie, Maggie and I went out. We went to the hip Adams Morgan section to a soul food place with great jazz called Madam's Organ.

I was truly enjoying myself as were Maggie and Joan. I couldn't tell about Marty because he was stoned when we met and he was in a stupor by 11:30 pm.

Fifteen minutes later, Katie began to weep and wail. She shouted at Booby at the top of her lungs, "It's your fault I'm not with my family. I miss my Mother. It's your fault they don't like me. And your Mother hates me and wants me out of your life. Maybe you don't love me anymore."

She ran to the ladies room crying and shrieking, "I'm all alone!"

Bobby was shocked as was everyone else. Where had that come from?

He looked at the other two women for help. "Can one of you go see if she's alright?"

As they were mulling it over, Katie came back and acted as if nothing had happened.

"What did I miss," she said.

All of us, including Bobby, were dumbfounded.

About 1:30 am, we were all ready to go. Katie refused to leave. When Bobby told her they were closing the place, she said she was not ready, she wanted another drink and that was that. A thirty minute scene ensued, with Bobby pleading and Katie shouting. Finally, the security guy came and forced her out of the place, wherein Bobby got in a shoving match with him. Another guy came and I started to get involved, but Maggie stood in front of me and held on to both my arms. The security guys escorted us all out the door.

I dropped Maggie off at Joan's house and went back to Bobby's. I walked in the door and heard Katie shouting, "Why did we have to go out with that bastard and that bitch? I want to go home now. I can't stay in this house another minute."

Bobby was trying to calm her down. His Mother came down to see what was going on.

Katie took one look at her and asked "Why don't you like me? Why is it you hate me?"

"I worry about the way you treat Bobby," Pat Gibbs said.

"Mom, you're not helping."

"See I told you she hates me. I want to go home."

"Ok, Ok, but we have to wait until the morning."

"You have to come with me. I'm afraid of my Father."

"Oh my heavens, you can't go Bobby!"

"I have to Mom. I'm the only one who will protect her."

Katie immediately settled down and said, "Come on Baby, let's go to bed."

I was standing in foyer when Mrs. Gibbs came down the stairs.

She looked at me and sighed, "What am I going to do Jimmy?"

"Mrs. Gibbs, I've been trying to figure that out for the last two years." In 24 hours I would be heading back to Charlottesville, but Mrs. Gibbs would still be worrying about her little boy.

I was determined to enjoy my last semester to the max and I did. Somehow, Maggie began to be a big part of my life and I enjoyed it. My classes went great and our lacrosse team had a terrific season. We went 15-2, won the ACC regular season championship and made it to the finals of the NCAA tournament. I told Ace (our coach Ace Adams) that he would win it all next year. It was actually 1994 before they won it all. I was sad about the outcome of the game, but was happy that Maggie, Trip and Mary Lynn were there to console me.

Trip very wisely said, "Only two teams made it this far. I think you are a champion."

"By the way Trip, I was accepted by the Harvard business school. I'm going there in the fall." Even though I was sweaty and dirty, I got a big hug from Trip and a nice tap on the head from Mary Lynn. But from Maggie, I got a big luscious kiss. I didn't want it to end. Mary Lynn winked at Trip who was beaming. He finally approved the direction my life was taking and so did I.

We were back at school about a week, when Maggie came charging into my room. "Jimmy Joe, guess what?" she said breathlessly.

"What?"

"I got a job at Putnam Investments in Boston. We can go there together. Me and you. We can room together."

"Hey Maggie, that is great. What are you going to be.........? Room together? Is that what I heard?"

"Yeah, isn't it great?"

I thought about it for a moment. "That will be terrific! Wow, we'll be roommates."

"We'll be more that. We'll be friends, we'll be lovers, and we'll be on the way. You're over most of your self-created traumas and it's time for us, you and me Jimmy Joe." She hugged me and gave me another of those luscious kisses.

To say I was stunned wouldn't quite capture how I felt, but on the other hand, it felt great to know that Maggie was more than just a good female friend. I was confused, but happy in my ignorance.

She and I were both tapped into Phi Beta Kappa and graduated summa cum laude. Trip, Mary Lynn and Allie were all there for the graduation activities.

Maggie's family was also present and the Jeter's were introduced to the Randolph's. Bill and Betsy meet Jim and Mary Lynn.

The **Randolph family** is a prominent Virginia political family, whose members contributed to the politics of Colonial Virginia and Virginia after it gained its statehood. They are descended from the Randolph's of Morton Morrell, Warwickshire, England. The first Randolph to come to America was Henry Randolph in 1643. His nephew, William Randolph later came to Virginia as an orphan in 1669. He made his home at Turkey Island along the James River. Because of their numerous progeny, William Randolph and his wife, Mary Isham Randolph, have been referred to as the "Adam and Eve of Virginia."

William Randolph was a member of the Virginia Burgesses for Henrico County and later Speaker of the Virginia House of Burgesses. He was a founding trustee of The College of William and Mary.

Thomas Jefferson, great-grandson of William Randolph, was a Virginia Burgess for Albemarle County and the principle author of the Declaration of Independence.

"Light Horse Harry" Lee, great-grandson of William Randolph, was an early American patriot who served as the ninth Governor of Virginia and as a Virginia Representative to Congress. During the Revolution, Lee served as a Calvary officer.

Robert E. Lee, 2nd great grandson of William Randolph, was an American career military officer best known for having commanded the Confederate Army of Northern Virginia. In post-bellum years, he was president of Washington College (later Washington and Lee University).

The early Randolph's were certainly a part of our nation's history, but after the civil war they were mostly lawyers and businessmen. Even though Maggie's family resided in a large townhouse in the Fan District of Richmond, her father was a VP and Trust Officer for First & Merchants Bank and her Mother taught English at St. Catherine's school. But they were part of the FFV (First Family of Virginia) group, as Bill was a direct descendant of William Randolph.

Trip was amused when Bill talked about his cousin's design of the University and how privileged his son was to have been chosen to live on the Lawn and be a member of the Jefferson Literary and Debating Society.

Trip suggested that he was simply thrilled to have me go to his Alma Mater even if was just for an MBA and how nice it was that Maggie had gotten a job.

Maggie said, "I truly get tired of the conversation about who has got the bigger one."

"Trip loves this sort of thing."

Meanwhile the two Moms were enjoying a nice conversation about children, schools and the merits of their respective cities. Mary Lynn was a died-in-the-wool Nashville lady, but folks from Tennessee have a slight inferiority complex, particularly when they have to deal with the FFV set.

We all went together for a meal at our favorite restaurant, The Saigon Café. All the waitresses were happy to see us and congratulated Maggie and I on our graduation. Trip and Mary Lyn were appalled. Bill and Betsy looked at the prices and were pleased. I told everyone to eat heartily; this meal was a treat from Big Jack Bradford, my grandfather.

"If we had known that, we should have chosen a better restaurant," whined Mary Lynn.

"These people got us through some tough nights. They are part of our family; mine and Jimmy Joe's," the retort from Maggie.

I was more confused than ever.

Chapter 7

Maggie was starting work in July, so that gave us about seven weeks to find a place to live and get our stuff up to Boston. She packed her things and took them back to Richmond. I decided to put all of my things in a storage unit and pick them up when I came back through to Richmond when we were actually moving to Boston.

I decided to fly to Nashville for a week. I could see Trip and Mary Lynn as well as Allie. Trip was interested in who was paying my tuition to Harvard.

"I'm paying for it. The firm had a good year and my share was significant."

"You're right; we did have a good year. We closed several corporate finance deals and a very large municipal finance deal. Retail was good. Absolutely, a good year."

"How about this year? Will the points be worth as much?"

"At least as much so you should be OK. What are you doing with the excess?"

"Erskine wanted me to put some into a rainy day fund. So I did. The rest I gave to Bill McLemore and he bought some stocks for me. I feel really good about it."

"Be careful with Erskine, he's not as sharp as he used to be. Don't get me wrong, you can trust him, but he's lost a few steps."

"I'm good with him. And I'm keeping things with the firm."

"You can't go wrong with Bill. He's really good!"

I called Bobby to check in and see how things were going.

"Well, I've decided to go to Vanderbilt Law. Katie is probably going to finish at GW in December and she is pretty sure she will be accepted in to the medical school at Vandy. Her Dad has some connections at the school."

"Don't count on him."

"Well, he seems to really want to help and he has apologized for all the hateful stuff he has done"

"I'm coming down next week to look for a place to live. Any thoughts?"

"I'm leaving on the 28th to fly back to Charlottesville to get my car and Maggie. But Mary Lynn would be glad to help I am sure. She has friends and so on that can get you what you need. I'll talk to her and we'll call you back."

"Thanks Jimmy Joe, you are a good friend."

Of course, Mary Lynn was more than happy to help. We called Bobby back and she talked to him about his situation. He told her that he and Katie would be down the following week and would give her a call. That never happened as Katie found something she liked and Bobby said OK.

I hooked up with some of my Nashville friends and we enjoyed several evenings together over a few beers. Allie and I were having lunch at the Sportsman's Grill when Janie walked in with several of her friends. She looked me in the eye and pretended I wasn't there.

"You want to leave?" Allie said with a worried look on her face.

"I'm OK, finish your sandwich. I'm going to enjoy mine. I don't think I'll get any burgers like this up north."

As I headed back to Charlottesville, I wondered if Nashville would ever feel like home again. I hoped so, since my family's firm was located here and I had a nice piece of the action.

I spent the night at the frat house in Charlottesville and then drove on to Richmond.

Maggie's family lived in the Fan District of Richmond. **The Fan** is so named because of the "fan" shape of the array of streets that extend west from Belvidere Street, on the eastern edge of Monroe Park, westward to the Boulevard. The Fan District is primarily a residential neighborhood consisting of late-nineteenth and early-twentieth century homes. It is also home to VCU's Monroe Park Campus, several parks, tree-lined avenues and three of the city's historical monuments. The District also has numerous houses of worship, and locally owned businesses and commercial establishments. The Fan borders and blends with the Boulevard, the Museum District, and the Carytown district.

Maggie lived in a three story old brick home on Grove Ave. It was built in the 19th century right after the War. The interior was beautiful with crown molding and chair rails everywhere. The furniture in the downstairs was beautiful with solid wood furnishings and ancestral portraits.

Mrs. Randolph fixed me a cup of coffee and a sweet roll. We sat at the kitchen table and talked about the things Maggie and I were planning to do in Boston. I told her that we were good; that we were looking for an apartment. She looked at me as if I were stupid and said: "I know that. I wondered what else you guys might be doing."

"I thought what we would do is look along the subway line and find out how to get around Boston."

"Yes Boston is pretty complicated."

Then she added another statement that sort of confused me. "Are you and Maggie an item now?"

Thankfully, Maggie came down the stairs and into the kitchen. Her mother looked at her and I stared at her as well. She got this self-conscious look on her face and said, "What's going on guys?"

"Your mom just asked me if we were an item."

"What was your answer?"

"I didn't have an answer, because I don't really know whether we are or not."

Maggie stood there without saying a word. Her mom looked at me and then she looked at Maggie. It was truly an awkward moment. Not so much for her mom, but Maggie was blushing and so was I. I guess we didn't have a clue about the nature of our relationship. We were simply two people moving to Boston and were going to live together. While we had been next-door neighbors at Virginia, and we had done a lot of things together, we had never slept with each other. It was an unusual situation and hard to explain. I truly liked Maggie a lot, she was absolutely beautiful and I enjoyed her company. But for some reason, I was gun-shy when it came to women given the outcome with Janie and her Mother. My luck over the past few years had not been that great and I wasn't sure if a relationship was the best thing for me.

Maggie looked at her mom and said, "Mom stop asking questions that don't have answers."

Then she looked at me and said, "Jimmy carry my bags to the car while I say goodbye to my mother."

I felt a little bit like a bellboy, but I grabbed her bags and headed to the car. I was happy to be out of the house and away from that conversation with her mother. It was a little tense.

Maggie finally made it to the car and we were on our way to Boston. We hit 95 N. and I began to relax.

"I guess the nature of our relationship is going to be that of neighbors again. After all, we plan to get a two-bedroom apartment, so you'll have a room and I'll have a room."

Maggie looked over at me with a strange look on her face and said, "Well, if that's the way you want it, then that's the way it will be. It's okay with me if we just stay friends and share the apartment."

"How about we just play it by ear for a while?"

"That's okay too."

We stopped several times on the way for gas, snacks and lunch. The food was so bad I don't know why we bothered.

Finally we arrived in Boston. Maggie was certain that she could direct us to her aunt's house, but I had this feeling that we were lost. It took us over an hour to find Back Bay and with that, she directed us to the house. These folks were not part of the impoverished aristocracy.

Caroline Randolph Warren had done well for herself as a wife, mother and realtor. Edward Warren was an executive with Putnam investments. Upon learning this bit of information, I understood how Maggie got her job. In this world, it truly is who you know.

Caroline was happy to see us, acknowledged that we must be exhausted and took us straight to our rooms. Notice the plural of rooms. Mine was very nice with a lovely view of the gardens in the back of the house.

I knocked on Maggie's door to see how she was doing. She said, "Let's go downstairs and see if we can find something to eat."

I was hungry so I was all in favor of that. Caroline was in the kitchen making some sandwiches when we arrived.

In a combination Virginia and Boston accent, Caroline said to us, "You both must be famished. It's a long drive from Richmond and most of it is boring."

I sat at the small round table in the kitchen munching on a corned beef sandwich as Maggie talked to her aunt about the plans for the next day. Apparently, one of her associates would pick us up around 9 AM tomorrow morning and take us to see several apartments that would be suitable for us. Maggie told her aunt that we would like something on the public transportation routes because we would probably only have one car in Boston. Also, she told her aunt that we would like something in the $1000 range.

"I don't think you can get a two-bedroom apartment in a nice neighborhood for that amount sweetheart," Caroline said.

I interjected a comment, "You can double that amount because nice is more important at this juncture. While I'll be in graduate school, I want to learn a little about living like a businessman."

Maggie looked at me and said, "Oh I forgot that you are the owner of the big brokerage firm in Nashville and have a nice income. Some of us don't have that."

"No need for sarcasm," I replied. "Don't worry about the money. You have a job and can contribute what you feel is appropriate. I'll cover the rest."

Caroline looked at Maggie and then looked at me, "That's very nice of you Jimmy. We will proceed with Jimmy's plan sweetie. It's a better plan than yours."

On that note, I took my leave of the two women, knowing that they had some things to talk about. I found my way to the stairs and headed for bed.

The next morning we were met by young woman named Margie. She had on a pink shirt, a gray skirt and a blue blazer. A businesswoman at 26. She had a lot of ideas about areas and apartments. She said she had talked to Caroline this morning early and had a very good idea where we should look. So we left Back Bay in search of a dwelling place somewhere between Harvard and the financial district in Boston.

By lunchtime, I was worn out. We had seen at least 10 apartments and none of them were quite up to Maggie's standard. I suggested we get a bite to eat and regroup.

"The next building I want to show you is on Quesenbury Street. It has two bedrooms and a bath, plus the laundry facility is on the same floor," Margie explained. "It's on the Red line so Jimmy can go one way and you can go the other. It's in a very nice neighborhood and there's plenty to do in Kenmore. I think you will just love it."

"Sounds great to me. I'm sold!" I said with a sense of enthusiasm in my voice.

We saw Margie's suggested apartment first. It was in a very nice building, clean and fresh looking and it had a small elevator that worked. It was a corner unit with lots of windows and light. It had two nice size bedrooms. The living room was large and the kitchen was more than adequate. I really liked it, but Maggie wasn't sure. Naturally, we set off to see some more units. We saw six more apartments before Margie dropped us off at Caroline's house. We agreed to meet the next morning at 9 AM for more looking.

Caroline greeted us at the door, "how did it go? Did you see anything you like?"

"We saw 16 apartments and of those, I liked 10. Maggie on the other hand liked one, maybe."

"It wasn't that bad. I liked three, maybe."

That night, Ed and Caroline took us to a steakhouse on Boylston Street called Abe and Louis's. I had a rib eye, baked potato and asparagus, which was delicious. Plus I had a great conversation with Ed about the brokerage business and money management. He was the national sales manager for Putnam and had actually visited JL Bradford. He said he had met my father and my grandfather and felt they were fine gentlemen. I was on my best behavior so that I wouldn't disabuse him of that notion. For some reason I thought I needed someone to put in a good word for me with Maggie's mother. The look she had given me in Richmond was still a little unsettling.

All in all, it was a great evening and Maggie seemed excited about the way things were going. So was I.

The next morning we met Margie and looked at about 10 more apartments. Over lunch, Maggie and I decided to take apartment G2 on Quesenberry. We signed all the papers and I gave Margie the deposit check. She then took us back to the apartment so that Maggie could decide about furniture. I have a desk that I was going to take and Mary Lynn said that I could have the sofa in the den since she needed a new one. Maggie was happy with that, but she seemed overly concerned about the beds. I said I wanted a king-size if it would fit and the two women decided that it would. Maggie said she would take the smaller of the two rooms, thus a queen-size would do for her.

Margie looked at us with a strange expression on her face, "You two are not a couple?"

"We have a strange relationship," Maggie said. "We are great friends and we are trying to figure out the rest of our relationship. For the moment, we're roommates. We'll have to see how it goes."

I just shrugged my shoulders, gave Margie a smile and let them both continue to talk about furniture and the way it should be arranged. For some reason, again not completely understood by me, I felt very good about the situation, that being my relationship with Maggie. I really liked her and was beginning to have true feelings for her.

That night, we again had dinner with Ed and Caroline. We had Italian at the Via Matta on the Boston Commons. Although the food was advertised as being straight from Tuscany, it was pretty ordinary Italian food. Nonetheless, it was a great evening. Ed filled me in on his time at Harvard and told me what to expect from the MBA program. It was very enlightening.

Maggie and Caroline talked about furniture. Caroline thought that Maggie should go to buy the beds and some of the other things we might need. These folks were really helpful. I liked them immensely and they seemed to like me. I was still hunting for that recommendation.

The next day we went furniture shopping, managed to spend several thousand dollars and arranged for the furniture to be delivered on July 1, when we took possession of the apartment.

Ed and Caroline were busy that evening, so Maggie and I were on our own. We found a small intimate restaurant on Columbus Avenue by the name of Coda. The service was slow which suited us just fine as we were in no hurry. We enjoyed an evening together without the pressure of school, parents, relatives, and friends. It was really refreshing, like we were really connecting.

"Today, it felt more like I was a new husband than a roommate."

"I know! The sales girl asked me how long we've been married. I told her we were not married, but we were moving in together. She smiled at me and wished me luck. I thought it was pretty funny."

"What was pretty funny? Was it the sales girl or was it the fact that we're just roommates?"

"The whole thing! Deciding to move in together, deciding we needed two bedrooms so we could pretend to be roommates, coming to Boston and staying with my aunt, looking at apartments together, buying furniture together; it was all just so bizarre."

"Can I go back to something you said? Pretending we're roommates; are we pretending?"

"Well Jimmy Joe, of course we're pretending. I couldn't very well tell my mother and my aunt that we were a couple, now could I."

"Your mother did pose the question."

"See what I mean."

"I really am glad that you cleared that up for me."

Of course I was really confused, but I decided that I would just go with the flow. Anytime I tried to control a relationship with a girl, it turned into a disaster. I really liked Maggie; I liked everything about her. She was smart, beautiful, opinionated, sometimes forceful and always ready to try something new. I would wait on the sex thing. It would happen when the time was right. The real question was whether this was actually me thinking about these things. The next few years in Boston were going to be truly great.

We got up early the next morning and drove back to Richmond. I needed to go back to Nashville to get a few things and to figure out the logistics of how we were going to get our stuff to Boston. I decided to rent a small U-Haul truck and tow my car behind it. Why not make it a real adventure. By the time I got my other things in Charlottesville, I would use about a quarter of the truck. I had this feeling that the remainder of the space would just barely accommodate all that Maggie wanted to bring.

I left on Friday, June 27 and truly looked like a vagabond. Trip and Mary Lynn were on hand to wish me a safe trip and off I went.

I was not used to driving a truck and I found it bumpy, uncomfortable and tedious. I had to remember that my car was tethered to the back of the truck. So for the first hundred miles of the trip I stayed in the right-hand lane. I was adventuresome only a few times. It was just too nerve-racking so I stayed in the right-hand lane. Finally I was in

Virginia and I stopped at a McDonald's with a large parking lot in the rear. I took up a few spaces so I wouldn't get blocked in and it would not be too difficult to set out again. I'd been driving for about seven hours and with the time change it was about 2:30.

I had a Big Mac, a quarter-pounder with cheese, a large fry and a Diet Coke. Then I got a large coffee to go. I was ready to get going by 3:30. Five hours later, I was at the junction of I-81 and I-64. I was exhausted and decided to spend the night in the Days Inn with a large parking lot. I ordered a pizza, ate most of it, and went to bed. The next day I pulled up in front of Maggie's house and found that there was no place to park.

The street was narrow, but Maggie's dad said to double-park and then we could load it. Maggie had arranged for a couple of big fellows to help with getting her stuff into the truck. As I expected, it took the remaining portion of the space in the truck. We had a few discussions about the necessity of bringing all the stuff, and I lost all of the skirmishes. Someday I would learn, but today was not the day.

Since we didn't have any place to park the truck with the car on the back and it was only 3 o'clock in the afternoon, we decided to drive a couple of hours to the outskirts of DC and find a motel with a large parking lot.

We spent the night in a Holiday Inn near Springfield, so there was every fast food restaurant imaginable. We walked to a Wendy's and ate burgers, fries, and salads. About the best I can say is that it was filling.

105

When we got back to the motel, I decided that it was very important for me to check the rig. Everything was locked up tight and looked to me as if it would be okay for the night.

As I walked to our room, I wondered what the sleeping arrangements would be given our conversation on the road. She had really not come out and said that we would become a couple, but there were certainly enough hints. Maybe it was just wishful thinking on my part. I really liked Maggie, more than any girl I had ever been with. We knew each other for the two semesters of our fourth year. In the spring semester, we were hanging together regularly.

I opened the door to the room. Maggie was nowhere in sight. She was probably in the bathroom.

"Maggie, are you in there?"

"Yes, do you need to get in here?"

"No, I just wondered where you were."

I settled on one of the beds, found the remote, and clicked on the television. Cheer's was on and I settled in to watch Sam and Diane go through their on-again off-again romance. My favorite character was the coach. I also liked the banter between Norm and Cliff. I watched the entire show. What was she doing in there?

Finally, she called to me through the door, "Jimmy Joe, turn off the light." Being an obedient man, I reached up and turned off the lamp as well as the television.

"Are they off?"

"Yes my love!"

She opened the door to the bathroom, the light was still on, and she had on a sheer negligée and a white bodysuit with lace. Was that a garter? Was she trying to seduce me? Stop asking yourself stupid questions. The slenderness of her waist emphasized the fullness of her breasts and her thighs were tanned and muscled. Her cheeks were very flushed and her eyelids dripped over eyes leaden with lust.

"You are the most beautiful creature on this earth. I am breathless, overwhelmed, at how beautiful you are."

She came toward me and I quickly shed every piece of clothing I had on. My penis was erect and pulsing with every beat of my heart. I stood to meet her. I put my arms around her and she folded into me so naturally that it seemed like we had been together for a lifetime. I was in new territory for me. I'd never felt these emotions before. We kissed and I was on fire.

I slowly removed the negligée and fumbled with the bodysuit before I found the zipper in the back. Her skin was like satin, her breasts were full and her nipples were erect. I couldn't help but kiss each one. As I slid the bodysuit down, I kissed her tummy, her navel, nuzzled the light hair covering her vagina and kissed her thighs.

We fell on the bed and kissed passionately.

"I want you now, right now," Maggie gasped.

"Slow down, we have all night. Let's enjoy this moment." Was I really saying this? I put my hand between her legs and she was wet.

I eased over, protection in place, and placed the tip of my penis into her vagina. "I don't want to hurt you Maggie, so please tell me if it hurts and I'll stop."

"It feels okay so far." I kept going ever so slowly. "Uh, that hurt. It feels wetter and warmer. It's stopped hurting."

I went further and deeper. Everything was okay. Maggie was holding on to me as if her life depended on it. I went faster and she got into the rhythm. It was glorious.

In the aftermath, I was exhausted, but Maggie was concerned about the mess. I thought the mess was wonderful and told her so. There was blood on the sheets.

"You like the mess because you didn't think I was a virgin?"

"Oh no, I knew you were a virgin or at least I thought you were, but you know, it's like a rite of passage, something that happens only once in life, and you have to enjoy every part of it, including the messy parts. I just love it!"

"Why Jimmy Joe that's very romantic. You seem to think we're going to be together forever."

"I do think that!"

Maggie moved to the other bed while I stayed in the mess for a while. I moved over to the other bed and we held on to each other the rest of the night.

Early in the morning, we made love again and this time I made sure that she had an orgasm. "So that's what all the fuss is about. That was wonderful. I want to have more of those." We fell back to sleep for another hour.

We were back on the road bumping along to Boston. It would take us about eight hours, perhaps a little longer due to the fact that we were in a truck hauling an automobile behind. I was getting a little more comfortable with the driving. We finally got to Boston around 7 PM. I called the moving guys who were going to help us unload the truck and they told me they would see me at 8 AM the next day. What was I going to do with the truck and my car for the next 13 hours?

Maggie called Caroline to ask her for advice. Ed got on the phone and told us to bring the truck to the church near their house in Back Bay. We could park the rig in the lot and walk over to their house. What wonderful people! We were saved again from our own poor planning.

Amazingly, three guys were at our building promptly at 8 AM. They had the truck unloaded by 10 AM and they helped me get my car off the trailer. By noon, I had turned in the truck and Maggie and I headed back to our new home. It was exciting to unpack our things and for Maggie to decide where things were to go.

All the items we had purchased earlier were delivered. Maggie had a list of all the stuff and she checked it twice. Two of the delivery guys set up our beds, Maggie found the linens, and made the beds. I was more than ready to try out this new mattress, but there was much left to be done. I was finding out very quickly that Maggie was a task master. Also, she was very fastidious. She really liked giving orders and when I looked at her beautiful face I was willing to take them. We actually had a good time playing house. I was truly in a relationship and didn't know how it happened. Talk about clueless, that was me.

Maggie started her job at Putnam which left me to my own devices. I puttered around the apartment for a few days; got back in to the routine of running; and found a few cool bars in the neighborhood. I also found a Chinese takeout that was pretty good.

Out of sheer boredom, I decided to go over to the business school to check things out. I located Aldrich Hall, which is the main classroom building for the MBA program. Every detail of its three floors of amphitheater-style classrooms was painstakingly designed to encourage interaction among students that is the hallmark of the case method at Harvard. Recent technology updates ensured the highest level of innovation within the classroom.

I also found Baker Library, with its signature bell tower and columned facade facing the Charles River, the physical and intellectual heart of the campus. The world's largest business library, with more than 700,000+ volumes spanning seven centuries, is a resource for the Harvard Business School community and scholars worldwide. I found myself comparing these sights with the Virginia I so loved. They had their differences, but the thrill of new insights and ways of thinking seemed to be as present here similarly to the University.

Batten Hall is home to the Harvard Innovation Lab, or i-lab, which is designed to foster team-based entrepreneurial activities and to deepen interactions among students, faculty, and entrepreneurs across Harvard University and the Boston business community. The i-lab hosts lectures, panel discussions, and presentations that are open to the public, as well as networking events for student teams, local businesses and interested individuals.

Section mates take their first-year classes together, sharing cases, classroom facilities, and their own dedicated team of faculty. Section faculties teach and manage the learning environment, using their own research and real-world experience to introduce innovative ideas and approaches to learning. In turn, students exercise their team-building and management skills to develop protocols for effective learning and shape the distinctive norms and personality of their sections.

First Year Classes:

Finance 1

Financial Reporting and Control

Leadership and Organizational Behavior

Marketing

Technology and Operations

Field 1

This was going to be a challenging year.

Maggie and I were both busy people. She found herself working until 6 or 6:30 every day and I was with my section mates until 7 or 8 working on cases and problems. Our schedule led to late dinners and falling into bed exhausted only to awaken at 6:30 AM to start another day. We made up for things on the week end, although we had chores to do such as wash clothes, change the bed and clean a little.

We didn't travel for Thanksgiving or Christmas since Maggie was still the low person on the totem pole. She did get a promotion in early January and became an inside sales person. She had to take several exams for various licenses. She fretted over them, but passed with flying colors. More credentials for my fabulous girlfriend. She could work for the firm in Nashville, unless she became my wife.

I was thinking more and more about nailing down our relationship, but fear kept me from doing anything at the moment. Still, I did not want to lose her and she was out in the environs of Boston meeting smart people who were doing business. I was just a student.

My section mates and I did well both the first and second semesters. Our projects were well received and our grades were excellent. We worked on a field project in the summer and got ready for a tougher environment in the fall. Maggie became the inside sales rep for the DC area which included Southern Maryland and Northern Virginia. She was really excited about this assignment. The field rep was also a woman by the name of Angie Clark. They seemed to instantly bond and worked extremely well together.

I went to Nashville in June to attend the spring partners meeting and check up on the value of my interest in the firm. Trip was pleased that I was doing well at school but he seemed to be particularly proud of Maggie for passing her exams and becoming a mutual fund wholesaler.

"I knew that girl had the business in her blood," Trip said.

"Actually, she has an uncle who works for Putnam," I replied.

"Yes, I know Ed Warren. He is a really good guy and knows his stuff. He's been to visit us several times. We actually do a lot of the Putnam funds. Our brokers seem to really like the wholesaler and their funds have performed well."

"Speaking of performance how is the firm doing?"

"Well, 1987 was a tough year. You probably noticed, because the partner point distribution was down about 50%. But 1988 is shaping up to be a much better year. We'll get close to the 1986 level of earnings. Maybe a little better if things go as I expect. I'm glad you're interested Jimmy. Have you made any plans about what you're going to do after graduate school?"

"Eventually I want to join the firm. But I want to do something first that will give me some experience so that these guys have a little respect for me and don't look at me just as the boss's son."

"When you get closer to graduation, give Bill Bonner a call. He'll hook you up with something in Washington that will give you some really great experience. Maybe you can even work for him."

"Bill is crazy Trip."

"Like a fox, but he can get things done that no other guy up there can. He'll teach you some things that no one else can."

"Thanks for the advice. I'll take it!"

After seeing the rest of my family, I went back to Boston with a plan for the future. Part of the plan was to ask Maggie to marry me. I had this vision of a truly great life that would only work if Maggie was part of it. It was a really worthwhile trip.

Ed Warren set me up with a friend in the wholesale jewelry business, who would give me a real good deal. He advised me to take Maggie with me so that I would end up with a ring she liked. The Randolph girls were sometimes hard to please, particularly in jewelry, and it would be better in the long run if she had a choice. All of this was great advice.

On a Saturday in late July, I asked Maggie to join me on an excursion to go look for some jewelry.

"Is it your mom's birthday?"

"Gosh I don't think I remember Mary Lynn's birthday."

"Well what's it for?"

"What does it matter? Let's just go and have some fun."

We went to the address that Ed had given me. It didn't look like any jewelry store I had ever seen. But I trusted Ed, so we went inside.

I asked for Benny LaRusso. He came out of the back and said, "Ah, you are Ed's friend."

"Yes I am. I'm Jim Jeter and this is Maggie Randolph."

"You want to see some wedding rings right and an engagement ring, right?"

Maggie took a step back, her eyes opened wide and her mouth opened, but no words came out.

Benny smiled. "A little surprise for the young lady."

"I guess so," I said.

"Well let's get started."

Maggie finally said something, "Can we have a moment?"

We moved back a couple of steps and she turned to me, "are you asking me to marry you?"

"Not yet, but I plan to do it soon. I just want to get an idea of what kind of ring you would like. I thought we would take that part of it out of the equation."

She actually smiled at me and we went back to talk to Benny LaRusso. After two hours or more, Maggie finally settled on a ring set that she liked very much. I asked Benny if he could size the rings to fit Maggie. He said he could, but I would need to pay him first. We settled on the price, I paid him, and he said I could pick up the rings Wednesday.

Maggie was home early on Wednesday and was waiting nervously for me. I gave her a kiss and acted as if it was just another day.

"Did you get them?"

"I did indeed!"

"Can I see them?"

"No! I haven't asked you to marry me yet."

"I'm waiting," Maggie said in a singsong sort of voice.

"This isn't a very romantic place to do it."

But I got down on one knee fumbled around in my pocket for the box and looked up at Maggie. She had tears in her eyes and a smile on her face.

I took the ring out of the box, took her hand in mine, and asked her, "Maggie Randolph will you marry me, will you be my wife?"

"Yes, yes, I will marry you Jimmy Joe Jeter!"

I placed the ring on her finger. It fit perfectly and looked beautiful on her hand. I was a very happy guy. Maggie gave me a long kiss and then ran to find her phone. She needed to call her mom and several other people..

I called Mary Lynn and told her the news. She was delighted and shouted the news to Allie and Trip. Everyone got on an extension to talk to me, but it was clear that they wanted to talk to Maggie as well. Finally she came on the phone and they talked for 15 minutes. It was a great day.

Chapter 8

I had been talking non-stop for 2 hours. Rex was obviously ready for a break. He was probably 15-18 years older than me, but he had spent twice as many years in prison. There is no doubt that confinement and limits on your freedom take a toll on your health.

"I take it we have a ways to go Jimmy Joe, so I need to take a piss. You watch our things. I need it worse than you. I'm surprised my bladder has lasted this long," Rex said.

"OK, I'll wait here, but I got to' go too, so don't take so long."

He gave me the finger and ambled off.

He returned finally and I got my chance. I was about to pee in my pants.

When we were facing each other again, he wanted to know all about my wedding to the lovely Maggie Randolph. He had met Maggie and was incredulous that I had cheated on her. I was incredulous as well.

■■■

I graduated from Harvard in May 1988. I had an MBA and had a job. It wasn't much of a job, but it was what I wanted before I went to the family firm. I promised Big Jack that I would join the business at the appropriate time. Since I didn't have any experience, I didn't think I would have much respect from the older partners in the firm. I know that I can't avoid the specter of nepotism, but I want to negate it is much as possible.

So I was going to go to work for Bill Bonner, the recently elected Mayor of Nashville. I knew Bill very well and was well aware that he was nuts. But somehow he kept getting elected despite himself.

But first, I had to deal with my marriage to Maggie Randolph. Our date was set for July 23, 2014 at the St. Paul's Episcopal Church in Richmond. Maggie, her Mother and a wedding coordinator named Missy Bird were handling all of the arrangements, with the exception of my family, relatives and friends. Mary Lynn was in charge of that. Thank the Lord they had given her a job that would keep me out of trouble.

Mary Lynn had booked the rehearsal dinner with the Jefferson Hotel, which was a lovely older hotel on Franklin Street quite close to the church. It seemed sensible to me, but somehow Missy wasn't quite satisfied. Mary Lynn told her politely to "fuck off."

This was my first "in the middle" experience. Maggie told me that my mother was being uncooperative.

"I thought you gave her the job of planning the rehearsal dinner and taking care of all the guests on our side of the family. Am I wrong?"

"You're right, but Missy doesn't like the Jefferson."

"Why?"

"She couldn't really tell me why, it just seemed that she thought it was rather pedestrian for our wedding."

"Well you see, anything that's old, seems very important to us. Folks native to Nashville have an inferiority complex when it comes to Virginia and anything that has historical significance. All we have is Davy Crockett and that's not much. So give Mary Lynn the benefit of the doubt. It will be tasteful and extravagant. She's very good at that. Just tell Miss Missy that you are going to concede this point to my mom. This is a very awkward position for me because I seldom defend Mary Lynn."

Maggie finally gave in and went off to tell Missy.

The day drew nearer and I simply was ready for it to be over. There were numerous bridal showers and several cocktail events that were in our honor. Some were even enjoyable, but most were kind of boring. Maggie seemed to enjoy the attention and I was grateful that she was going to be my wife and the mother of my children. I have grown to love her with all my being. I had met her by chance on the Lawn of the University and our friendship grew from there. I considered it a miracle and I wasn't going to do anything to harm this beautiful romance.

Finally Saturday, July 23 dawned with beautiful sunshine and a cloudless sky. I had made it through an unbelievable bachelor's party. A number of my fraternity brothers were there along with my good friends Billy Corbett and Bobby Gibbs. To this day I don't remember getting back to my hotel room but when I came to on the morning of my marriage, I found that the front of my body had been dyed purple and obscene words were written all over my back. My fraternity brother, Eddie Underwood, was in his third year of medical school at Medical College of Virginia. He was the source of the purple dye. I would remember him for weeks.

As expected, the rehearsal dinner was spectacular. Mary Lynn had done an excellent job with the venue, the decoration of the room and the menu. Her seating chart put people in just the right places. Maggie told Mary Lynn that no one could've done a better job than she and I was delighted. The two of them seemed to bond after that event.

The wedding itself went off without a hitch. St. Paul's Church was filled with the Randolph family and friends as well as a number of people from Nashville who were friends of Mary Lynn and Trip. Of course my fraternity brothers were there in force along with girlfriends and several wives. I was happy to see them all, even Eddie Underwood. He took one look at me in my morning suit and gave a great guffaw.

"I can't wait for Maggie to see my art work," Eddie said.

"I'm sure she'll love it," I replied with a wink.

My sister Allie was a bridesmaid and her friend, Katie, was lurking in the background. Bobby Gibbs was following her around like a lost puppy. While that made me sad, I didn't reflect on it very much and didn't let it spoil my happiness.

Trip was my best man; after all he is my father. He seemed delighted with the task and I was happy I had not disappointed him.

As we stood at the front of the church, I was nervous with the anticipation of seeing my beautiful bride. When she appeared at the back of the church, it took my breath away. She was absolutely the most beautiful creature I had ever seen in my life. All were standing as she walked down the aisle and everyone saw how beautiful she was. It was truly exhilarating and I couldn't believe my good fortune for having fallen in love with this lovely woman.

In about 30 minutes, we were married and were walking down the aisle as man and wife to the congratulations from all around us. What a wonderful day; what a wonderful day indeed.

The rest of the happenings was a blur. There was the obligatory reception and dinner held at the Commonwealth Club. We had all the appropriate toasts, including a few drunken ones that were hilarious. For myself I avoided all alcohol. My stomach was still a little queasy from my adventure the night before. We also had the traditional dance and Maggie danced with both her father and mine. We finally left for the bridal suite at the Jefferson Hotel.

"Your body is purple! How did that happen?"

"My Sigma Chi brothers got overly creative."

"With all those words on your back, I'm not swimming with you."

"But you'll do everything else?"

"Oh, yes!"

Maggie and I left Richmond the next day, bound for Jamaica. We were booked for 6 days at the Couples San Souci, an all-inclusive resort in Ocho Rios. We had a great time. Top shelf whiskey, good food and plenty of it, and an absolutely gorgeous beach made for a wonderful honeymoon. We had a room that was fairly close to the ocean, at least we could hear the waves hitting the beach, and we made love with our door open and the gentle breeze blowing over us. Now that we were married, our intimacy was more serene and gentle. I liked it very much, I felt fortunate to be married to Maggie Randolph.

We flew back to Nashville and arrived at my parents' house late in the afternoon on Saturday. We were going to stay with them for a couple of weeks while we looked for an apartment or a small house. Maggie was going to assume that responsibility since I was going to be busy getting acclimated to Bill Bonner and my job as liaison to the Nashville/Davidson County Council. Bill told me that he didn't know much about being mayor, so it was okay if I didn't know much about being liaison to the Council.

We were hoping that all of our things from Boston were in storage somewhere in Nashville. I had one suit with me and a navy blazer that would have to serve as my business attire for the next week or so. I was pretty sure I could squeeze in some time to do a little suit shopping in downtown Nashville over the next two weeks. I was truly looking forward to working with Bill Bonner. Trip actually liked Bonner and was happy that I was working for him. Bill was in a little hot water over the past several years and Trip continued to support him.

Chapter 9

William Henry Bonner, Jr. was a native of Nashville and loved the city. He went to college at Middle Tennessee State University in Murfreesboro and received his Masters' degree from Peabody College in Nashville. He served as a member of the Tennessee House of Representatives and both taught and coached at Nashville's Trevecca Nazarene College. He also received his law degree from the YMCA Night Law School of Nashville in 1978. In that same year, he decided to run in the Democratic primary against Fifth District Congressman Clifford Allen. He won the election and was subsequently reelected four times to Congress.

In 1987, Bill decided to run for the mayor's job in Nashville. However, there had been recent disclosures about his personal finances and his relationship with a government contractor, named James W. Parham. In fact, there was talk of amending the city charter so that current mayor Richard Fuller, Bill's main mentor, could run for a fourth term. But the truth is, Fuller wanted to be governor and he wanted Bill to be mayor.

"There are those who are comfortable with Bonner in Congress, but they don't want him as mayor," said James J Jeter, senior partner at JL Bradford & Company. "I guess they feel that he can't do much harm as one of 435 yo-yos up in Congress as he can if he were in charge of running the city."

Bill is a gifted politician who never seems to tire of campaigning, even when there's no one to campaign against. He is noted as a highly conscientious problem solver for residents of his district.

One person who asked for help was the aforementioned James Parham, a flashy, red bearded businessman who owned American Specialty Products, a Nashville company that supplied material to the Defense Department. Bill acknowledged that he untangled some red tape in 1980 to expedite an overdue $70,000 payment that the Defense Department owed ASP. After that, the two men and their wives became good friends. Parham asked for other favors, and the congressmen complied.

Bill acknowledged that he flew to Philadelphia and Los Angeles with Parham at the contractor's expense to introduce them to an Army general and to executives of Hughes Aircraft Corporation. Furthermore, he said that he had accepted expensive goods from Parham, including a $1200 tailor-made suit.

Parham has told federal prosecutors that he channeled more than $2000 a month in bribes to Bonner through his wife over a 23 month time frame for the congressmen's help in getting business for his company. He gave that version of events in 1983, when he was under investigation for supplying the Defense Department with substandard metals that were used for doors on underground silos at a nuclear weapons testing site in New Mexico. The information was reportedly given in exchange for a promise that he would not have to go to prison.

What few people knew was that Bonner who earned a mere $10,500 in 1978, the year he was elected to Congress, was on his way to becoming a millionaire, at least on paper. That information came out of a newspaper article by the Nashville Tennessean. The article suggests that Bill acquired real estate holdings worth at least $2 million. In one instance, for a five dollar investment, Bonner was given an interest potentially worth $3.6 million in an $18 million Radisson hotel development. In another case for a $50 investment, he was given a 5% interest worth $250,000 in a $5 million restaurant development by Shoney's Inc., a national restaurant company headquartered in Nashville. Other allegations are that he funneled more than $300,000 in campaign contributions to companies he created and owned. Supposedly, the payments were made under a deal in which the campaign leased computer equipment and rented an office building from the firms that he owned. The last allegation was that he accepted $50,000 from Parham.

"The reaction in the public mind is that Bonner has been hassled, hounded, and mistreated," said prominent Nashville attorney Joseph Lambert. "But right now, if an indictment comes along, then I think Bonner is through. I don't think he could get elected to anything in this town. That's a hard way to put it but I think it's true."

Bill may have been crippled, but he wasn't dead. He began to fight back in the only way he knew. He appealed directly to the people. At a news conference, Bonner denied the bribery charges. He indicated that his wife, Beverly Fowler Bonner, received $50,000 from Parham for some legal work that she did for his firm. He went on to say that Parham had threatened to make bribery allegations unless Bonner put pressure on authorities to end the substandard metals probe.

"He wanted help, he demanded help and then made the threats," Bonner said. "Neither my wife nor I had done anything wrong. With those threats we both became aware that he had serious problems," insisted Bonner.

Bill did divest himself of the interests in the hotel and restaurant, and then released his tax returns. They showed his net worth to be $165,500.

Charges never materialized and an indictment was not handed down. The people of Nashville were relieved. Bill won the job of mayor by defeating Phil Breeden in a runoff election. Six people ran for the job initially, Bill was the leading vote getter, but he didn't have 50% of the vote. Thus, the runoff.

He was sworn in on January 19, 1988. He put together a small team that had been with him in Congress, but he needed someone who was from Nashville, who was young and energetic, and had connections in the community. I think my dad whispered in Bonner's ear that I would be available in the summer after finishing my degree and getting married. My dad kept me apprised of all the shenanigans going on in Nashville around Bill. For some reason, Trip really liked him. I was surprised at myself for that fact alone didn't turn me off.

But I really liked Bill myself and thought he could teach me a lot about people and how to deal with them. This was not my strong suit, although I didn't tell him that because he wanted me to schmooze the council. I could learn.

"Hell Jimmy, were all learning as we go. And we actually are doing a pretty good job. But I need a Nashville guy with your connections."

I took the job without batting an eye and was going to have quite an adventure.

On June 28, 1962, the voters of the city and the county voted in favor of the creation of a metropolitan government. Beverly Briley was elected the first Mayor in November and the Metropolitan Government of Nashville and Davidson County was implemented on April 1, 1963.

Nashville became the national pioneer in metropolitan organization. Although other cities had partial consolidation, Nashville was the first city in the country to achieve true consolidation. Today, there are some 14 consolidated governments in the United States out of over 3,100 county units. Each successful consolidation has used the 1962 Nashville charter as a model.

Metropolitan government is a consolidation of two governments rather than the county taking over the city or the city taking over the county government. It is, in reality, a third form of local government with a range of options and flexibility to provide for population shifts to the suburbs. The Metropolitan Charter provides a mechanism for changes to be made in the document through the Charter Revision Commission. Since 1962, the Charter has been amended for several housekeeping measures, but there has not been a major, comprehensive revision of the Charter since its adoption.

The Mayor is the chief executive. There are thirty-two or so departments that report to the mayor. Also, all legislation passed by the council is sent to the Mayor for approval. The Mayor must approve or disapprove legislation before the next Council meeting. If the Mayor does not veto a bill the Mayor's signature is the final step of the legislative process before the bill becomes effective. If a piece of legislation is passed by the Council, but the Mayor simply refuses to sign it, the legislation becomes effective without his signature. The Mayor can veto a bill.

Legislation originates from three different sources: the Metropolitan Department of Law, the Council Office, and other departments within the city. The Council Office prepares legislation that is requested directly by a Council member. Regardless of its origination, at least one member of the Council must sign the bill or resolution before it can be filed with the Metropolitan Clerk's Office.

My official title was Special Assistant to the Mayor for Legislative Affairs. This meant that I had to get to know all 40 members of the Metropolitan Council. There are 5 at-large members and 35 district members. The presiding officer is the Vice Mayor, who is elected at-large by the citizens of Nashville and Davidson County. Members are elected to serve a term of four years. I also had to be aware of legislation that was moving through the process so the mayor could determine his position in advance. I would learn that sometimes he liked to veto a bill just to jerk someone's chain.

By Charter the regular meetings of the Council are held on the first and third Tuesdays of every month. The meetings are held in the David Scobey Council Chamber in the Historic Metro Courthouse.

When I arrived on Monday morning, I was met by Jason Holdeman, the Mayor's Chief of Staff. He took me to my office, gave me a brief lesson on how to use the phone, and then introduced me to Janet Whitaker, who served as the administrative assistant to Jason and myself. She would be someone to know well, since she had been with the city for 15 years. Jason told me that I would have a brief meeting with Bill at around 10 o'clock and then I would have lunch with Chris Harman, the vice Mayor. This was a lot to absorb, but I was ready.

"Welcome Jimmy Joe, it's great to see you again," said a grinning Bill Bonner. "Are you getting settled in?"

"Yes I am. It looks like I'll have plenty to do."

"That's true! Tomorrow night will be your first Council meeting and you'll learn a lot there. Take Janet with you and she will introduce you to people. She knows a lot about what goes on down there and will be happy to explain it all to you. Then you can begin to use your connections to help us out for some of the things we want to get accomplished. We need to fight drugs, crime and do something about all the people that are hungry in this town. Lots of work to do Jimmy Joe and sometimes the Council is not very cooperative. It'll be your job to get them all to buy into what we're trying to accomplish. Don't get intimidated, they'll respect you, maybe more than me."

"I doubt that Mr. Mayor. You are very popular with people and I know the Council recognizes that."

Jason and I left the meeting and walked back to my office. "Bill really likes you Jim."

"I think it's my dad that he really likes. He may be a little disappointed there, because my dad only does things that benefit him and the firm. He's a pretty typical self-centered businessman. I'm pretty realistic when it comes to him. But I'll give it all I have."

My lunch with the Vice Mayor went very well. He explained to me how his office worked as well as how he functioned in his role as the presiding officer of the Council. This was truly a powerful position since he enforced the rules and decided all procedural issues. These were major factors in legislation getting to a vote. My education had begun.

When I found my office again, Janet had put a lot of reading material on my desk.

"You should read all of this, study it thoroughly and then tomorrow we can discuss it all."

"Janet, the mayor said that you would be attending the Council meeting with me tomorrow night to explain to me what was going on."

"Okay that'll be fine."

"You know it seems to me that you are more qualified for this job than I am."

"It's nice of you to say that, but I don't have the connections you have and my name is not Jeter. Your grandfather and your father are well respected and well known in this town. And you will be well known soon."

"Well I really appreciate your help Janet."

My first evening at the council meeting was very exciting for me. Chris Harman, the vice-Mayor, introduced me to a group of six members. All of them knew my father and several new my grandfather. They all had kind things to say about my family and they welcomed me to the trenches of city government.

Then Janet took over and we met at least a dozen members of the Council. Also, I met several people who served as Chief of Staff for the members. Janet told me that I would need to know all 40 of the Chiefs. They control access to their members and have a great deal of influence. Those were the folks that I really wanted to meet and get to know well. I asked Janet if we had a list of all these people and she said we did.

"The next thing I need to find out is where all these people hang out and drink," I said to Janet.

She smiled at me and said, "That would be Dick's Last Resort or Rock-Bottom Brewery. Rock-bottom is the favorite, but it's close to the arenas so it depends on who's playing. If there is a game, then Dick's becomes the favorite."

"You are a wealth of information. You're going to be my best friend and confidant. That is, if it's all right with you."

Again I got that nice smile. "I think that will work."

By the next Council meeting I had studied the names of all the Chiefs and which member they were associated with.

I'd also been drinking with 5 to 6 of this group and was getting to know them pretty well. They seemed to accept me into their group, particularly when I was buying the beer. I was really going to like this job.

On the home front, Maggie, with Mary Lynn's help, had found two places she really liked, both of them in Green Hills. One was in the Hillsboro Village Area and one was on Woodmont Blvd.

"I will not make this decision without you. Remember your pledge that we were going to be a team. I'm holding you to it. That's the end of the discussion."

"Okay, I get it; when do you want to go see them?"

"We have an appointment with the realtor at 2 PM to see both units. Once we decide which one we want, then we'll have to give them a down payment or at least a deposit until we close. One of the places is empty, so we could probably close on that pretty fast."

"Well I like that one best already. I'm already tired of living with Trip and Mary Lynn. I'll see you at 2 o'clock. Where do we meet?" She told me.

We both decided that we liked the one on Woodmont Boulevard. The realtor was happy with the choice because this was the unit that was empty. Mary Lynn approved of the address and was already offering decorating ideas. Why do all women seem to think they are great decorators? I hoped this was not going to lead to any hurt feelings or arguments. Mary Lynn could be very pushy, but I felt like that Maggie could hold her own if this resulted in a tug-of-war. This was going to be a good place to live with over 1200sf, which was much bigger than our Boston apartment.

I could not believe my life. I was married to a beautiful woman and I had a job that I loved. I was working for a powerful man who was nuts and provided a new dawn every day. My wife was exciting, intelligent, sexy and caring. Lots would happen to me in the future, but this was a great part of my life.

One afternoon in early 1989 I got a call from Bill Bonner. "Jimmy, can you come up to my office about 5:30 PM? I have something I want to talk to you about. Don't tell anyone else about this meeting."

"I'll see you then." To say that I was intrigued was clearly an understatement. Bill was strange and often had bizarre requests, but I expected this one to be a little better than usual.

At the appointed time, I went to meet the Mayor. "Jimmy, have I ever told you about that time I went undercover when I was in Congress. I was concerned about poverty. So on one of the recesses we had in Congress, I grew me a beard. It didn't take very long. I put on some old tattered clothes and went out to be among the poor. I went to the rescue mission over on Lafayette Street. I had a meal there among the folks; I listened to what they had to say; and then I spent the night. I had breakfast with everybody the next morning and then I went out on the streets to hang out. I learned a lot about how people think that I have done. From then on I waged a battle against poverty."

"That was truly brave. I'm sure you did learn a lot"

"Well Jimmy, I feel as if I have to come "face to face" with the enemy again. I want to go undercover to see how easy it is to buy illegal drugs in our city. I'll wear a fake beard and dark glasses and I'll be accompanied on the trip by a police informant and his girlfriend, who are drug addicts. You're a young guy and can assume the role of an addict pretty easily. So I want you to come with me. A couple of undercover cops will be covering our back."

"Well I guess I have to do it. It's my job to support the Mayor. When are we going to do it?"

"Saturday night!"

I was a little uneasy as I headed home that evening. Maggie commented on my being a little late. I told her about my meeting with Bill.

"You are going to do what? Have you lost your mind? I know he is crazy, but are you buying into his insanity? You could be killed."

I assured her that we would be fine. She was still telling me that I was an idiot when Bill arrived to pick me up. He drove an old pickup truck and there were several Nashville vice officers behind us.

We meet Bear and Tammy in a joint over in East Nashville. Bear had on a Tennessee Orange hoodie. He was average size, had a runny nose that he wiped on his sleeve and he kept looking around to see if anyone was watching. Tammy had stringy, dirty blond hair, had on a blue long sleeve t-shirt and twitched constantly. I had the look of a typical urban drug buyer with jeans, flip flops and a

Grateful Dead t-shirt. The only one out of place was Bill with that stupid fake beard and wraparound sunglasses.

"There's a dude that's gonna' meet us out back. I want him to do the talking." He pointed at me. "You've done this before. I can tell it."

"I'm taking the 5th."

"Don't blame you."

"I have to be there!" Bill says excitedly.

"Yeah man, don't get excited. You can be there. Just stand sort of behind your man here. That beard doesn't look so good."

I gave Bill the eye and then asked, "What time is this guy supposed to show?"

"He'll be here in about five minutes. Pour me another beer from that pitcher. I am thirsty and pour Tammy another one."

We waited a good 15 minutes. Finally, a guy came in the back door and pulled on his earlobe. Apparently that was our sign. We got up and headed to the back door.

Outside there were three black dudes and I could see one at the end of the alley that was the lookout.

I stood with Bear at the front of our little group and looked the three guys over. For a short time, it was a staring match.

The short muscular black guy looked at me and said, "what are you looking for?"

"Smack!"

"Ain't got any smack."

"I told Bear that I was looking for smack."

"Well look man all I got is blow."

"Any good?"

"What you think man, I'd sell bad shit?"

"No not at all. You got four bags?'

"You got $180?"

The transaction was completed and we all walked back in the bar. As I sat down in my chair, I began to tremble a little. We finished the pitcher, bought another for Bear and Tammy, and left.

"Where are the vice-cops Bill. I want to get this shit out of my pockets?"

"No I want to keep it to show the press. I got to have some evidence or they won't believe me."

"Take off that beard, okay, you take the blow."

About that time, flashing lights appeared in my rearview mirror and the cops pulled us over. Two uniforms got out of the car, drew their guns, and started to shout, "Get out of the car! Get out of the car!"

"This is not good Bill!!"

"They will recognize me and know that I'm the Mayor."

As we were both cuffed and bent over the back of the car: over the trunk of the car actually, I could hear Bill saying, "I'm the Mayor, I'm the Mayor!"

"And I'm the governor," responded the cop.

Finally the vice-cops showed up and we got everything cleared up. I didn't have to kill the Mayor this time.

Chapter 10

In May 1989, Maggie called me to tell me she had some news to share and could I come home soon. I tried to get her to tell me what the news was, but she wanted to share it in person. I didn't waste any time, I left the office immediately.

I came rushing through the door of our home. Maggie was sitting on the sofa in the living room. She had a smile on her face.

"Come sit on the sofa Jimmy Joe."

She never called me Jimmy Joe. My mind was racing through everything that could happen. But I didn't guess this, the actual event that Maggie was going to spring on me.

"Jimmy, you remember when we were talking about my birth control pills, that they were making me feel bloated and I wanted to stop taking them. You said it was all right with you; just let you know that I'd stopped. Well I stopped and I'm letting you know. Actually I stopped three months ago and you have been very passionate. Our sex life has been wonderful and plentiful. You even told me my scent was better."

I must be dense because I still didn't get it. Then it struck me!

"Oh my God don't tell me you're…."

"That's right Jimmy Joe, the love of my life: I'm pregnant with your baby. Actually it's our baby."

"Oh Maggie, spectacular, that's wonderful, that's the best news I've ever had. I love you Maggie with all my heart."

I stood and helped her up from the sofa, then held her tight. I was the happiest man in Nashville. I kissed her passionately and then I touched her tummy.

"You're not showing anything. There's no little baby bump there yet. Do we know what it is?"

"It'll be another month or two before I start showing. Let's not tell anyone until we get through the next month or so just to make absolutely certain. Okay."

"It's fine with me sweetheart. Anything you want, I will do."

"And Jimmy Joe, let's agree to no more undercover work with the Mayor now that you are going to be a father, okay?" I smiled and agreed.

I was the luckiest man in Nashville as well.

In July of 1989, Bill asked me to join him in his office. We exchanged pleasantries and then he told he had served divorce papers on his third wife, Betty.

"Jimmy Joe, I have met the love of my life, Staci Deal. She's a country star and she can sing and do other things."

"Where did you meet her?"

"Chris introduced me. We were down at Spiffy's."

"Bill, you are making my job very difficult. You have to get serious about being Mayor. Harman wants to run for Mayor. He's making you look bad enough as it is."

"I'm in love Jimmy Joe and anyway, I'm not going to run again. I want you to come down to Spiffy's with me"

"I'll have to check with Maggie. She's pregnant you know and I don't like to leave her alone."

"Call her; I really want you to meet Staci. I'm going to give her this ring before the 7:30 show."

I called Maggie and told her the short version.

"Please don't get roped into anything dangerous."

"You mean more than going to Spiffys'"

We got there around 7. Bill went backstage. I found a table near the stage.

I was sipping a scotch and ice. Bill ordered a beer. The waitress was very solicitous to "Mr. Mayor."

"How'd it go?"

"It went fine. She's wearing the ring."

"Isn't this going to have an impact on your divorce? Isn't Betty embarrassed about this?"

"Aw, Betty's good. She's the one that wanted the divorce. She's got some hot young attorney friend that she's hooked up with. She wants out. He's got family money."

The Anorexic Assassin

The emcee came on stage and announced, "Our country crooner, Staci Deal, the Real Deal in country music."

Staci Deal, a 34 year-old country crooner, was sporting a spanking new 2.2-carat diamond, and announced to the world that she was going to marry the Mayor of Nashville, Mr. Bill Bonner.

With that Bill leapt onto the stage and as Staci began to sing he accompanied her on the harmonica.

There was a reporter there from the *Nashville Scene* as well as a photographer. They were taking pictures and notes as fast as they could.

But no one in Nashville was singing along. And when the reporter phoned her at home, Peel joked that he had caught the lovebirds at a "bad time," and she boasted of the Mayor's sexual stamina. During the telephone interview, she giggled and joked about their sexual prowess. At one point, Peel said Bonner remained amorous as long as seven hours.

"He's got great stamina. That's pretty good for a 46-year-old man," Deal said.

"Forty-five," Bonner corrected, talking on an extension.

Staci said publicity from her romance with Bill, who was still married, may be hurting her bookings. "If you think that I have become a big draw with all the publicity, that's not the case," she said. "If anything, I've probably lost some dates."

That did it. Like the strings on a country fiddle, the public could only be stretched so far. The Nashville Banner charged that Bonner had "turned the Mayor's office into a joke" and urged him to resign. Citizens appeared in ribald T-shirts about the pair's relationship. Nashville Tennessean columnist Larry Daughtrey wrote, "We were cheered by the seven-hour thing ourselves, since many skeptics...doubted that Bill Bonner ever worked at anything for as long as seven hours." And humorist Mike Price cracked, "If Nashville is a circus, why shouldn't the Mayor be a clown?"

Despite the uproar, Bill refused to step down, though he did announce at a press conference that he wouldn't run again next year. "The only people who don't make mistakes are in the cemetery," Bill told reporters. Staci was standing by his side as he also noted that they plan to marry in a private ceremony in Hawaii when his divorce comes through. Says Staci to anyone listening: "I don't need any votes, and he doesn't need any votes anymore, either." Staci also reiterated that her bookings had been hurt by the controversy. "If you think that I have become a big draw with all the publicity, that's not the case," she said. "Why can't you just leave us alone so we can enjoy the love we have for each other?"

Then the final straw blew into Nashville. Bill and Staci made a controversial appearance on the October 15, 1990 episode of *The Phil Donahue Show*. Staci was sporting the large rock, making their romance controversial, since Bill was still married to his third wife. He and Betty were still wrangling over some property. That was the reason Donahue wanted them on the show. Of course he asked Staci about the seven hours of intercourse she talked about with a Nashville reporter.

"My Billy boy is quite the stud. He has more stamina than any guy I've been with and that's saying a lot." Bill gave us that big Tennessee grin. Every person in Nashville cringed. But it only got worse.

The next part of the act was Bill playing harmonica, while Staci sang "Rocky Top," the state anthem of Tennessee.

This one was clearly on me since I had flown with them to LA. Jason Holderman had resigned six months earlier and Bill had appointed me his Chief of Staff. Janet Whitaker took my job, something that should've happened years earlier.

Chris Harman, who wanted to run for mayor, called me on the phone, "Jimmy Joe, how you let him be on that show is beyond me? He made every person in Nashville look like a bumpkin."

"He had his mind set on it. I told him not to let Staci talk so much and I certainly didn't want them to sing and play. I tell you Chris, I'll be happy when you're Mayor. This is my first and last foray into politics. I'm going to the private sector as fast as my legs will carry me."

After this disaster, my friend Bobby Gibbs called to give me a hard time. Bobby had finished his law school education at Vanderbilt University and was now working as an associate at Walker Landsman, Porter and Jones plc in the healthcare litigation group.

"Did you come up for air just to give me a hard time?" I asked.

"Who could pass up an opportunity like this? I have never met the guy, but he must be nuts. I couldn't believe the harmonica bit. Donahue was cracking up."

"Well Bobby, Bill is in love and he's also nuts. The combination is driving me crazy. I mean I thought the undercover drug buy was crazy enough, but the show put the finishing touches on this administration. But I'll tell you, the show at Spiffy's was even better."

"Enough of that stuff; when are you going into the private sector, "Bobby asked.

"I'm gonna start the new year 1991 at the fine firm of JL Bradford & Co. Our baby should be here in early January and I'll join the firm a week or so after that. I'm really looking forward to it. How's Katie doing?"

"Did you know that Katie has quit med school?"

"No I hadn't heard that. Why did she do that?"

"Well, at the end of the third year, she said it just wasn't for her. She didn't like the 18 hour days, she didn't like the 36 hour rotations, and she truly did not like sleeping at the hospital. She said she got the creeps every time she was there. Plus she said she missed me too much."

"I really thought she wanted to be a doctor. What's her dad say about all that?" I asked.

"Apparently, he threw a fit, really went into a rage. He complained about all the money he spent on her schooling and he had wasted time and effort in giving her new tits."

"I thought he'd given her new boobs when she was in college?" I said.

"New and better products came on the market, so he took the old ones out and put in new ones."

"How do they feel Bobby?"

"It's none of your business, Jimmy Joe."

"Have you guys set the date for the wedding?"

"Yes we have. It's going to be on June 22 at the Brentwood Baptist Church. I think she's leaning toward a 4 PM wedding, but that could change. With Katie, anything can change in an instant. I'm getting used to it but it's hard. By the way, that card you sent regarding the baby was really nice. But you know I am your best friend so you could just pick up the phone and tell me about it."

"You are right Bobby. I've been a little self-centered of late and I haven't been reaching out to many people. I've been a little embarrassed about my job and I've tried to focus on Maggie. Her baby bump is getting bigger and she is a little self-conscious about it. To me she's more beautiful than ever and I tell her that all the time. Just wait until you and Katie start having babies—you'll understand what I'm talking about.

"Yeah I can't wait. I hope Katie doesn't change her mind between now and June."

We hung up. I couldn't help but thinking that I felt sorry for Bobby. He was so smitten with Katie that he could forgive her for almost anything. I wish she loved him as much as he loved her. I'd have to talk to my sister Allie about the situation and get her take on Katie's thinking.

I called Allie and she picked up after several rings. "I just got off the phone with Bobby. He told me that he and Katie are getting married in June. And he told me that Katie had quit med school. It's her third year. What's going on with all that?"

"Typical Katie is all I can say," Allie replied. "She told me that she had a big fight with her father about Bobby and the fact that she wanted to marry him. She was afraid that Bobby was gonna get tired of waiting and marry someone else. You know, I don't believe she loves him, but he's been around so long that she would be embarrassed if he married someone else."

"Poor Bobby; he's marrying someone with his eyes closed."

"You've never gotten how Katie thinks. She's not normal. It took me until our sophomore year in college to figure that out. I hate to say you've been right, but she is crazy. I thought several times she was going to kill herself over grades, over her father who she fantasizes about, or some guy."

"She fantasizes about her father?"

"She has orgasms with his picture in her bed along with a vibrator."

"That's more information than I wanted. Thanks Allie."

"Love to Maggie, Jimmy Joe."

That was a disconcerting conversation with my little sister. My friend Bobby was in real trouble and I didn't know what to do.

Chapter 11

"I think my water just broke. I think it's time Jimmy Joe. We should go, we should go!"

"Okay Maggie, here put on your coat and start to the car. I'm right behind you with the bag."

We were on our way to St. Thomas Hospital. I used my car phone to call Mary Lynn and tell her to put out the word that we were on our way to the hospital. I told her to call Maggie's mother first and then she could go down the list as she chose.

Maggie's contractions were getting closer together and the breathing we learned in Lamaze classes didn't seem to be working. Finally we reached St. Thomas and I made an illegal left turn to go into the hospital entrance. I got out of the car and headed for the door of the hospital; I forgot something, my wife. I went back and got Maggie, all the while shouting "my wife is having a baby." Luckily, an orderly followed me out with a wheelchair. Maggie had gotten out of the car and was screaming at me, "you forgot me, how could you forget me, I'm the one having the baby, remember!"

The orderly said to me, "give me her bag, go park your car and then come back to admissions for the paperwork, and I'll take your wife to the obstetrics unit. Okay?"

I followed the instructions perfectly.

By the time I got all of the administrative stuff out of the way and found Maggie, she was in bed, sweating, her hair was wet and askew and she was groaning, maybe even screaming.

The nurse winked at me. "You got a screamer on your hands! She's been yelling and cursing for a good 15 minutes. Her contractions are about 2 minutes apart. It will not be long."

"Maggie remember the training, sweetheart. Screaming and shouting makes the pain worse. Let's start the breathing. Take a deep cleansing breath. That's good, now do the breathing exercise."

"Don't patronize me Jimmy Joe, it hurts!"

"I know it does but it's not long before our baby is here. Your contractions are getting closer together and you are dilating. So hang on let's get this done."

"Jimmy Joe you are so romantic and you're a prick, but I love you."

I could hear Mary Lynn in the hallway, but I decided to stay with my wife. I didn't want to miss a minute of my child's birth. The doc and nurse came in to have a look and pronounced us ready to go to the birthing room. They put a hospital gown and mask on me.

Mary Lynn was giving Maggie a hand squeeze and a kiss. My sister Allie stood right beside her. Trip was coming down the hall. My family showed up. It was great. With tears in my eyes, I moved down the hall behind the gurney.

About an hour later my son was born.

Maggie was exhausted. I had never seen her sweat so much. She was determined to have our child naturally. I asked her several times if she wanted some help through this, but she declined saying that our baby would have every chance to be healthy and normal.

As I was gazing into her eyes, she looked at me and said, "Well Jimmy Joe, I guess we have to give him the name. He'll be number 5 won't he?"

"Yes, but we can call him Jay or Joe or Josiah or JJ or James."

"So those are my choices? Well then, I'll choose Josiah. That's a very strong name and Josiah Jeter has a nice southern ring to it; in fact I really love that name for our son."

The nurse handed the baby to me and I said to him, "Josiah I am your father and I love you."

They were going to take Maggie to the recovery area, clean her up a little bit and do a few things for Josiah and then she would be in a room. I took off my gown and headed out to see the family.

They were in the waiting area and all stood up to greet me. "Everything went well, Maggie's doing great and so is Josiah."

A big smile crossed Trip's face. "So he's going to be the fifth. Thank you Jimmy for honoring your family."

I stepped toward Trip and gave him a big hug. Then I had a group hug with all my family.

"When can we see him?" Mary Lynn wanted to know.

"Let's go to the nursery!" I said and off we went.

"Thank God," Allie said. "He looks like Maggie and he is beautiful."

I called Betsy Randolph to let her know that Maggie was doing well and that my sister said that Josiah Jeter looked like Maggie. She was thrilled and was looking forward to talking to Maggie. She also asked when she could come see Josiah. I told her to talk to Maggie; it was all good with me.

I joined my firm on January 21, 1991. It was good to walk in the doors of JL Bradford & Co. There was a lot of my family's history contained in these walls. I looked forward to building some history of my own. The one thing that my time with Billy Bonner gave me was contacts. Whether you loved him or hated him, everyone knew who Billy was and who his people were. So I had a few things in my kit of tricks that would get me off to a good start at the firm.

One of the people I met during my tenure was Willy Wayne Bonner, Bill's dad. He was an interesting country character, but he was in the midst of developing a very good business. Willy started out as an oil jobber and through the years he had acquired several gas stations on interstate highway exchanges or exits. To improve the cash flow of these locations, he added a gift shop and then a country cooking restaurant. Soon the gift shop and the restaurant were outpacing the gas station.

Being a good businessman he decided to test his theory that the gas station may not matter. He built a standalone restaurant/gift shop at the exit for his hometown of Lebanon Tennessee which was off Interstate 40. The Apple Barrel Country Diner was born, the ABCs of good home cooking. It was extremely successful. At the present, Willy had eight standalone restaurants/gift shops along the 40 corridor from Johnson City to Memphis. He also had four gas stops with restaurant/gift shops along this corridor. He had made land acquisitions along I-24 from Nashville to Chattanooga and along I-65 from Nashville to Huntsville Alabama. Three of these restaurants would be in Nashville/Davidson County and the fourth would be in nearby Franklin Tennessee. There would be one restaurant in Chattanooga and another in Huntsville with the remainder spread along each of the interstates.

Before the holidays, Willy and I sat down to discuss his business plan with his accountant and lawyer. Willy needed to raise some money to build out this dream. The restaurants, which were fairly large given the need for gift shop space, cost about $1 million apiece. Willy was a stickler for details and was very conscience of the need for quality. He also paid his managers well and had an incentive bonus system in place based on the profitability and quality controls of each restaurant. With all of this, the profitability of his operation was higher than that of the industry. As he grew, he would have to tweak his distribution system, but his business plan dealt favorably with that issue.

Tim O'Hara, who is head of corporate finance at JLB, met me in the hallway leading to the corporate finance section.

"Hey Jimmy Joe, it's good to see you. I was just heading to the conference room for the morning call. Put your stuff inside the area there and join me in the conference room. I'll save you a space."

I joined them in the conference room and took my seat. My dad was there and so were some of the department heads and associates. Tim introduced me to several people, including Tim Dibelius, Eddie Calhoun and Dottie Graham; they would be my corporate finance cohorts. My dad tried his best to ignore me, but I kept my stare on him until he recognized me. This was not Trip's favorite day and I understood that, but I considered this my birthright and was not about to let go.

Tim showed me to a desk next to Dottie in the bullpen. Tim had a nice office as did Alex and Eddie. There were also several empty offices along the inside wall. I guess my dad and Tim wanted to add a little humility to my fare, but I wasn't going to settle for it very easily. While I was only 27 years old, I had been through a lot of stuff with the Mayor and the Councilmen. I learned to recognize bullshit when I saw it and this was as pure as it gets.

Around lunchtime, I wandered down the hall to find Trip.

"You have lunch plans today?" I asked.

"Don't you have lunch plans with your colleagues?" he replied.

"No I don't, I wanted to have lunch with you.'

"But I was just going over to the City Club and eat at the group table. Does that suit you?"

"That'll be great. Let's go."

When we got there, Trip asked, "Should we get our own table? You look awfully serious, like you have something to say."

"I do have something to say, so that is probably a good idea."

Trip had a standing order for lunch which the waiter knew about, so I ordered a club sandwich and iced tea.

"What's on your mind Jimmy?"

"I'm sorry we're having this conversation. I thought you might get it, but alas you're still looking at me like I'm your little boy. I stayed away from the firm after Harvard, so I could get a little experience and maybe some credibility. But now, I'm ready to take my role in the firm. You need to get the ball rolling to name me a partner of the firm. I have partnership points that exceed a number of the existing partners and when you combine that with the proxies I hold for my sister and my cousins, it gives me a pretty good position."

"I didn't want it to appear that I was playing favorites. You're my son and some will believe that it's nepotism at play."

"It is nepotism at play. I'm Big Jack's grandson and his name is still on the door. His blood is coursing through my veins and he asked me to become a part of this firm as his heir since I'm the only male. So I don't really care what others think. This is my rightful place and I'm ready to assume my role. And you needn't worry, I'll carry my weight. I've developed some great contacts and I'll have a very good piece of business sooner than you think."

Trip didn't like my speech, but deep down he knew I was right. With the invocation of Big Jack's name, he seemed to wilt a little bit. He knew without a doubt that big Jack loved me beyond compare and knew that he was watching everything that was going on. Trip was more than a little superstitious.

"I guess you talked to your mother about this?" Trip said.

"No, I haven't talked to her. This is between the two of us."

"What about your sister and your cousins?"

"They trust me to do the right thing and are well aware that our generation of the Bradford family has to stick together so that our interests are protected."

"Don't you trust me Jimmy Joe?" Trip said with a startled look on his face.

"No I don't trust you Trip. I think you're out to protect yourself and your status within this firm. I'm comfortable with the way things are at the moment, with the exception of my not being named a partner. But at some point things will change and you may not be too happy about it."

"I'm your father; how can you not trust me?"

"All's fair in business, isn't that the watchword for you and the firm?"

155

Our meal came and there was a quiet interlude while we ate a bit.

Trip put his fork down. "Okay, I'll get together with the executive committee this afternoon and will name you a partner. I'll tell Tim that you're being named a partner and you'll be taking one of the spare offices as your space. I don't suppose you want me to kick anyone out of their existing office do you?"

"No, one of the existing offices will do just fine."

I went back to my sandwich and enjoyed it a good deal more than just a few minutes ago.

I looked at Trip and said, "I have a potential piece of business and I want to talk to you about it. You know Willy Wayne Bonner?"

"Of course we know him. We have been trying to get in to see him for a couple months now. For some reason, he hasn't wanted to see us."

"He's been waiting for me to join the firm. I have been talking to him for the last three or four months. He wants to expand pretty rapidly. He has 12 stores along the I-40 corridor and wants to add at least 12 more along the two other interstates out of Nashville. The stores cost about $1 million each to build and furnish. He has the spots picked out and he has a couple of contractors that understand how to build stores to Willy Wayne's specs. He has a Nashville engineering firm that does the layout. He also has some good people working for him, but he may need a CFO. That's something for you or Tim to think about and help

Willy Wayne with the idea. I'll tell you Trip, it is a pretty slick operation."

"That's truly great Jimmy Joe. When can we go see him?"

"I thought I'd go over on Wednesday to see Willy Wayne. You want to go with me?"

"No, you should probably take Tim. He's gonna be put out a little bit and I would rather not step on his toes too many times this week. It'll be good for the two of you to get to know each other. You have any other contacts in your hip pocket?"

"That's enough for today. You should stop by sometime and see Josiah. He's really developing a personality."

"Your mom and I will be over on the weekend if that's okay. I know Maggie is very tired and very busy."

"Yes she is. I've been trying to help out, but she says that I just get in the way. And since she's nursing I can't do the middle of the night feeding. But I do run errands for her and try to keep things organized around the house. It's amazing how small the house has become with the addition of our little guy."

We went back to the firm and everything happened as it was supposed to and I was a happy man.

I moved into one of the vacant offices. I didn't have much stuff in the office, but I was happy with the spartan look and all I needed was for my telephone to work. Luckily there was a telephone guy in the building.

Tim O'Hara came into my office around 4:30 PM and congratulated me on being named partner. Then he asked me about Willy Wayne Bonner and I described Willy Wayne to him. We then talked about the company, their plans, the profitability of the units and how to structure a deal. We then talked about the Wednesday meeting. I told him that this was a meet and greet; that we shouldn't get into specifics until Willy Wayne got comfortable with Tim. Then we should ask them to come down to Nashville to visit the firm, see what we're all about and then talk about some specifics. Tim agreed that this was a good plan and he was on board. He thanked me for wanting him on board.

"Well, Tim, you are my boss and I respect what you've accomplished. I hope to learn from you and I don't want your job. You will do it far better than me."

Tim shook my hand, gave me a quizzical look and left the room. He was thinking about whose job I wanted. I didn't see any reason to explain it to him.

I went home that night a very happy man. I had a wife that I loved, a new son and my birthright was being established.

Chapter 12

I was sitting in the original Apple Barrel Country Diner in Lebanon Tennessee. With me were my wife Maggie, Bobby Gibbs and his fiancée, the ever crazy Katie Morgan.

"I can't believe we're eating at a place like this in a place like this. I mean Lebanon is the end of the world," Katie said.

Lebanon is the county seat of Wilson County, Tennessee. Many people think it is a country in the Middle East, but those of us who live near here think of it as nice little town.

Lebanon is located approximately 25 miles east of downtown Nashville. The city was incorporated in 1801 and was named for the biblical cedars of Lebanon. Local residents have called Lebanon "Cedar-City", mostly a reference to the abundance of cedar trees in the area. The city is home to Cumberland University, a small, private four-year liberal arts institution. The University, founded in 1842, has a rich heritage and has produced over eighty Congressmen and Senators such as Albert Gore, Sr. and Thomas Gore. The institution has also produced a Nobel Peace Prize recipient, Cordell Hull, who served as Secretary of State from March 1933 - November 1944.

Lebanon is host to the annual Wilson County Fair, which is considered by Busy Bee Trader Magazine (based in Greenbrier, TN) to be the best County Fair in Tennessee. The Wilson County Fair has been listed as one of the top 50 fairs in North America by attendance.

"Well Jimmy Joe has been obsessed with Apple Barrel for the last few months. He has been dying for me to eat at one of these restaurants. He thinks it's the best thing to come along in a long time. This is my first night out since Josiah was born so I'm just happy to be anywhere. And of course Mary Lynn is having the time of her life taking care of Josiah," Maggie said.

"You did have a lot of class Jimmy Joe," Katie said with a sneer on her face. "But why Lebanon? We could've eaten at this place in Nashville."

Bobby looked at her and smiled, "But we wouldn't have had the experience of eating in the original Apple Barrel."

"Plus we wouldn't be meeting Willy Wayne Bonner."

"Willy Wayne? You've got to be kidding me. Who names their kid Willy Wayne?" Katie sneered again.

"My Mama!" Willy Wayne was standing by our table.

"Willy Wayne," I said as I jumped up from the table. "How are you doing? Let me introduce you to my friends and my lovely wife." I made the introductions and sat back down.

Willy Wayne looked at Maggie and said, "Jimmy has told me about you and he didn't do you justice. You're as pretty as any picture I've ever seen. And you little lady," he said as he looked at Katie, "I hope you like my food a lot better than you like my name."

"We were just looking over the menu Willy Wayne."

"Don't bother with the menu," Willy said, "I got a little bit of everything going back in the kitchen, so we'll just serve it up."

"Will we be able to tell what each dish is?" Katie said with a scowl.

"You sound skeptical little lady, but I hope you will enjoy it."

He left the table and Katie stared after him and said, "I doubt it."

I looked at Katie and said, "Willy Wayne is a client of my firm. Could you hold off on the snide comments?"

"You want me to be dishonest?"

"Come on you two, cut it out. We haven't seen each other in a while and we should enjoy the chance we have," Bobby said.

Maggie chimed in, "I agree with Bobby. I haven't been out in a while and I just want to enjoy someone else doing the cooking and cleaning and changing diapers."

Willy Wayne reappeared with several waitresses holding trays of food, and the aroma was wonderful. There was a smorgasbord of many of the offerings of the restaurant.

Meatloaf

Fried chicken tenderloin

Fried catfish

Chicken n' dumplings

Pinto beans with ham

Turnip greens with ham

Green beans

Creamed corn

Corn muffins

Buttermilk biscuits

Butter, jam and apple butter

It was enough food to feed an army. "Wow Willy Wayne," Maggie said with delight. "You have outdone yourself! This looks terrific." She scooped some turnip greens on to her plate along with some pinto beans and meatloaf.

"Tastes good too!"

Being the polite guy that I am, I offered Katie some of the food.

"You really don't expect me to eat that stuff do you? I mean that's the stuff our maid eats. It's all fried and cooked with ham. I just can't bring myself to eat that. At the very least, I should have a steak."

Willy Wayne turned around and headed back to the kitchen.

"Well that's just great Katie!"

The waitress said, "He just forgot something, he'll be back."

Bobby looked at me and said, "Well I'm going to enjoy this food. Pass the biscuits please." He helped himself to something of everything. I did as well. And Maggie refilled her plate. She was eating as if she was starved and it was great to see her enjoy the food.

About 10 minutes later, Willy Wayne reappeared with a sizzling 12 ounce rib eye steak cooked medium rare.

"This was cooked especially for you little darlin'."

Katie was forced to muster a smile and said to him, "Willy Wayne you're as nice and good as they say you are," she said pointing to us. Then she attacked the steak with gusto. Willy Wayne smiled from ear to ear, slapped me on the back and said, "Y'all enjoy!"

Willy Wayne saved the day. From that point on, we engaged in small talk with Bobby, Maggie and I doing the talking. Katie enjoyed her steak in silence. She had this air of superiority about her since she had made her point and gotten some special treatment. I felt sorry for Bobby, but he looked at her with such love that he was more than willing to overlook the occasional outburst. The absolute silence was weird, but it suited me since I enjoyed both Bobby and Maggie.

We all enjoyed dessert except for Katie who excused herself to go to the restroom. After about 5 minutes, Maggie decided to join her. Bobby and I were both attacking Baked Apple Dumplings with Vanilla Ice Cream and Maggie had a Double Chocolate Coca Cola Brownie waiting.

Bobby looked at Katie and asked, "Want some of my apple dumplings?"

"Ugh, that looks awful. Yuck!" She was back in form.

We said our goodbyes to Bobby and Katie without any incident. Maggie and I went looking for Willy Wayne who was in the manager's office.

"Well, how was it?"

Maggie stepped forward and took Willy Wayne's outstretched hand, "It was wonderful. The beans and greens were better than my grandma's. I suppose the recipe is secret. And that brownie was awesome. I'm sold. I'll be a customer for life."

"That's a great endorsement, Maggie. How about the other little lady? She seemed real critical."

Again Maggie replied, "She ate every morsel of that steak. I think that says it all."

I looked at Willy Wayne and said, "Thank you Willy. We're on schedule with everything, but I'll give you a list of events early next week." Maggie hugged Willy Wayne and we had a man-hug.

On the way home Maggie said, "A strange thing happened in the rest room. Katie was in one of the stalls gagging and throwing up. I asked her if she was OK and she told me to mind my own business. I think she is bulimic. She couldn't weigh more than 95 pounds."

"She's always been concerned with her weight and has been thin."

"That's true, but when I saw her at UVA and at our wedding she wasn't that thin."

"She's probably getting in shape for her wedding."

"Do you think I should talk to Allie about it?'

"Let's not escalate things. The less I think about Katie Morgan the better."

We would not see Katie again until the rehearsal dinner in late June, but I would see Bobby on several occasions in the next few months.

Willy Wayne grew to really like Tim O'Hara and Trip. After a lengthy discussion, he agreed to add a CFO to his team. We made several suggestions, but Willy finally decided on a guy in Knoxville who was a CPA and the assistant finance director for the Tennessee Valley Authority. The guy was very competent.

We brought the deal in May and raised $15 million for the company. The symbol was ABCD and the stock started trading at $10.50 per share. It was a success and everyone was happy. It was my first deal, but now I had to find the next one. I had some irons in the fire and I was going to hold my own.

Bobby and I agreed to meet at Cheekwood at 4 o'clock. We were being fitted for our wedding clothes. Since Bobby's dad would be best man, I was one of six groomsmen. Cheekwood was the chosen venue for the extravaganza, the Baptist Church having been discarded some months ago.

The history and origin of Cheekwood are intimately interwoven with the growth of Nashville, the Maxwell House coffee brand and the Cheeks, one of the city's early entrepreneurial families.

Christopher T. Cheek moved to Nashville in the 1880's and founded a wholesale grocery business. His son, Leslie Cheek, joined him as a partner.

In 1896, Leslie Cheek married Mabel Wood of Clarksville, Tennessee. Their son, Leslie Jr., was born in 1908 and their daughter, Huldah, in 1915. By that year, Leslie Cheek was president of the family firm.

During these same years, the elder Cheeks cousin, Joel Cheek, developed a superior blend of coffee that was marketed through the best hotel in Nashville, the Maxwell House. His extended family, including Leslie and Mabel Cheek, were investors. In 1928, Postum (now General Foods) purchased Maxwell House's parent company, Cheek-Neal Coffee, for more than $40 million.

With their income secured by the proceeds from the sale, the Cheeks bought 100 acres of what was then woodland in West Nashville for a country estate. To design and build the house and grounds, they hired New York residential and landscape architect, Bryant Fleming, and gave him control over every detail - from landscaping to interior furnishings. The result was a limestone mansion and extensive formal gardens inspired by the grand English houses of the 18th century. Fleming's masterpiece, Cheekwood, was completed in 1932.

Leslie and Mabel Cheek moved into the mansion in January 1933. Leslie Cheek lived at Cheekwood for just two years before his death at 61.

In 1943, Mabel Cheek deeded the house to her daughter, Huldah Cheek Sharp, and her husband, Walter Sharp. The Sharps lived at Cheekwood until the 1950s, when they offered it as a site for a botanical garden and art museum.

The development of the property was spearheaded by the Exchange Club of Nashville, the Horticultural Society of Middle Tennessee and many other civic groups. The Nashville Museum of Art donated its permanent collections and proceeds from the sale of its building to the effort. The new Cheekwood opened to the public in 1960.

The Cheekwood Museum of Art is housed in the 30,000-square foot Georgian-style mansion. It has a world-class collections of American and contemporary paintings and sculpture, English and American decorative arts and traveling exhibitions. Collections also include silver, and the most comprehensive collection of Worcester porcelain in America.

There are ten separate botanical gardens on the grounds. The extravaganza will be held in the Wills Perennial Garden because it will accommodate 200 folks properly seated. It's going to be hot in June, but a little sweat won't keep the crowds away. Everyone among the knowledgeable crowd wants to be at all the Cheekwood events. Below the formal gardens of the mansion, overlooking the mustard meadow and the ponds of the Robinson Family Water Garden is the Wills Perennial Garden. It is dedicated to iris breeder and author, Jesse Wills and displays both new and traditional perennials and many bearded irises. A steep limestone wall provides both habitat and background for this colorful, full-sun garden.

My sister Allie was a bridesmaid. Even though she and Katie had been friends since kindergarten, the disagreement that occurred when they were seniors in college caused a gulf to develop between the two. Accordingly, Allison Cartwright was the maid of honor. Allie was relieved that she did not have all the duties that Katie would assign the maid of honor.

The day of the wedding was sunny and 85. The crowd looked to be about 220 people as some folks had to stand around the perimeter of the Wills Perennial Garden. I had the honor of walking Katie's mother down to her seat. Her father would walk her down the aisle. I looked at the crowd and it seemed to me that every seat was filled.

As luck would have it, I was aligned with Allie and got to walk with her during the procession of bridesmaids and groomsmen. Bobby and his dad walked down the aisle and stood in front of us near the priest. I looked out in the crowd, caught Maggie's eye and gave her my best smile. Katie and her dad came down the aisle as the traditional wedding March was played by a violinist and a harpist. I have to admit, the music was beautiful and so was Katie. Her white wedding dress had many layers, a large head piece and veil and the longest train I have ever seen. The dress, which was beautiful, added size and volume to Katie's 90 pound body.

When Katie and her father reached the priest, he was asked, "Who gives this woman away?"

He replied, "I do, but only temporarily as I have more work to do."

There was a murmur through the crowd as many people didn't realize how crazy Perry Morgan was.

The priest gave him an angry stare and Dr. Morgan said, "Just kidding Father. Her mother and I both give her away to this wonderful young man."

There was another murmur through the crowd, a little laughter arose, and the priest moved along with the service. Poor Bobby was in for a long and arduous life. I looked at his mother sitting on the front row and saw the look of sadness on her face as she knew as well that Bobby was in over his head. The rest of the service went off without a hitch and before I knew it, the bride and the groom were kissing and then walking down the aisle and into the bright sunshine. I was very happy because the outfit I was wearing had gained about 5 pounds with sweat. Everyone sitting in the chairs seemed to be relieved that they were heading inside to the art museum where the air-conditioning would be on high. We all knew that the reception would be quite lavish with plenty of champagne and any other drink that you desired plus enough food to feed a small country. I for one had passed on lunch because I knew that the food would be plentiful and absolutely delicious. I walked my sister down the aisle and both of us headed straight for the Museum. Allison Cartwright caught us both and reminded us that pictures were to be taken in the area just outside the garden.

After the pictures, I set off to find my bride, the lovely Maggie Jeter. I found her holding a glass of champagne talking to Mary Lynn. Bobby's mother was standing nearby so I walked over to her and started to chat.

"It was a lovely wedding. Your husband looked quite dashing in his outfit. He looked to be totally in control. It was a good thing because Bobby was a little scattered."

She gave me a very serious look. "Maybe it finally dawned on him that these people are crazy. You know Jimmy Joe I wouldn't say that to anyone else but you. But I know that you and Bobby have had a lot of disagreements on this issue. You understand more than anyone else what he's gotten himself into. You're the only one who will look out for him in all of Nashville. No matter what he says or does please don't abandon him." She had tears in her eyes and she meant every word she said.

"I promise you I won't abandon him, but sometimes he is his own worst enemy when it comes to Katie."

"I know. His dad keeps telling me that I have to let it go, but he's one of my babies. I just can't let him go and walk away. I know I can't control the situation and I'm not supposed to interfere, but damn that's a hard thing to do."

About that time, the champagne came by and I grabbed two glasses off of it. "This will make us both feel a little better."

She turned the flute up and drained every drop. "I'm going to find my husband." And off she went.

Maggie was off in another group of women chatting away. I turned around and saw Dr. Morgan talking to a very lovely woman dressed in a pretty yellow frock with a large brimmed hat covering her beautifully flowing blonde hair.

Dr. Morgan was saying, "An augmentation and lift is very easy to accomplish and all of my patients are very satisfied with the results."

The lovely lady replied, "I'm sure they are. Do you have any pictures or other examples of your work?"

"Well you can go over and take a closer look at Katie. You can tell how nicely her breasts look in the dress and see just a touch of cleavage; just enough to tell they are breasts, but not enough to be classified as a slut."

"You did the procedure on Katie?" She seemed a little startled by this revelation.

"Oh sure; in fact Katie's my best advertisement. I'm sure she'd be glad to show you the results. Wait till things calm down and then get her to take you into the bride's room to show you how perfect my work is."

"I don't know; that seems a little brash and forward to me."

"Oh no she's happy to do it. She likes to show off the improvements in her body."

The woman drifted away and Dr. Morgan watched her make her way over to Katie who was standing next to

Bobby and talking to friends and family. The DOC had a satisfied look on his face. I was astounded that he offered up his daughter in this way on her wedding day. What an asshole! First of all, it bothered me that he did this work on his daughter, but it seemed like he was a pimp not a doctor.

Chapter 13

Time flies when you're having fun. I became adept at finding companies that needed to raise capital or to go public. Middle Tennessee was a pretty fertile ground for interesting new businesses, but the southeast was growing and companies were springing up all over the place. We had a good network of retail offices in most of the states considered part of the southeast plus we had some offices in northern Florida. Trip often said that he couldn't understand the rest of Florida, so we had better stay out of that area. But along the redneck Riviera from Pensacola to Mobile we had a pretty good presence. The competition was often fierce, but we could hold our own and managed to find our share of nuggets.

Maggie and I had our second child in 1994, a beautiful little girl that we named Abigail. It was love at first sight for me. A third child appeared in 1997, a boy that we named Christopher. With the expansion of our family, we also had to find a new home. Neither Maggie nor I wanted to move into Belle Meade. We decided to move into the lovely Hillwood neighborhood and bought a house on Fleetwood drive. It was a lovely one-story house that seemed to meander forever and had plenty of room with five bedrooms, three baths, a nice large kitchen and a family room plus a large yard. I wasn't too keen on the large yard because I knew I would have to take care of it, but Maggie loved the new house and was looking forward to the redecoration process.

Bobby and Katie moved along as well. Bobby was named a partner in his firm after only six years. Bobby had become an able litigator and was extremely well regarded in Nashville legal circles. They had two boys and a girl. They avoided the glare of Belle Meade living as well. They bought a beautiful home on Bowling Avenue in Green Hills. Although Katie worked at the Medical Examiner's Office when they were first married, she became a stay-at-home mom as their first child was born in early 1993. Judging from outward appearances alone, the two had the makings of a beaming, happy couple. We saw the two of them at functions from time to time but seldom did the four of us get together just as couples.

However, Bobby and I had lunch together every couple of weeks and got together for drinks every Friday. We were regulars at Bar Louie on 11th Ave. As time moved along Bobby began to confide in me. All was not well in the Gibbs household. Since being named a partner in his firm, Booby's stature in the Nashville legal community had risen further and his earning power had gone up considerably. I was very happy for them.

One evening in 1998, just after their third child was born, we were sitting at the bar sipping scotch whiskey when Bobby said, "Katie is hearing voices in or through the intercom system. The voices told Katie that Robbie, our oldest, was colluding with them. She accused him of working with the voices in her head, verbally abusing him until our nanny whisked him away upstairs. He cried for an hour. He's only six."

"Wow, that's scary. Is this happening often?"

"It's happening more than I'd like to admit," Bobby said.

I turned to Bobby and looked him in the eye. "Do you think she is schizophrenic?"

"I don't know. It's frightening to think that your wife is going over the edge, but it's something that I might have to face."

Katie began to see a psychiatrist and a psychologist that seemed to help her for a while. Bobby told me that the psychiatrist had diagnosed Katie as a mild schizophrenic. He gave Katie some medication that seemed to help although Katie complained that it made her feel sluggish and lethargic. She had always been active and she was very aggravated by the whole process.

On another occasion, months later Bobby said, "I think my wife is a drug addict and I don't know what to do. I think she's dangerous for my children and maybe even for me."

"She wouldn't hurt those children Bobby. I just couldn't believe she would do anything to harm any of you," I said to him.

"She's a schizophrenic who refuses to take her medication. What she has done instead is to begin a pattern of prescription drug abuse—targeting drugstores in Belle Meade and Green Hills to fill multiple prescriptions for Percocet and OxyContin to squelch pain for back problems she doesn't have. She's in a rehab center right now called Ocean Breeze which is in Pompano Beach. It was recommended by her psychologist. She's been there for a week and will likely stay another week or so I hope. It's difficult to say whether she'll stick it out or not. She calls me every night to tell me how much she misses her babies.

I keep telling her that she can't take care of the kids in the shape she's in. I think it pisses her off that my mom and sister are here taking care of the kids along with the nanny. The sad thing is the kids are happier than they've been in months."

"Bobby I really feel for you. I don't know what to say. I hope the rehab works and that she gets herself straightened out."

In early 2001, Bobby filed an injunction outlining Katie's strange, psychotic behavior. The filing to keep Katie out of the family home established that she was in and out of drug rehab facilities and psychiatric hospitals for three years. The document detailed one stint at Vanderbilt Medical Center following an alleged suicide attempt and an emergency room visit where she received IV fluids because of her drug-induced weight loss. Bobby said that she used drugs in front of their children. At one time, after screaming and becoming combative with the Metro police officers and paramedics enlisted to haul her off to treatment, Katie had to be restrained by police and put in physical lockdown for days on end at a local drug treatment center.

Bobby claimed that she was physically, verbally and emotionally abusive to him and their children. Police arrested Katie twice for an aggravated assault against Bobby in 2000 and for reckless endangerment, domestic violence and evading arrest this May of 2001. According to another police report in early 2002, Katie called police after an argument with Bobby. During the call, the operator heard Bobby tell Katie to "put the knife down." Though Bobby didn't want to prosecute, he later admitted that Katie cornered him with a knife.

Katie's May arrest also stemmed from an argument with Bobby, who smelled alcohol on her breath when they were fighting. Katie had taken the couple's youngest child, a female toddler, placed her in an SUV and rammed her husband's car to push it out of her way. She then exited her car and tried to force past Bobby to get to the other children, ripping his shirt and pinching his right bicep to the point of bruising.

As Katie pulled out of the driveway with her young daughter in tow, a police officer approached, made eye contact with her and activated his lights and sirens. Still, Katie sped off, reaching speeds of well over 70 mph in a 30-mph zone before the officer stopped pursuing her. She disappeared for two weeks. Katie told Bobby she was with a girlfriend in Birmingham.

My sister Allie called in May of 2002 and asked if we could meet for a drink at Dalts on White Bridge Road. I immediately said yes since this was a most unusual occurrence for her to even call me. We had never met for a drink that I could recall—just the two of us.

When I arrived she was nursing a martini in a huge goblet. I ordered my usual Dewar's scotch on the rocks—sometimes I am so boring.

After the usual pleasantries, she said, "I want to talk to you about your friend Bobby. I know that you think highly of him and that he may be your best friend, but I don't think he's the guy you think he is."

177

"Well you're right, he is my best friend. Has been for a long, long time. I know Bobby pretty well I think. I really feel for him given everything that's gone on with Katie."

"Jimmy Joe, I know you think it's all Katie's fault, but it isn't. Bobby has a lot to do with it. He pokes at Katie and eggs her on. In fact, that incident with the knife, Bobby started it and told her that she didn't have the nerve to kill him. Then when she called the cops, he started yelling for her to put down the knife and then of course she did corner him with it, and who are the police going to believe."

"What's this all about Allie? Why are you defending Katie and blaming Bobby?"

"This animosity that they have for one another all started right after Robbie was born. They got into an argument because Katie wouldn't go out to a function for some business deal. She was breast-feeding and didn't want to do whatever you do to store some breast milk. Bobby got so mad that he smacked her and bloodied her lip."

"Where are you getting all the stuff Allie? I just can't believe that Bobby would do something like that."

"Lots of times when they got into it and Katie needed a safe haven, she came to my house. Sometimes she would stay as long as a week and when the police got involved she would stay even longer. I'm telling you, Bobby isn't the saint you think he is."

"Why are you telling me this? There's nothing I can do. I mean I talk to Bobby, he even confides in me, but I don't have much to add in terms of advice for his situation. I love Maggie and I love my kids and I love my life. I'm as happy as I've ever been. Frankly, the only thing I can do is screw it up. So when it comes to being a referee or a counselor or Rabbi, I'm not the man for the job."

"You did it for the governor and you seemed to be pretty good at it."

"That was different. It wasn't real life."

"Mark my words Jimmy Joe, something bad is gonna happen if somebody doesn't intervene."

"I continue to talk to Bobby, but I don't think I'm the man to intervene. I'm too close to Bobby and frankly, I can't stand Katie. By the way, I thought you two were on the outs with each other."

"We were, but I just couldn't abandon her when she reached out to me for help. We have just been part of each other's lives far too long for that."

"Let's hope things get sorted out somehow. Let's have one more drink. It's been a long time since we've talked about anything. Anyone new in your life?"

"Well, I've been dating someone that was very much a part of your past."

"My past; who on earth could that be?"

"Cora Jane Davis!"

My mouth dropped open. I was stunned on two fronts. One was the fact that the name Cora Jane Davis resurfaced; the second was that Cora Jane was a woman. Was my sister a lesbian? How could that be; she always dated guys when I was around.

My sister sat there smiling at me knowing full well that I had no idea that she liked women better than men.

I looked at her and said, "are you a...?" I just couldn't quite get it out.

"Yes Jimmy Joe, I'm a lesbian. Does that make you feel any differently towards me?"

"Do Trip and Mary Lynn know that?"

"Of course! And all of my friends."

"Why am I always the last person to know? I just don't get it. And for heaven sakes, how in the hell did you get involved with Cora Jane?"

"I got to know her real well the last two years of high school. Then we ran into each other again in law school. We both were at American University law school and we spent a lot of time studying together. Then I got the job with the Big Jack Foundation and she went to work for a women's advocacy group. We lost touch with each other for a while and then she called me one day out of the blue and asked if I could have a drink. I said yes of course because I really like Cora Jane and she likes me. We've been seeing each other for about a year."

"A year; are you kidding me, an entire year?"

"Yep, an entire year! Jimmy Joe you are so wrapped up in Maggie, your kids, and the investment business that you don't have time for anything else."

"I may not know what's going on with my best friend, but I should know what's going on with my sister. I just can't get over the fact that your partner is Cora Jane Davis."

"You drove her to the other side Jimmy Joe. Me, I got there naturally; I just like girls better than men. That fiasco with you had a big impact on her and it took her several years to get over it. In college at Rhodes, she just dated other girls and ran with the pack. If we end up at some function together, I hope you will be nice to her and extend to her any courtesy that you would a family member."

"Of course, that goes without saying."

"I'm saying it so you won't forget it!"

"I've got to say Allie that this has been a hell of a conversation. I haven't been staggered like this since the other fiasco with Janie and Jeannette Watson. What in the world is next? I love you baby sister and only want the best for you."

We had a nice hug and left Dalt's. Was I living in a cave somewhere in the wilderness? There was a lot I was missing out on. Am I selfish and self-centered in the extreme? Am I all I think about? I know one thing, I need another drink. In fact, I need several more. I went back into Dalt's and sat at the bar. My best friend was in a terrible situation and my sister was in a lesbian relationship with a former lover of mine. This was the stuff of daytime television and I was one of the leading characters.

Maggie was reading in bed by the time I got home. She told me my dinner was in the fridge and followed me into the kitchen.

I was a little drunk but I could still get the words out. "Did you know that Allie is a lesbian?"

"Of course I did. It's obvious to anyone that she's always with a woman in social situations and Mary Lynn told me that she only has relationships with women."

"It wasn't too obvious to me! I had no idea. Why didn't someone clue me in? I felt like a dope tonight. Just another selfish prick. Do you think I'm selfish?"

"I think you love your job and I think you love your family and that doesn't make you selfish. Have something to eat; it will make you feel much better. I think you had a little too much scotch for one evening."

"She thinks Bobby is the reason that he and Katie are having so many problems. She says Bobby is the instigator."

"Well she and Katie have become close again. I think Katie stays with Allie sometimes when things get out of hand."

"You knew about that too?"

"Don't be so hard on yourself Jimmy Joe. I've been assuming too much. I thought you knew about all these things that were going on. It's my fault. I haven't been doing a very good job of keeping you abreast of all the things going on."

"Don't tell me anything else tonight please."

For the next few weeks, I tried to be more engaged with Maggie, my children and my dad. I went into Trip's office, sat down and just looked at him.

"Something wrong?" He gave me a quizzical look. I continued to stare at him. "What's going on Jimmy Joe?"

"I'm really out of touch with my family and my friends. Things are happening and I don't know about them and it bothers me. Allie is a lesbian. I didn't know that until a couple of nights ago. What type of man doesn't know that about his grown sister? I feel terrible about that. Then she tells me that Bobby is smacking Katie around and is in part responsible for all the stuff going on there. And here at the firm all I know about is what's going on in corporate finance and with my little team. What's going on here? Are we doing okay? The markets have been a little choppy of late. Is this impacting retail? And how is Marty doing in municipal finance?"

"Municipal finance just closed the deal for Shelbyville and is doing a small deal for Jackson. Retail is doing well; we are in the middle of a bull market run. We're gonna have a really good year. The thing with your sister is not something we run around waving a flag about. Mary Lynn probably told Maggie about it. Anyway it is what it is and there's nothing you can do about it nor should you try."

"You know she's dating Cora Jane Davis?"

"That's what Mary Lynn told me. I think that's funny as hell. I told Mary Lynn we should have a party, invite Cora Jane and Allie, you and Maggie and the Davises."

"You know, Trip, you have a perverse sense of humor."

"Well Jim you have provided a lot of fodder for humor."

"I guess I have if you consider my whole body of work. I am so fortunate to have found Maggie. So it's all for the good."

"Go home and talk to Maggie" She's the best thing that has ever happened to you. Big Jack would love her, by the way."

"Thanks for the talk Trip."

I went home and talked to Maggie.

"I have decided that I'm going to throw a 40th birthday party for you and Bobby. He and Katie are back together for the moment and this looks like a good time to have a party. I called Jesse over at the Bluebird and we have it booked for March 23 which is a Tuesday night, kind of a slow night for the Bluebird."

"I don't know if Bobby will be up for that, particularly if Katie's involved. I don't think he wants to be in the limelight. I get the feeling that he's about to do something that will precipitate a lot of anger."

"Well Mr. Jeter it's up to you to convince him to put it off for a little while so we can have this party. This is something I really want to do this and Allie has agreed to help me. By the way Jimmy, you never told me that her current girlfriend is someone you used to date."

"It was just a high school thing. Not much to it. I'll talk to Bobby and get them on board with this party idea."

"Nicely done Jim. You avoided that thing very well. Allie says you turned Cora Jane into a lesbian."

"I think her mother had more to do with it than me."

I called Bobby as soon as I got to the office. "Hey partner, Maggie has cooked up this idea of throwing a birthday party for the two of us. She wants to do it at the Bluebird on 23 March. She's gonna take care of everything."

"Yeah Katie said something to me about it this morning. Your sister's involved and I guess Katie and Maggie will be the ringleaders."

"So you're gonna do it?"

"I don't have much choice at the moment. I'm doing this for you because I'll probably need your help in the near future. Katie was gone recently for about three weeks, and I had no idea where she was. The credit card bills say she was in Birmingham, although I don't have any idea why she would be there. It's probably some Doctor she met while in med school. And he probably gave her some prescriptions. She gets a bunch of pain medications. You know she's a full-blown drug addict don't you?"

"I believe what you tell me Bobby. Maybe Allie knows what she was doing, but I think she's sort of like me and she doesn't want to get caught in the crossfire."

"Well you're going to have to choose sides sometime!"

"Bobby you're my friend and I'm always on your side."

I would guess that at least 100 people showed up at the Bluebird by 7 o'clock. The drinks were flowing and a buffet of all the Bluebird's culinary offerings was available. The food was delicious. An all-female country and western swing band was playing music that sometimes made it hard to hear, but I got my share of birthday wishes.

"Happy birthday Jimmy Joe! Remember me?"

"Of course I remember you. It's good to see you Cora Jane. Allie must be here."

"I just met your wife Maggie. She's a lovely person. What did you do to deserve somebody as beautiful as her? It can't be your charm or sensitivity."

"Some things are just inexplicable Cora Jane."

Allie walked up just in time, "I see you two are getting acquainted. Happy birthday Jimmy Joe. Come with me Cora I have somebody I want you to meet." Allie gave me a wink as she moved on.

I decided to stick by Maggie's side for the rest of the evening and let her protect me. After about an hour of this serenity, I noticed that Bobby was sitting at the end of the bar by himself.

I ambled over to where he was sitting and ordered another drink that I didn't need. Bobby looked at me and said, "By

Thursday I should have everything in place to get Katie out of the house and have full custody of the children."

"Does Katie know anything about this?" I asked.

"She has chosen not to come to any of the hearings, although her lawyer has been there. I don't know how much he's talking to Katie, but it doesn't seem like she really cares at this point."

"When the reality hits her in the face, she'll care."

"I've had enough of this frivolity. Happy birthday to you my friend. I'm going home. I haven't seen Katie lately, but I'm sure she's stoned and I won't see her for a while. Just as well."

Maggie and I said goodbye to most of our guests and then she said, "I'm heading home, how about you?"

"I'm going to sit at the bar for a little while and revel in the fact that I'm now 40."

"Okay, don't wait too long and be careful when you're driving home."

A little period of introspection never hurt anyone, unless it morphs into self-pity. I am 40 today; does that mean I've reached middle-age? I guess it does in many ways. But when I look back at the last 15 years or so, I have to be happy with what I see. I am fulfilling the destiny set for me by my grandfather, I have a beautiful wife and three wonderful children, and things are really going my way. The only thing I can do is screw it up.

"Fancy meeting you here," Katie said as she slid onto the seat beside me. "Buy a girl a drink?"

I wasn't too happy to see Katie. I had been talking to Bobby a lot lately about how crazy she was and about her addiction to alcohol and prescription drugs. But she was Bobby's wife and even though I couldn't understand her or abide her, I could at least be polite.

I motioned for the bartender and ordered another Dewar's on the rocks plus a dirty martini. Our drinks came and we saluted one another.

"Jim I want to ask you a serious question. Please try to give me a serious answer. You have never liked me and I've often wondered why. I did a lot of things growing up to aggravate you, but I did it to get your attention. I've been a secret admirer of yours for years. I married Bobby because I knew that would keep me in touch with you. You know, I'd get to see you on a regular basis, because I knew you would never cut Bobby out of your life. Jimmy I love you."

"Don't say that Katie! That is really scary. It's probably the whiskey talking. I love Maggie and I love Bobby. I don't love you Katie. You've always been there, part of Allie's life and part of mine I guess. The things you said really got under my skin and you've always looked like a little girl to me; so skinny and small, like a little person."

"I need another drink," she said.

I ordered another round. I thought to myself that I was getting really drunk and I was. I could hear this buzz in my right ear and turned to see what it was; Katie was babbling away and I couldn't understand a word she was saying.

My glass was empty so I ordered another round. The bartender brought them to us and I think I heard her say, "That's it, no more for you two."

I took a sip of Scotch and my head began to spin. I tried to shake it off, but all I could do was put my head on the bar and pass into oblivion.

When I came to, I was sitting in a car in a place that was very dark. I was in the backseat, my pants and underwear were nowhere to be found and I didn't have on a shirt. I was stark naked. Katie was sitting next to me with her arm around my shoulders and was nibbling my neck. She was naked as well.

"You want to do it again Jimmy Joe?" Katie said in a whisper.

I was still drunk but I mumbled, "Do what again?"

"Screw!. We screwed Jimmy Joe and it was great. Let's do it again."

"Do what again?'

She leaned over and began to suck on my penis. Natural reflexes took hold and I got a huge erection. Katie climbed over, sat down on my erection and I slid into her vagina. I could feel her squeezing by tightening her muscles and it produced a wonderful feeling. I leaned my head back on the seat, let her be in control and did nothing to stop it. Before long she was bouncing up and down pressing on my shoulders and all of a sudden I was having a gigantic orgasm. Katie kept going and she had one as well.

Sometime later I came around and had enough sense to look at my watch. It was 3 AM. Katie was curled up in a fetal position beside me and she was sound asleep. I was still drunk, but I had enough sense to know that I had to find my clothes and somehow escape from this situation. I would feel the guilt and remorse later, but now it was a case of survival.

I found my underwear and my slacks. My shirt was on the shelf behind the seat. Where were my shoes? They didn't seem to be anywhere in the backseat. I leaned over the middle console and found them on the floor on the passenger side.

I had no idea where we were. It was dark and looked to be a dense forest. Maybe it was Percy Warner Park. I could almost walk home from here, but what would I do with Katie? I couldn't leave her naked, asleep in the backseat of her car with no protection whatsoever. I decided to call my sister.

She answered the phone with a grumble, "This better be good."

"It's me and I'm in deep shit." I explained everything that I could remember, although I left out the sex part.

But Allie is shrewd. "Did you have sex with her?"

"Well I woke up naked; so probably in the blackout I did."

"You are in deep shit. That's what you get Jimmy Joe when you think with your dick. You haven't done that in a while, so I guess you're due. You know she has a thing for you."

"Allie please don't lecture me now. There is plenty of time for that later. A lecture doesn't help me at this point."

"Where are you?"

"I'm in the woods somewhere. Probably Percy Warner Park; although I can't be sure"

"I know exactly where you are. Katie has a favorite spot in sort of a picnic area that's very secluded. I'll come get you and we will deal with Katie. After that you're on your own. I hope Maggie never finds out about this; I'm only helping you because I love her and I love our family. For a guy that's so smart, you surely are a screw-up."

Man, was she right! I am a screw-up. This is the kind of thing that just seeps out of the woodwork. It won't stay hidden, no matter how I try. I should probably go home and confess everything to Maggie-- throw myself on the proverbial sword. Yes, that's what I should do. Will I have the courage to do the right thing?

Allie arrived, and how she found where we were I'll never know. She had Cora Jane with her. I knew my chances of keeping this quiet were between slim and none.

"I see you're up to your old tricks Jimmy Joe," Cora Jane said. I managed to say nothing which was the smartest thing I'd done all day.

"Get in the car Jimmy Joe," Allie commanded. "I'm gonna get Katie in the car after I dress her. Cora Jane is going to drive Katie's car to my house. We just can't leave it here. She won't say anything."

I thought to myself that Allie better keep her happy or Cora Jane would hang me out to dry. What an opportunity she has to drive a nail right into my heart-- revenge is such an aphrodisiac.

The back door of the car opened, Katie fell into the backseat and immediately went back to sleep. She was really out of it.

Allie took me home first. I looked at my watch and couldn't believe it was 4:30 AM. I was still a little buzzed, so I went into the den and poured myself a finger of Scotch. Then I put my head on the sofa pillow and went sound asleep.

About 6 AM, Maggie was shaking my shoulder, "Jimmy, why didn't you let me know you were here? I have been worried sick about you. I called the Bluebird and the bartender said you left about 1 o'clock with Katie. What were you doing with her?"

"What time is it? Is my car here?"

"It doesn't matter what the time is and no your car is not here. The bartender said you were really drunk. What were you doing with Katie?"

"She just showed up at the bar. I don't know why or what she wanted. We talked a little bit, disagreed as usual and were generally uncivil to each other. I had a few more drinks and frankly I don't remember much else. I don't remember leaving the Bluebird, but I came around as we were turning in the drive here and Katie was driving. I guess it was her car she was driving, since my car isn't here. I didn't think that I could make it as far as the bedroom so I just collapsed in here. I feel terrible. Please never leave me alone in a bar again."

She put her arm around my shoulders and said, "You poor thing. Come on. You go upstairs, take a shower, get in bed and I'll bring you some toast, Alka-Seltzer and orange juice. I'll call the office and tell them that you won't be in until the afternoon. Oh sweetheart, I hurt just looking at you."

I stumbled upstairs feeling like a complete jerk. My wife, who I loved dearly, was treating me with such compassion and I had just lied to her about something that was at the core of marriage—fidelity. How low can you go? I was a snake. I was even worse—I was a CHEATER.

I stood in the shower hoping to wash away the stink of the evening. Maybe it really hadn't happened. Maybe it was a dream. I pounded my fist into the wall of the shower knowing full well that it had happened and somehow this was going to come back to bite me.

As I got out of the shower, Allie called me, "Katie is still asleep. She must've taken something that knocked her out. Cora Jane has promised me faithfully that she will keep this quiet, but I'm worried because she's enjoying it just a little too much. I just want to make sure you know that Katie will not leave this alone. You have to know Jimmy that she is going to use this in some way that is gonna damage you.

You think you dislike her, but it doesn't hold a candle to the hatred stemming from unrequited loves. I mean she really hates Bobby, but you are in second place and she wants to hurt you both. You fell into the trap buddy boy, so be ready."

"Gee sis, thanks for the positive reinforcement."

"You can be sarcastic all you want, but I am speaking truth here and you should pay attention."

"You're right of course, I am in deep trouble. There are too many people involved, but I didn't have a choice. Thanks for your help Allie."

As we hung up, Maggie entered the room carrying a tray with coffee, juice, some fruit, and coffee. I didn't deserve her. Maybe I should just tell her everything right now. I decided not to act on my first thought and postpone any decision on coming forth with the truth. The truth will set you free, but it will take a lot of pain to get there.

Maggie put the tray down in the middle of the bed and sat down. She poured some coffee and handed me the carafe. Maggie didn't say a word. She was eating a piece of toast and sipping coffee with a blank stare on her face.

After finishing a piece of toast and a cup of coffee, I looked at her and said, "Thanks for the breakfast and for being so kind to me. I really appreciate it, probably don't deserve it. Anyway, I think I'll catch a couple of hours sleep and then go into the office."

"Who was that on the phone Jimmy?"

"It was Allie. She wanted to see how it went last night after they left."

"Does she know that Katie brought you home last night?"

"She didn't, but I told her. Are you upset about that Maggie?"

"It just seems odd that she would bring you home, actually do something nice for you. I mean she professes to hate you with a passion."

"I admit it's strange but I was in no shape to drive home. I'm ashamed of having gotten myself into a situation like that."

"And what time was it you said you got in?"

"I didn't say and I really don't know. I would assume that it was around one-thirty, but who knows. I certainly don't."

"I'm sorry I'm asking so many questions Jimmy, but as I said it doesn't make any sense to me that she would bring you home unless she had some ulterior motive. She is a cunning woman who will stop at nothing to get what she wants. Mary Lynn told me all about her and about her parents; that they are very strange people and the doctor uses both his wife and his daughter as examples of his fine surgical work. Katie had a restraining order against her father last year and he has been arrested several times for physical abuse of his wife. Katie is nuts and you don't need to be hanging around her. She is Bobby's problem, not yours Jimmy. I know you love Bobby, but you need to leave his relationship with Katie alone. It's none of your business."

"You're right Maggie. I had a couple of extra drinks last night, because I got into it with Katie when she made some derogatory remarks about Bobby."

"Jimmy, promise me you will stay away from Katie and Bobby and not get involved in their situation. Promise me right now."

I looked her in the eyes. She was so beautiful. I raised my right hand and said, "As God is my witness, I promise you I will not get involved."

She stared into my eyes and said, "Please, please keep that promise."

I wanted to keep that promise. I really did.

Chapter 14

My life had become a bad Lifetime movie.

I was sitting in my office trying to familiarize myself with the company whose management team we were meeting tomorrow, when my phone rang, "You are going to want to watch the local news at five. Katie got arrested earlier in the day. Apparently she was involved in threatening Bobby with a knife."

"Allie how do you get all this stuff?"

"Katie's lawyer called me from the lockup and let me talk to Katie. She was coming off something, you know, strung out like. She's in deep trouble. Watch yourself Jimmy."

I had a TV in my office so it wouldn't be a problem to watch the news and I did. According to the news report, Katie's arrest stemmed from an argument with Bobby. Apparently Katie called the police, but during the call the operator heard Bobby tell Katie to "put the knife down." When the police got there a minute or so later, she had him cornered with the knife as two of their three children watched.

When the police tried to get her to stand down she immediately became combative, threatened them with a knife and started screaming that the voices were telling her to resist. She told police that they could ask her seven-year-old son, because he had conveyed the message from the voices. The police finally restrained her and took her into custody.

I couldn't believe what I was hearing and found it impossible to resist calling Bobby. We had been friends for a long time and he was probably tired of talking to police and reporters.

"It's great to hear a friendly voice Jimmy Joe. I've just been in court getting a temporary injunction to keep this bitch away from me and the children. She is really toxic at the moment and volatile. I thought she was gonna kill me last evening. The look in her eyes was really frightening."

"Are they gonna keep her in jail?"

"She is going to a drug rehab center and is going to be under psychiatric lockdown. She has stopped taking her medications for schizophrenia and has been taking some sort of drug to induce weight loss which she doesn't need. I mean she weighs 95 pounds."

"How are you holding up Bobby?"

"I'm worried about my kids. I'm particularly worried about Robbie because he has been the center of a lot of her craziness. It's hard to believe Jimmy that I'm a victim of spousal abuse. She has been physically, verbally and emotionally abusive to me and to the children. You don't know this Jimmy, but over the last two years she's been arrested twice for aggravated assault."

"You've got to get out of here Bobby. Aren't you afraid that she will do something to hurt one of your kids or you?"

"Where would I go Jimmy? This is home now. My business is here, all of my friends are here and absent all the shenanigans that Katie has pulled, I like it here. It's way better than being in Bethesda or Chevy Chase."

"What about the cops and the judges, can't they do something?"

"I have the injunction that keeps her from getting the kids. I'm working on the divorce papers and a restraining order that keeps her away from my house and the kids. But you know, it's amazing that she just ignores them all even if that means she's gonna get arrested again. She's crazy dangerous. I'm just going to do all I can to protect my kids and myself."

"Well I'm here for you man! Just call me and I'll be there. You're the best friend I've ever had and I love you. I don't want to see anything bad happen to any of you."

"Don't think I don't know that Jimmy Joe. You warned me early on about Katie. I wish I had listened."

I had broken my promise.

Several weeks passed with no new developments in the continuing saga of Bobby and Katie. As far as I knew, Katie remained in lockdown at a drug treatment center. It would be fine with me if she remained there for a long period of time. Somehow I knew that when she got out, she would make my life miserable. I tried to keep my role in the situation out of my thoughts, but there was a lingering feeling of guilt and remorse. My home life returned to some semblance of normalcy and I was working on a very lucrative deal at work. The firm overall was doing very well.

 Maggie and I double dated with Trip and Mary Lynn for dinner at Jimmy Kelley's. It was very pleasant. Afterwards, Maggie and I made love for the first time since the birthday party (six weeks or so) and it was wonderful. Maybe Maggie had put all this behind her.

"Hey, it's me! Katie! I just got out of rehab. Can you believe that I was in solitary confinement for 10 days? The only human contact I had was the guy bringing my meds. I need someone to talk to me. Allie is unavailable, so it's your turn."

In less than 30 seconds my life went from some semblance of normalcy to absolute shit. It has always amazed me how quickly my life can change. This doesn't seem to be normal for most people, but it is my normal.

"My turn for what? I'm not on your list of people who you can talk to about your problems."

"Sorry Jimmy Joe, you're at the top of the list. I'm sure poor little Maggie would not like to hear the awesome story of Jimmy Joe and Katie. You know, how you like having your dick in my pussy. You remember that-- right Jimmy Joe?"

"Actually I don't remember most of it, but I will admit that I was naked with you in the back of your car."

"Look I am staying at the Four Points Sheraton which is on old Hickory Boulevard in Brentwood. Down the way a little bit is the Cross Corner Bar on Franklin Road. It is 4 o'clock now, so I'll meet you about five at the Cross Corner. We'll have a drink and I'll talk. Okay?"

"Yeah, yeah okay, I'll see you there in about an hour." I broke my promise a second time.

When you start digging a hole, the best way to get out of it is to stop digging. I was in a pretty deep hole and I couldn't seem to stop digging. I called Maggie and told her I wouldn't be home until seven. She said that was fine because she had several things to do before even thinking about dinner. There was soccer practice and piano lessons for two of the kids and the third was going to be a copilot.

This would give me a lot to think about all the way to Brentwood. My kids were such a treasure and my wife was a blessing. And it was clear that I was putting all of this at risk. I was still digging.

I arrived at the bar a little early, but Katie was already there. She was sitting at the bar nursing a drink. She turned and looked at me as I walked in, "Well you didn't get lost in this part of town. Have you ever been over here? You are such a Belle Meade guy."

"Yep, you're right; I am a Belle Meade guy, and kind of proud of it. What do you have on your mind Katie?"

"That piece of shit you call a friend is blocking me from seeing my children. He has this restraining order against me and if I go near the house they can arrest me and put me in jail."

"I thought that had been in effect for a while?"

"My lawyer tells me this one has more teeth and I could go to jail for a longer period of time. I really miss my children. I don't miss him at all. Maybe if I just got rid of him everything would be okay."

"Well you could always file for divorce."

"Divorce wouldn't settle our problems, because he has convinced the courts that I am a bad person. So you see, they would never allow me to have my children. Bobby would always be in control. I think I may have to get rid of him permanently."

About that time, the bartender was standing in front of us asking if he could get us another round. I nodded yes, told him what I wanted and he left to get the drinks.

"Katie you have to be careful what you say. Somebody might misinterpret your meaning. The wrong person could hear you and start all kinds of rumors."

"Have you lost your balls Jimmy Joe? Where is the guy that used to be so daring?"

"That guy has gone. He exited stage right forever! I have too much going Katie to risk it anymore."

"I could ruin that for you very quickly. I don't think Maggie is the forgiving type. I think she would be pretty pissed off at you."

"Maybe, maybe not!"

"I may need your help Jimmy Joe. Don't let me down or Maggie will know all the graphic details."

"What do you need my help for? I'm not gonna help you do anything. You may as well tell Maggie now."

"I'll be calling on you soon Jimmy Joe, even if it is just to put that big dick of yours inside me. Now run along home and be a good husband."

I got out of there quickly and breathed a sigh of relief in the cold air outside. I sat in my car for a while thinking. The thought came that if I simply told Maggie the truth I could stop digging this hole. I decided that when I got home that would be the course of action. But when I was sitting in my garage, I lost my nerve. I could not muster the courage, so I went inside and lost the opportunity.

A few days later, Katie called me and asked me to meet her again at the Four Points Sheraton. I told her I was not going to sleep with her, so if that was the reason she could forget it. She said she had something of a financial nature to talk to me about.

I drove out to Brentwood, walked into the hotel and headed for Katie's room. When I got there she was dressed in a business suit that was probably a size or two too big, but she looked very professional.

"I am going to go get my children and take them to Birmingham where my friend lives. Bobby has not cut off my funds at the bank. If the account is just in my name, can he close it?"

"Is his name on the account in any way?"

"I am pretty sure it isn't."

"Then he can't close it, but he doesn't have to put any more money in it. Katie you will be guilty of kidnapping. Bobby will certainly come after you as will the police. Moreover it will involve crossing state lines if you go to Birmingham. Your children will simply see you carted off to jail again. This is really a dumb idea and you should give it up immediately. You have just got to stop this craziness Katie."

"Katie, have you talked to Allie about this at all?"

"She's not taking my calls."

My sister is doing exactly what I should do. I have escaped two meetings with Katie without getting seriously damaged. I'm already pressing my luck; so from now on I'm not taking her calls. The chips can fall where they may, but I'm stopping the digging.

So much for that plan. I met Katie for the third time, this meeting at a Hampton Inn off I-40 West.

"My only option is to kill him."

"You can't do that Katie. The first person they look at is the spouse. With your record, they'll find a way to convict you."

"What do you think of this plan, Jimmy Joe? I'll wait until he is drunk, which is every night, sneak into the house and strangle him with a cord."

"I think it's crazy. You aren't strong enough, you weigh only 95 ponds. Bobby is much stronger. Secondly, the police will come straight to you. Third, you just can't kill your children's father. It's just wrong."

"None of those are very good reasons. Nope, just a matter of timing now."

"Waiting until he is drunk is a good idea."

We talked a little longer and I left. I stiffened my resolve to not take her calls again! But I didn't tell anyone about our conversation.

A week later, Bobby called me and asked if he could have lunch. We agreed to meet at the Cumberland club around 1:30 PM.

We were seated in a quiet corner of the club and Bobby said to me, "Katie is driving me crazy. She calls me at all hours of the day and night, tries to get in the house when I'm not there, and is generally terrorizing my nanny. I am at my ropes end. I have a restraining order against her, but she doesn't pay any attention to that. I'm going to file for divorce, but I don't see what that would do to keep her from harassing me and the children. The children are basically afraid of her, particularly Robbie. I just need someone to talk to and you are my oldest and dearest friend."

I guess I had become the sounding board and the designated listener for the Gibbs family. I felt guilty about talking to Bobby without disclosing that I had been talking to Katie as well, but I just didn't seem to be able to get the words out.

"I know this is going to sound harsh, but have you ever thought of moving to somewhere else. A place you would have more support. Here you have friends who are supporting you, but it's not like having family to defend you and help you. Bobby let's face it, you moved to Nashville because of Katie. Maybe you would have gone to Vanderbilt, but I don't think you would have stayed here if it were not for Katie. I believe she has really damaged Robbie with this voice thing and it might be nice for him to have a loving grandma and granddad around. I'm just afraid that you and maybe your children are going to get hurt, not emotionally but physically."

"Have you been talking to Allie about Katie? "

"Some, but I think Allie has become afraid of Katie. She tells me that she's no longer talking to Katie or taking her calls. Katie, according to Allie, is on so many drugs that often she doesn't make sense. By the way, you will be interested to know that Allie's partner is Cora Jane Davis, a girl I dated in high school and I probably turned her against men."

"I didn't know the specifics of her relationship, but I did know she was into women. Jimmy, this is my home, it's where all my friends are, my business interests are here, I'm in the midst of buying an interest in a medical accounting firm and am probably going to become part of the management team and I just couldn't imagine going back to Maryland and starting all over again."

"I understand that perfectly well. I remember looking into that medical business for you and you should do really well at that. So you're gonna give up the law?"

"It looks that way. The law business in Nashville has been very good to me. But I think my partners are a little embarrassed about my personal life and clients are a little wary as well. I won't be making as much money for a while, but it will be enough for the children and me to continue living as we have been. I'll be growing something for myself and the kids, and I've been able to protect it from Katie."

"My advice to you is to divorce her as soon as you can, get the strongest restraining orders possible and put as much distance between you and Katie as you can."

"Thanks Jimmy Joe! I know I can count on you to be in my corner when all this stuff gets out. The way Katie goes about things; I think the newshounds sort of follow her around from time to time hoping for a good story. She usually gives it to them."

April showers bring May flowers. As the flowers began to emerge, Katie came out from her seclusion. Apparently, Katie came to Bobby's house and became engaged in a shouting match with the nanny about her daughter. She wanted to take the young girl with her and was planning to go to the other children's school. The nanny called Bobby who left work immediately. As the nanny and Katie were playing tug-of-war with Laurie, the other children came home and immediately joined the nanny in trying to keep Laurie from their mother. Katie began to scream at them as well as the nanny and eventually got Laurie away from the nanny.

She took the girl to her SUV and buckled her into the backseat. This was the second time she had tried to take Laurie. Bobby arrived home and parked his car in back of Katie's car trying to block her exit. He immediately went inside and saw Katie going for the other children. He got in between Katie and the children: she hit him square in the nose and blood went everywhere. She tried to scratch his eyes, but he managed to shove her away. The children were hysterical.

She gave up the struggle and headed for her SUV. She got into her car, pulled forward a little bit and rammed Bobby's car creating a huge dent in the side panel this time. As Katie pulled out of the driveway with her youngest child in tow, a police officer approached, as neighbors apparently reported the fight and activated his lights and siren. Katie sped off, reaching speeds of at least 70 miles an hour on Estes Road. Because of the danger involved, the police officer did not pursue her. He did, however, put out a bulletin giving her license number and model of car plus a warning that a child was involved and could be in danger.

Finally, Katie was spotted on Old Hickory Boulevard and several police cars in the area converged on her. She was forced to stop, but she did try to get Laurie out of the car so she could run. It was too late so she turned and fought with the police officers. They arrested her for resisting arrest, child endangerment and violating the restraining order. One of the police officers said, "This woman is crazy!"

She spent about 2 weeks in jail before her lawyer, Mary Langford, a dynamic advocate on women's issues, convinced the judge to grant bail, a mere $500,000 bond.. Her father posted the bail with a bondsman.

I called Bobby. "I hear she's out on bond."

"Yeah she is. It was so peaceful for those two weeks she was in jail. That crazy father of hers did say that part of the agreement for the bail was that she stays a month in rehab. She'll be in lockdown, thank heavens."

"Rest easy for a month."

"I think I'm gonna take the kids to the beach for a couple of weeks when school is over in 2 weeks."

"Sounds like a good plan. Keep in touch Bobby."

I truly felt sorry for my long-time friend, but I didn't know what to do for him except to be there for him when he needed to talk. I began to think about my own situation. My life was back to normal. I was about to take a due diligence trip with John Ferber of Advertising.com, Maggie and I were back to our normal sex life and more importantly, we were talking again like always. I hoped Maggie wouldn't hear gossip about me, before I could be truthful with her. I just didn't want to spoil things.

Chapter 15

"Jimmy Joe are you okay," Trip said as he came rushing, breathlessly into my office.

"Why wouldn't I be?"

"Jimmy, Bobby Gibbs is dead. It's all over local TV. Turn it on!"

One of the local talking heads was reporting on Bobby's death. "Attorney Robert Gibbs was found dead in a closet in his Green Hills home today June 24, 2004. Police arrested his wife, Katie Gibbs, and charged her with violating a protection order that prevented her from seeing her children and husband. Robert Gibbs had custody of their three children."

"The couple had been going through a bitter divorce and custody battle."

"When police began investigating Robert Gibbs' death, his children were not at the home. They were with Katie Gibbs at a local hotel, the Renaissance. "

"Katie Gibbs told police the night her husband was killed that she had been at the house. She said the back door was open, so she walked in the house. She also said she saw a few lights on. She allegedly tried to see if Robert was inside, and even called his name several times."

"Then Gibbs said she heard one of the children crying in a bedroom. Since she couldn't find Robert, Ms. Gibbs said she took the children back to her hotel, which is not too far away from the scene of the crime."

"Detectives asked her why she didn't call police. She said she feared for her children, but didn't feel the need to call authorities."

I sat there with my mouth wide open. I couldn't believe it! "Oh my God, she killed him, she really did kill him!"

"Who killed him?" Trip said.

"Katie!" I shouted. "I know it was her. She said it was the only way she could keep her children."

"You talked with her about this? Are you crazy Jimmy Joe?" Trip said as he shut my office door. "Were you screwing her?"

"Well, no not exactly."

"Not exactly! What the hell does that mean? Either you did or you didn't."

"I wasn't having an affair with her, but she was blackmailing me with something. After the 40th birthday party, I stayed at the bar for a while. Katie joined me and I got really drunk. She took me from the bar with the help of the bartender. They put me in Katie's car and the next thing I remember is coming to in the back seat of Katie's car, naked, with her, also naked, straddling me and pumping up and down for all she's worth."

"Jesus, Joseph and Mary! Where were you?"

"As it turns out we were in Percy Warner Park. I had to call Allie to come rescue me."

"Allie knows about this?"

"And Cora Jane Davis. She came to help Allie. She promised to keep it quiet."

Trip laughed in a snide way, "Every gay woman in Nashville knows it now. You, my only son, are screwed, literally and figuratively. Does Maggie know about this?"

"No, not really. She knows I came in late and thinks Katie brought me home."

"My advice is to tell her the whole thing now before she hears about it from Allie. Bobby's death will move Allie to protect Maggie. She loves you Jimmy, but she has a sisterhood with Maggie, a very strong bond. She'll sell you out in a New York minute."

"That's good advice. I'm going home after I call Pat Gibbs."

After all these years I still had Bobby's mom's number in my book. I finally got Pat on the phone.

"Pat, I am so sorry that this has happened. It's devastating!"

"Jimmy, I knew she would kill him, I just knew it. There was nothing I could do," she said as she gasped to cover her tears. For several minutes she wept, then said, "I have to get control of myself. We have a fight ahead of us and I need to be in control to protect my poor grandchildren. At least we will have a piece of Bobby through his lovely children. I need to be there for them."

"They need you Pat. In all of this, they have suffered a great deal and without your help they will be lost. I am here for you and I'm here for them. I loved Bobby as the brother I never had. Are you going to be traveling down here soon?"

"My daughter Delores has already booked flights to Nashville out of Baltimore for herself and her husband, Larry Fleming. They will be there late in the day and will sort things out for the children. They will also find a place to stay."

"Don't worry about that. We have several good-sized, nice rental properties. We'll find a place for you and don't worry about the cost."

I got Delores's number before we hung up. Then I called the people who handled the real estate end of our investments and made arrangements for a large three-bedroom house with plenty of room to spread out. I called Delores and gave her the information she would need to get in the house. By the time she got to Nashville, the house would be furnished and fully functional.

I left the firm and headed home. It was time for me to have a discussion with Maggie. I had the feeling that my life would never be the same after today. Maggie was an understanding and forgiving person, but I was asking a lot of her to forgive me.

"Oh Jimmy Joe, I am heartbroken. I can't believe that Bobby is dead. How could this all happen?"

"I know that it's hard to believe, but I had the feeling that she was gonna do something drastic. Bobby was doing

213

everything he could from a legal standpoint, but those roadblocks just didn't seem to get in her way. She did get arrested, do her time in jail or in rehab, get out and do the same thing all over again. It's just pure insanity."

"I'm glad you're home. You know Allie has the same take on it as you do. She thinks Katie's crazy, but that's still no excuse."

"You talk to Allie today?"

"Of course and Mary Lynn too. We had a good cry together, Allie and I."

"Listen, there's something I'd like to talk to you about. Let's get some coffee and go into the den." So that's what we did.

"It's about that night of the birthday party at the Bluebird. I wasn't fully forthcoming about that."

"At the time, it didn't sound right to me either, but I figured you'd tell me when you were ready. I guess that's now, although I don't know if I'm ready for it or can take it given all that's going on. But if you have to do it now, get on with it."

"I did stay at the bar and Katie did join me at the bar. We talked about a variety of things and even argued about stuff, Bobby mostly. I did get sloppy drunk and the bartender did help Katie get me to her car. But I don't remember much after that, but Katie didn't bring me home that night and I didn't get home until about 4:30 AM. Allie brought me home."

"ALLIE BROUGHT YOU HOME!" she said in a very loud voice. "How did that happen?"

"I called her and she came to get me. I didn't have a clue where I was, but when I explained to Allie the circumstances, she knew exactly where I was."

"You know you have a wife Jimmy Joe. I would, I would've come and gotten you."

"I know, but you wouldn't have known where I was and Allie did. You see I was in Percy Warner Park with Katie."

Maggie's eyes widened, her jaw dropped and she made a little whining sound. I could see tears forming in her eyes.

"When I came to, Katie and I were in the backseat of her car. We were both naked, she was straddling me, and we were having sex. I am so sorry Maggie! I can say that I didn't know what I was doing and for some of the time I didn't. But when I did recognize what was happening, I didn't stop. I am so sorry. I feel terrible, but I had to tell you the truth."

Tears were flowing from Maggie's eyes.

"I thought we had a good marriage Jimmy Joe. I have loved you since the first day I laid eyes on you. I thought you loved me."

"I do love you Maggie. This is all killing me, but if I didn't tell you and someone else did, it would be worse.

She stood, turned toward me, looked me straight in the eye and said, "The thing I hate the most Jimmy Joe is that you lied to me. You lied to me in my own house. I never expected you to be so cruel." She left the room and was as graceful as she had ever been.

I sat in that room for over an hour, sipping cold coffee and thinking about my life. Sexual relationships had caused most of my problems, but this one took the cake. I'm sure my grandfather, Big Jack, was looking down on me with pure disgust. I had no clue what my wife was going to do next and my best friend was dead, probably killed by his wife.

My phone rang and I answered. It was Allie. "So you talked to your wife. That was a good move. She's very hurt at the moment and she probably won't trust you for a long while, but I think she's going to stay with you come hell or high water."

"That's good news, I hope you're right. I feel awful; I really love her and our children. I just can't imagine life without them. Did you tell her anything I ought to know?"

"I told her what my role in it was and that I advised you to tell her everything."

"Yeah, Trip told me today to tell her before you did. I think he was right and so are you. I really appreciate the love you have for Maggie."

"It's all up to you now big brother!"

As I hung up from Allie, Delores Fleming called. She was at the condo and wondered if we could talk. I told her I'd be there in half an hour.

Delores wanted to thank me for making the arrangements for them. She also wanted to go over to the house so that she could get Bobby's car which the police had released to her.

One of the things I did was to keep a running account of the newspaper and TV stories on this tragic event. It helped me keep my sanity. The reporting all seemed to point to Katie as the culprit and the lawyers seemed to love the TV time and seeing their names in print.

A housekeeper discovered Bobby Gibb's dead body stuffed into an upstairs bedroom closet at his Green Hills home. Relatives and friends began pointing the finger at Katie, even though police publicly had not named her as a suspect or even a person of interest in the homicide. The cause of Bobby's death was widely reported as strangulation, though police didn't release the cause of death early on. Authorities reportedly have only questioned Katie, adding fuel to a real-life murder mystery that had Bobby's quiet West End neighborhood buzzing.

It was a marriage out of soap opera hell. A series of police reports coupled with the divorce papers Bobby filed— which had been largely ignored by the press—documented claims of psychotic episodes and portrayed a toxic, unstable relationship marred by volatile arguments and Katie's alleged drug abuse.

In March, a Davidson County judge awarded Bobby temporary custody of the children and issued restraining orders and an injunction that would prevent Katie from coming into contact with Bobby or the children. Since

Bobby's death, police arrested her for violating that order. Bobby also had an injunction that prevented Katie from entering the family's home.

But someone did enter the home to strangle Bobby sometime before 10:15 a.m. on June 23, when a housekeeper called 911 after discovering his lifeless body in one of the home's closets, leaving neighbors and friends to grapple with a sensational "Who done it?" In the center of the media storm stood Katie Gibbs, a crazed woman. I could testify to that fact.

Mark Hartfield, an attorney who represented Bobby in his divorce and who had been a close personal friend with him for more than 20 years, described the couple's relationship as chaotic. He characterized Bobby as "one of the good guys," and Katie as explosive and aggressive. "I'm just trying in my little mind...to understand why this happened," Hartfield said. He was distraught and still a little stunned after returning from Bobby's memorial service. "He put up with hell for 13 years living with her and tried to make it work and went above and beyond what most husbands would ever do...."

And Katie seems to have been quite devoted to him, too. In a surprising move, she filed a motion last week to stop the cremation of Bobby's body. His sister, Delores Gibbs Fleming, who has control of what happened to her brother's remains, wanted him cremated. An attorney for Katie, Jeffrey Levy argued that she had been excluded from visitation and had not had the opportunity to see her husband's remains. The judge ruled that Fleming should keep control of her brother's remains and awarded Katie an hour-and-a-half to visit his body.

The battle to see Bobby's body was a little odd, but it seemed to be on par with how the relationship was all along. An emergency injunction Bobby filed against Katie earlier this year outlines a pattern of psychotic behavior. She was a schizophrenic who refused to take her medication, divorce papers read. She opted instead to begin a pattern of prescription drug abuse—targeting drug stores in Belle Meade and Green Hills to fill multiple prescriptions for Percocet and OxyContin to squelch pain for back problems Bobby said she never had.

Bobby and Katie's tumultuous 11-year marriage had all the trappings of a suspense novel—one that ends in horrific tragedy. But judging from outward appearances alone, the two also had the makings of a beaming, happy couple. Bobby was a well-liked businessman and attorney who was buying a business in the medical field with several other partners. Hartfield says that Bobby was "just like a little boy" who loved to hunt fish and have fun. In fact, the man had just returned from a weeklong beach vacation with his three children days before his death. And Katie, a graduate of Harpeth Hall, was a housewife, the kind of woman who classmates remember as the popular cheerleader, a real looker whose former love interest was, indeed, the high school football star.

Katie has retained two attorneys: criminal attorney Jeffrey Levy and Mary Langford, who will represent her in custody matters and in hearings regarding Bobby's will, among other matters.

Both Levy and Langford categorize Bobby's divorce filings as one-sided. In fact, Langford says Katie did not file a response to the claim because it was always her intention to reunite with Bobby. Langford says Bobby called Katie almost on a daily basis because the two were discussing their future and a possible reconciliation. Katie was even named as the executrix of Bobby's will, Langford says. Her mother was the alternate executrix. "If you look at that divorce file, it's a totally one-sided file—basically what you have is what's created by Mr. Gibbs and Mr. Hartfield without any response," Levy says. "There are always two sides to the story, but a lot of those allegations are unfounded."

Langford says the way Katie has been portrayed in the media since Bobby's death is a shame. Langford says she's been dubbed "a mad woman" who is guilty of killing Bobby, but she quickly explains that it's simply not the case.

"Basically, her history is that she was part of this town and she was a hard worker," Langford says. "She worked her way through college and on into post-graduate work, some pretty high-profile things." She says Katie worked as deputy press secretary for former Gov. Ned Ray McWherter, for NASA at the Marshall Space Center in Huntsville, Ala., and for a time as a nanny to three children in France. Katie even worked in the local medical examiner's office.

Katie started dating Bobby while she was at George Washington University and he was at University of Virginia, Levy says, as the two had met through their friendship with Jim Jeter IV, whose sister Allie and Katie have been friends since elementary school at Ensworth School. "They married and her focus turned from the medical school to children, and that was her life."

"Katie is a person," Levy says. "She's a hard worker but the most important thing is she's a mom. It seems like everybody's trying to paint a different picture.... The people I've spoken with say that her children adored her and tell me stories of how they followed her around like little puppies and how they would pile in her bed and watch movies—things that mothers who love their children do."

The attorneys now say that Katie intends to fight for full custody of the children. "She's obviously devastated to be separated from her children and to have lost her husband under these bizarre circumstances, but she's trying to put one foot in front of the other and take care of these matters," Langford says.

Bobby's filing to keep Katie out of the family home shows that Katie was in and out of drug rehab facilities and psychiatric hospitals for years. The document details one stint at Vanderbilt Medical Center following an alleged suicide attempt. He even claimed that she used drugs in front of their children. According to police reports, after screaming and becoming combative with the Metro police officers and paramedics enlisted to haul her off to treatment, Katie had to be restrained by police and put in physical lockdown for days on end at a local drug treatment center.

Back when Katie lived in that home, Bobby claimed that she was physically, verbally and emotionally abusive to him and their children. In fact, police arrested Katie twice in the last few years for an aggravated assault against her husband in 2003 and for reckless endangerment, domestic violence and evading arrest this May.

Hartfield says it wouldn't be far-fetched to call Bobby a victim of spousal abuse. "We had every possible court order we could possibly get against her to keep her away from him and the children and the house—and she violated every one of them," Hartfield says.

Claims made by Katie's family and friends on online blogs speculate that Bobby was no saint himself. Others have said that the couple was patching things up. But Hartfield says Bobby was considering nothing of the like and that he didn't know Bobby to have any serious personal issues, other than his troubled marriage. That was more than enough for anyone.

In fact, when he spoke to Bobby on the Friday before his death, Hartfield says Bobby was ready to reconstruct a life that had been chaotic for so long. "Bobby had come to terms with the fact that the divorce was going to go forward, and he was at peace with that," he said. "He had struggled—he didn't want a divorce.... But she simply wouldn't stay straight. He decided that was the best thing for the children."

Hartfield says Bobby was rebuilding relationships and reconnecting with old friends. He didn't want to be a single dad, but in that final conversation, Hartfield says Bobby asked about the quickest way to get his divorce resolved before his children started school again in the fall.

Katie wasn't coping with the divorce quite as well, Hartfield says. "From what I could tell from talking to him, she was very angry at Bobby because we obtained court orders keeping her away from the children and from the house."

Still, the thought of Katie as a potential suspect is a little hard for some to swallow. After all, according to an injunction, earlier this year Katie weighed a measly 90 pounds because of her alcohol and drug use. Friends wonder if a woman of her stature could overpower any man—even Bobby, who at about 5 feet 7 inches and 180 pounds was not exactly large.

Police are releasing little information about the crime scene. Was there any sign of forced entry? Was Bobby drugged or beaten? The medical examiner won't release his full report for a few more weeks. And police will only say there were no visible signs of what might have killed him.

Then there is the matter of the children. Police say the children were spotted with Bobby the night of his death. They had gone to the Sportsman Grill for dinner. As far as Hartfield and other friends and family can tell, the three children were at the family's home when he was killed. Yet the morning after Bobby's death, when police went to the hotel Bobby paid for Katie to live in, the kids were with their mother.

Such contact was strictly prohibited. Days later, police arrested Katie on charges that she violated the order of protection. She has since been released after posting $45,000 bond.

Of course, Katie had violated that order and others again and again since the very beginning. And Hartfield says that, as far as he knows, Bobby never slipped or caved and allowed Katie to take the children after he obtained the court orders.

Court hearings aside, all of us who were friends or family were left to grapple with more questions than answers.

In court documents, Bobby said he feared for his safety and the safety of his children. "He never told me he was afraid that she would try to kill him," Hartfield says.

"I've gone over in my mind a million times since last week: What could I have done or what could we have done differently to prevent this?" Hartfield says. "And I don't know of anything we could have done. We obtained every possible court order we could through the legal system to protect him and the children from her. And if you have somebody who's going to commit a homicide, a court order is just not going to stop them. There's nothing by law you can do if someone is going to harm somebody."

Avidly defending his client, Levy seems surprised that Hartfield, among many others, has tagged Katie as a killer. "I think it's a little irresponsible for my friend to form those kinds of judgments and conclusions," Levy says. "The police will conduct an investigation and go where the facts lead them...."

The turbulent nature of the Gibbs marriage was not lost on Bobby's family and friends. Hartfield fought Katie in court to ensure that Bobby's side of the family kept temporary custody of the couple's children. And the battle now has literally spilled onto the front lawn of what was once the Gibbs family home.

Patricia Gibbs called police to the Gibbs' home because Katie's attorney was supervising a locksmith who was changing the locks to the family home. Officers arrived on the scene to ensure that the verbal argument between Patricia and Katie's lawyers did not get out of hand. Police then instructed both sides to allow attorneys to solve the dispute, or if necessary, to take the civil matter to court.

Langford says that the home has been in Katie's name since 2005, and that she advised her client to change the locks to prevent Bobby's family from removing items from the home. She says the man's family entered the property sometime last week and took Bobby's Mercedes and other contents from the home. I know all about that since I was there.

This was something that the best of romance novel writers could never imagine!

Chapter 16

Police arrested Katie exactly two weeks after the housekeeper found her husband's body in the master bedroom closet in the couple's house. She was not arrested on murder charges, but on three counts of criminal contempt for violating an order of protection. On the morning Bobby Gibb's body was found the children were found in Katie Gibbs' possession at her hotel in Downtown Nashville.

She appeared in a Nashville courtroom on the charges two days later. Afterwards, she told a group of reporters, "I'm devastated by all this."

Police did not name any suspects in Bobby's death at that point in time. According to Delores Fleming, Katie told police the night his body was found that she had been at the house. She said the back door was open, so she walked in the house. She also said she saw a few lights on. She tried to see if Bobby was inside, and even called his name several times.

Then, according to Delores, she said she heard one of the children crying in a bedroom. Since she couldn't find Bobby, Katie found the children and took them back to her hotel.

Detectives asked her why she didn't call police. She said she feared for her children, but didn't feel the need to call authorities. Her attorney, Jeffrey Levy, further explained Katie's situation by saying "Anytime you have a spouse that passes away under suspicious circumstances, the other spouse is always going to be considered a person of interest." Levy went on to say his client is claiming innocence when it comes to the death of her husband and even defended why police discovered the couple's children with her. Her instincts as a mother were overwhelming and she felt a need to protect her children, since she believed they were unattended.

Delores looked at me and said, "Does that sound convincing to you Jimmy?"

"Doesn't convince me!"

Delores looked a little flustered. Her husband, Larry, had returned to Bethesda for work. She and Larry didn't have kids and the three young ones that she and Pat were looking after were taking a lot of attention and care. Two were back in school, but were very shaky given all the news about their mom.

"What is she thinking? Do you truly believe that she believes she will get away with this murder?"

My response was easy, "I do. She believes she is smarter than anyone. I have known her for most of my life and have seen her full blown superiority complex emerge more than once."

"Well, I hope she is wrong!"

"She is this time."

"By the way, Larry and I have been appointed guardians for the children. Dianne Crozet has been very helpful. Larry has a friend in Chevy Chase that is an estate/domestic relations attorney. As it happens he is licensed to practice in Tennessee and he is going to help us in all of this along with Mark and Dianne. His name is Harry Steinbeck. We just need someone we know."

"Makes sense to me."

"Her attorneys are going after the estate for their fees."

"Why am I not surprised?"

Several months later it was revealed that the attorneys were indeed after the estate. On behalf of Katie, Mary Langford had gone to court over matters ranging from access to the family home, possession of personal property and financial assets, and even who gets to keep the family dog, a Bichon Frisé named "Sugar."

Langford also petitioned successfully to have the court disqualify Nashville attorney Lawrence Haskins from representing Delores Fleming on the grounds that Haskin's prior representation of Bobby Gibbs made him ineligible to act as counsel in this case. And he represented her interests as the estate sold its shares of Medical Systems of Tennessee, a company Bobby Gibbs had just invested in and planned to join before his death. They sold his portion for $6 million.

In addition to those proceeds, an estate inventory has showed other assets totaling almost $1.9 million. If Katie Gibbs is ever convicted of her husband's murder, state law would prevent her from inheriting any of his property.

Meanwhile, Katie was trying to find out the status of and gain access to some of that property. Another lawyer,

David Hale, sought court approval for the estate to loan Katie $132,000.

Last month, Hale obtained a court order requiring Equitable Trust Co. to turn over a full accounting of a Gibbs family trust that it administers. Equitable had refused to provide information on the trust, citing the potential that Katie Gibbs would be barred from inheriting its funds. Equitable, saying it had no knowledge that Katie was seeking such an order until after it was issued, has asked Probate Judge Randolph Kern to rescind it.

I asked Delores if she felt she was getting good representation. She told me, "When Larry was thrown off the case, we just decided to bring in Harry to help us with all of these estate issues. There's a lot of money here and we need to protect it for the children. I can be very combative and this is something that just makes my blood boil. I have lost my baby brother and these children have lost their father."

While police had not identified Katie as a suspect in the case, her attorney, Jeffrey Levy, said investigators have called her a person of interest.

"Anytime you have a spouse that passes away under suspicious circumstances, the other spouse is always going to be considered a person of interest," he said.

My situation with Maggie was still very tense even though several months had passed, and we were rapidly approaching the holidays. Maggie told me that she had invited her father and mother to come for Thanksgiving and they had agreed. I was actually happy about that and told her so.

We also had a talk about everything that's going on. She looked me squarely in the eyes and said, "Jimmy Joe, I don't think our relationship will ever be like it was and I have been praying for the strength to forgive you. All I can tell you is that it's getting better. Is there anything else that's going to blindside me again? I need to tell you that I've talked to Allie at some length about all of this and she has been very helpful in giving me perspective."

"There's nothing else that will blind side you. If I had been smart, I would have left the bar with you. I wanted to think and gain some perspective about being 40, you know, half my life being over and all that. My self-centered nature surely came into play. That's a problem for me and I'm working on it. Allie is very truthful and forthright when it comes to my character. I've often thought that she was downright judgmental. But she'll give you an accurate assessment of that night and what it means."

"She already has done that for me. She told me that you truly didn't know where you were and why you were there. I know from my experience that Katie is a manipulator and Allie says you were clearly manipulated and drunk. She and Cora Jane have remained silent as they promised with the exception that Allie has talked to me. I feel better about things, but I haven't totally healed. I thought having my mom here would help and you could talk to my dad some. He isn't the brightest bulb in the lamp, but he does have a number of good qualities. One is that he loves my mom unconditionally."

"Maggie please never have doubts about whether I love you. I truly love you and the best day of my life was the day I met you. I think the Thanksgiving idea is perfect."

Thanksgiving was perfect. Maggie and her mother fixed a wonderful meal complete with duck and a Virginia ham that the Randolph's brought with them from Richmond. My favorite thing of all was the sweet potato casserole that Maggie made. My second favorite thing was that Mary Lynn, Trip, Allie and Cora Jane were invited as well. I did have several discussions with Maggie's father about long-term relationships, patience and tolerance along with faithfulness. His thoughts really resonated with me and my whole opinion about the man changed. He was a man of courage and strength along with integrity and I wanted everything he had along those lines.

In mid-January 2005, Katie Gibbs was arrested for the murder of Bobby Gibbs. Amazingly, after a week in jail, she was granted bail and only $75,000. She tried to get custody of her three children, but Delores got an order of protection against her and that ended that quest. Katie was free on bond for several months after her arrest, but Allie called me with startling news, "Guess what? Katie's missing. She has just disappeared." I couldn't believe that she had just disappeared and didn't seem to be anywhere in Nashville. The police seemed very inept in their search for Katie.

Six days later, she was found in Gulf Shores, Alabama at the home of her friend Brett Carlson. She had met him in medical school and he now works for a hospital in lower Alabama. He told police that Katie showed up at his hospital dehydrated and very sick. He took her to his home and began to treat her for these problems. He said he didn't realize she was a fugitive until one of his friends told him about it. Carlson immediately called the police and that's how they found Katie.

Judge Dianne Cosgrove ordered her jailed after she violated the terms of her release by removing an electronic tracking device that she wore as a condition of her bond. Katie remained incarcerated, awaiting a trial set to begin July 8.

The Gibbs children and their guardians filed a wrongful death lawsuit against her for $40 million.

The trial began on Friday, July 8, 2005. Why the judge started a trial on Friday was beyond me, but she noted that she didn't want any nonsense and expected the trial to move with dispatch. Plus she indicated that while she was allowing the press and videographers in the courtroom, she expected no shenanigans. She also said she wanted the defendant referred to by name and not by the appellation "the Anorexic Assassin." The press had taken to referring to Katie by that so-called "handle."

After much wrangling and maneuvering, the jury was finally seated. There were seven women and five men on the jury plus two alternatives. Katie's attorney called to tell me that I was on his list of witnesses and should not attend the trial. He also asked if I needed to be subpoenaed. I thought that was strange. I called my friend Doug Hazelwood and asked him if that question was unusual. He told me to be prepared for some off-the-wall questioning. He recommended Patrick Bramlege and his partner Elizabeth

Oliver. Two days later, I met with them and explained my situation thoroughly. I had a problem and they knew it. Keep out of sight and don't go near the courtroom. They planned to find out where the defense was going.

I told Maggie about the call I received from Katie's attorney and Doug Hazelwood's advice. Maggie was distraught. "I cannot believe that you are being dragged into this situation. You didn't have anything to do with this, did you?"

"Of course not! You already know about my involvement with Katie."

She shrugged, "I guess all of that will be public."

The actual trial started.

On the morning of June 24, 2004, a housekeeper, Rose Jones, found 40-year-old Bobby Gibbs's body in an upstairs closet of his home in Green Hills. The prosecution claims his estranged wife, 39-year-old Katie Gibbs, entered the home on Bowling Avenue the night before his body was found and wearing latex gloves, strangled him with an electrical cord used for recharging a cell phone.

Witnesses called by the prosecution testified about forensic evidence that police believe links Katie to the murder scene including the tip of a latex glove that contained her DNA. James Hart was the lead investigator in the murder case. He told the jury Tuesday that he found a box of gloves at Katie's hotel the day after Bobby was found dead.

"I noticed a box of latex gloves, and the name brand was Walgreens. The corner of the box was missing," said Hall.

Hart said the tip of glove found at the crime scene contains Katie's DNA on the inside, and her husband's on the outside. The jury also saw surveillance video showing Katie stealing a box of gloves from a nearby Walgreens the same night as the murder.

Hart continued, "The fact that she stole the gloves is an indication that the murder was premeditated."

In a phone conversation played to the jury Wednesday, Katie explained to a friend that she used the gloves when coloring her hair.

Bobby Gibbs was strangled to death, with bleach poured on his body. Hart showed the jury the pants Katie had been wearing that night and part of her pants appeared discolored by bleach.

"Detective Hart, how many murders have you investigated? " Associate DA McNally was asking the questions.

"I have closed 93 and have 5 unsolved cases."

"Do you consider yourself an experienced homicide detective and something of an expert?"

"Yes, you could say that."

"Your honor, we would like Detective Hart to use the evidence that we have and let him tell us how he thinks this crime occurred based on said evidence."

"Objection, your honor! I commend the detective's record, but there is no such thing as an expert on murder." Jeffrey Levy was beside himself.

"I am going to allow the question to be asked, but you have no latitude Detective Hart. Stick to the evidence."

"Detective Hart, can you review the evidence in this murder and tell us what it shows to have happened in this situation."

"I'll start off with the gloves. Ms. Gibbs stole a box of sterile gloves from a Walgreens in Green Hills. This indicates to me that she was going to the home with the intent to kill her husband. She had talked about strangulation as a method with others and we saw on her computer that she had visited websites that show strangulation techniques. She had her cell phone cord that had nice size plugs on each end that could serve as handles. She went upstairs to the bedroom and found Mr. Gibbs passed out on the bed. Based on his blood alcohol level, he had quite a bit to drink. She climbed on the bed and pushed him on his side facing away from her, but toward the closet. We have these photographs of the bed showing the indentation from her knees."

The pictures were displayed on a screen.

Hart continued. "The cell phone cord is a fiber wire that is strong and is the most efficient and discreet method of silently strangling someone. She slid the wire under and around his neck; pulled the cord very tight using the plug-ins as handles. Upon tightening the wire, she cut deeply into his neck, severely constricting Mr. Gibb's trachea and also the supply of oxygenated blood to the brain through the carotid artery, which caused unconsciousness and death in a very short timeframe. Also, the target's windpipe was fractured and crushed. She then sat him up on the side of the bed; placing her arms under his armpits, she dragged him to the closet and dumped him inside. She didn't lift his whole body."

Jeffrey Levy rose and faced the detective. "Anyone could have done that, right?

"Yes, but her DNA was in the piece of the glove and everywhere else"

"Yes or no please."

"Yes."

Tuesday afternoon Rick Brunis testified. He was Katie's lover at the time her husband was killed. He said he pressed Katie about the murder of her husband. "I said look me in the eye and tell me you didn't know his body was in the closet," said Brunis. She said "Rick, I can't tell you anything because I don't want you to have to lie."

Billy Claiborne, a bartender, told the jury he heard Katie talk about her husband while waiting on her at a restaurant in Brentwood. "She said her husband was flying in women from all over, including Florida. They were bimbos and not good for her kids. She told one dude that she would kill her husband if he tried to take her babies away."

"Did you know the dude?" McNally asked.

"Never seen him before, but she called him Jimmy. I remember because that comment really shook him up."

The prosecution had a very strong circumstantial case. In addition to the DNA evidence at the scene, the jury would have to consider whether Katie was strong enough to strangle her husband with a cell phone charger cord. Her attorney Jeffrey Levy, said at 5' 3" and around 95 pounds, she was simply too weak to commit the crime.

The jury also learned on Thursday that at the time of his death, Bobby's blood alcohol content was double the legal limit. The prosecution argued that with this level of alcohol in his system, Bobby could have been easily moved. The adrenalin rush would have given the additional strength needed to make the easy move.

The prosecution also suggested she had additional knowledge the average person would not have. She worked in the Medical Examiner's office often assisting with autopsies. She learned how to easily manipulate bodies.

The defense has long said there is no way she could've physically killed her larger, taller husband. Levy also tried to convince the jury that police did a sloppy job investigating the case. He argued they didn't check thoroughly on other potential suspects, and did not proceed carefully enough in evidence gathering.

After the prosecution wrapped up its case earlier Thursday morning, the defense called five witnesses, including my sister Allie, a woman Katie met while in Huntsville, her psychiatrist, a forensic scientist and me, Jimmy Joe Jeter IV. Katie did not testify.

Amanda Jo Bishop met Katie in 1987 when the two worked together in Huntsville, Alabama. Two years later, Katie moved back to Nashville to pursue a career in the medical field and attend medical school. Bishop, 54, testified she was a bridesmaid when Katie married Bobby and the two remained friends through the years.

Bishop said she came to stay with Katie in a Nashville hotel for a few days after she was removed from the family home due to what prosecutors say was a drug problem and history of previous violence. Bishop testified that Katie was skinny and sick and during her visit, Bobby Gibbs called his wife several times. "I was mystified by all the calls."

"She said, 'No, do not come and get me'," Bishop testified. "He was saying he would come get her in the morning. She was crying and she said, 'Bobby, why are you doing this? Why are you putting me through this?' and he just kept saying it would be alright. 'I'll just come get you in the morning.' I believe he was purposely tormenting her," Bishop said.

Allie was called to the stand next. She indicated that she had known Katie for 35 years or so and had known Bobby for 18 years or so. Asked to describe her relationship with Katie, Allie said, "We were inseparable in our early years, but in college and thereafter we went our separate ways. We are still friendly and I have given her shelter several times when she was separated from Bobby. When Bobby would find her staying with me, he would come to my house to see her even when he had the restraining order. He told me that he loved her and wanted her back. It was strange."

Jeffrey Levy asked Allie if she thought Katie could kill Bobby.

Allie responded, "Katie could say that she would kill Bobby, particularly when it came to her children, but she would never follow through. She did not kill Bobby in my opinion."

The second chair for the prosecution, Dianne Crozet, asked, "Who did then?"

Allie said, "I don't know. The police should be out looking for the person now."

Dr. Elise Bondurant, Katie's psychiatrist testified she was treating her for depression, anxiety and panic disorder. She said Katie's life was in a state of "chaos" because she was separated and moving from hotel to hotel and she was on several medications including Adderall and antidepressants.

"Katie has so much anxiety that she would never be able to kill her husband."

The defense also called Dr. Jonathon Sparks, a forensic pathologist, who testified "there was a substantial amount of force, a very large amount of force" used to kill Robert Gibbs.

"My opinion is that it would take a strong person. Somebody with substantial strength was performing that act at the time," Dr. Sparks said.

Crozet asked if an adrenaline rush could account for the force exhibited. Dr. Sparks answered; it's possible, but unlikely.

I was the next witness called. Jeffrey Levy stood to examine me for the defense.

"Your honor, I would ask for permission to treat Mr. Jeter as a hostile witness."

'Counselor, he is your witness. Isn't this a little unusual?"

"Your honor, we plan to ask Mr. Jeter some sensitive, personal questions and he may become evasive. Public disclosure of some of these items could prove embarrassing and damaging."

"Permission granted. Mr. Jeter, I expect you to be forthcoming and truthful."

Levy looked at me over the top of his glasses, "Tell the court about your relationship with Robert Gibbs."

"Bobby was my best friend. We met as first year students at the University of Virginia and have been friends ever since. We visited our respective homes in Bethesda and Nashville. We formed a strong bond over the years. I loved Bobby."

"Did you introduce Katie Gibbs to Bobby Gibbs?"

"Yes, I suppose I did. I invited my sister for a weekend at UVA and she brought Katie with her. Bobby met her that weekend and instantly fell for her. He was smitten."

"You have known Katie Gibbs for a long time as well, isn't that true?"

"Yes, she was a friend of my sister. She was at our house a lot as a child. So I have known her for over 30 years."

"Is it fair to say that you have been in love with Katie Gibbs for 20 years or more and that you would do anything for her?"

"That is not fair to say. For most of the years I have known her she has aggravated me purposely. I wondered why you would call me as a witness, because I actually detest her. I begged Bobby not to date her and certainly not to marry her. I chose my wife when Katie was still single. I never, ever considered her as a wife or lover."

"Really, I find that odd. Have you ever had sex with Ms. Gibbs?"

Trapped and being hoisted on my own petard was not very comfortable. "Yes, but I was not capable of making a decision about it."

"Just yes or no."

"Yes."

"When was that?"

"In March of 2004."

"So you had sex with your best friend's wife before his death and while she was in turmoil over her marriage."

I didn't respond. What could I say? I did notice that the news hounds were taking notes and were paying rapt attention.

241

"No answer to that question Mr. Jeter."

"I thought it was a statement, not a question"

The judge said, "I agree with Mr. Jeter." But Levy had made his point, so he moved on.

"Did you meet with Ms. Gibbs at the Corner Bar in Brentwood before her husband's death?"

"Yes I did."

"What did you talk about?"

"She was very upset about not seeing her children. She was also certain that Bobby was seeing others. She missed her son Robbie because he had messages for her from the voices. She was real concerned about those voices."

"Did you discuss murdering Robert Gibbs?"

"Katie mentioned the possibility. I told her not to think in those terms. It was just idle talk on her part.

"Did you meet with Ms. Gibbs in her hotel room at the Four Points Sheraton in Brentwood?"

"Yes I did."

"Did you have sex again?"

"No we did not have sex. We talked about her situation with Bobby. She was angry and combative. I left feeling that she might do anything to get her kids back."

"Did you talk about murder again?"

"She posed it as a possibility, but I told her to forget that notion."

"Did you call Bobby Gibbs to warn him?"

"No I did not do that and I regret it. But I knew he was doing everything he could to protect himself."

"He was your best friend and you didn't warn him?"

"No I wanted to stop being involved with the situation."

"You actually agreed at that meeting to kill Robert Gibbs didn't you?"

"That's preposterous!" I shouted. "I did not agree to kill Bobby and I, in fact, did not kill him. Are you out of your mind?"

"You wanted Katie and so you killed Bobby, isn't that right Mr. Jeter?""

"I am happily married to Maggie Jeter and wanted nothing to do with Katie Gibbs. She threatened to tell my wife about having sex, so I met with her, but I told my wife the whole truth and that was that."

"That's all your honor; I am through with this witness." Levy looked at me with disgust.

I left the courthouse and walked all the way to the Hermitage Hotel. I booked a room, called room service, asked for two fifths of Dewar's and proceeded to drink myself into oblivion. My sister found me three days later.

Jurors Thursday afternoon began deliberating the fate of Katie on the charge of first degree murder. The closing arguments were a rehash of the evidence, with the exception that the defense offered me as the alternative theory of the case. They suggested that it was possible that I had killed Bobby, because I was in love with his wife.

Katie was convicted of strangling her husband to death. The jury handed down a conviction Thursday afternoon of first degree premeditated murder, which comes with a life sentence. She will be eligible for parole in 51 years. The jury deliberated for about an hour before returning a verdict. Headlines read: THE ANOREXIC ASSASSIN GUILTY.

After the verdict was announced, Katie's mother, Adelaide Morgan, said her daughter didn't murder Robert Gibbs and that she was a wonderful wife with "a hard rope to tow." As for who did murder Gibbs, Morgan said she had an idea but didn't want to name anyone, saying "it's too sordid."

In a prepared statement released through the District Attorney's office, Bobby's family wrote, "We are grateful to have this behind us. We feel that justice has been served and thank the members of the jury for their careful attention to the facts of the case. Our family appreciates the efforts of the local authorities and the support and well-wishes of everyone as we return our focus onto our family and these three wonderful children."

Asked about the guilty verdict, Assistant District Attorney Dianne Crozet told reporters, "Well, whenever a death is involved and three children have lost their father, I'm not sure I would call it a victory. I think justice has been done, but it's still a sad day all the way around." Crozet said evidence of Katie's DNA inside the tip of a latex glove with her dead husband's blood on the outside of the glove was too difficult to get around.

Katie is spending the rest of her life in the Tennessee Prison for Women, the state's primary women's correctional facility, which houses women of all custody levels. It is located in Nashville. The state classifies the prison as a maximum security institution. It's a pretty dreary place.

Chapter 17

I sat in my room at the Hermitage, watched television, passed out from time-to-time, and drank Dewar's scotch. The hotel staff was only too happy to keep me well-supplied. One guy brought me a bottle of Glen Fiddich and I made a game of alternating drinks between the two whiskeys.

I heard some conversation in the room, but I couldn't figure out who was doing the talking.

"Oh thank God! That's him. Thank you very much, we will take it from here."

"He stinks to high heavens. It looks like he has pissed all over himself and the bed. There is nothing worse than a drunk, particularly one that has been drunk for three days."

"Have some compassion Cora Jane. After all, his life is not gonna be the same. Do you want to help me or not?"

"Yes yes I want to help you because I love you and for some reason you love this brother of yours. So I'm gonna help, but I don't have to like it. After all, he did create a lot of grief for me and ruined one of my high school years. But he did help me in one regard; I found that I liked women much more than men. In fact, I became aware of my dislike of men when I was dating him: odd isn't it?"

It was very interesting to listen to these two people, whoever they were, talk about me. One of them seems to care for me quite a bit and the other one didn't seem to care for me at all. At least, they can order me another bottle of Dewar's.

I sat up for a minute, but my head started to spin something awful, so I laid back down. "Whoa, that was not good. Watch out I'm going to throw up," I said with slurred words. I then began to vomit all over myself and everything around me. The two women were disgusted.

One screamed, "Watch out, he really is going to vomit. Ewwwww, it got on my shoes. These are Ferragamos. This is awful."

Of course, it was Allie and Cora Jane who came to my rescue. They ordered some coffee, soup, some bread and additional towels and soap from housekeeping.

Then Allie was on the phone; "Dad, I need your help. Can you get Jerome to come over to the Hermitage Hotel and give me a hand? Just do it. Daddy, why are giving me such a hard time. Yes, I am saving my brother, yet again. I seem to be the only one that cares. Room 622. Thanks."

"Sometimes that man drives me to distraction!!"

Allie looked at Cora Jane, "First, thanks for helping. You don't have to do it, but you are and I'm grateful."

"Allie I love you. We are partners. I hope someday we can be married. Partners help each other. Too bad he doesn't get it."

Allie looked my way, "He's just a man."

"That says it all," Cora Jane said as she hugged Allie.

"I need to go buy Jimmy some clothes. Can you stay with him until Jerome gets here? He'll know what to do."

"I've got it covered," Cora Jane said.

There was a loud knock at the door that even I could hear. Jerome was standing in the hallway beside a waiter that had the coffee and food. He took one tray and Cora took the other. She took the check from the waiter in the hallway and signed it, giving the guy a $100 tip. The bill was only $61.

Looking at the waiter she said, "I've always wanted to do that. Another dream satisfied thanks to the J-man."

"Oh man he smells awful. That's the worst; peeing all over yourself and then vomiting on yourself; don't get no worse than that. You going to be helping me missy?

"I am. What we do first?"

"Let's get the bed sheet off of him. Then we'll get the shorts and T-shirt off of him. Watch you don't get any of that puke on you. Oh God, that shit smells."

They set me up on the side of the bed. I was alive, but I felt bad. My head began to spin like a tilt-a-whirl. "My head's spinning like a top. I'm gonna be sick."

Jerome jumped back, "Watch out missy, he's going to project again."

I fell on the floor and vomited all over myself again. Jerome looked at Cora Jane and said, "Hand me one of them big towels." He cleaned me off as best he could and then grabbed my legs at the ankle. Jerome dragged me to the bathroom leaving a trail of vomit behind. Cora Jane was already in the bathroom adjusting the shower to the right temperature. They got me to a sitting position and I felt the rug burn on my back.

"Man could you be a little gentler?" I pleaded.

"Ain't no way I'm going to be gentle with you when I'm doing this foul job for your daddy and your sister and her friend. Just ain't no way I'm going to do that."

They stood me up. I was making progress because I didn't have to vomit. Cora Jane looked at me and said, "Jimmy Joe that thing has gotten bigger since the last time I saw it. Have you been doing some sort of exercise or taking something?" Jerome laughed.

"Missy could you please get that gym bag I brought?"

He took a huge bottle of body wash out of the bag and poured a bunch of it over my head and down my body. He took a washcloth and started to scrub me all over.

"Damn man, first I get rug burn and now you're killing me with that washcloth."

"Shut up and take it like a man."

By that time Allie was back and was, along with Cora Jane, thoroughly enjoying my humiliation. How had I let this happen? What I needed now was a drink. I wonder if there's any left. The problem will be getting it without these people knowing it. Interesting that I thought a drink would solve everything.

I was standing in the bathroom with Jerome who was helping me dry off. "You know Jerome I think I'm going to give up on the vagina. I DREAD the vagina just like King Lear. His description of the vagina went something like this; 'there's hell, there's darkness, there is the sulphurous pit; burning, scalding, stench, consumption!' Yes, he had it right. Every time I've had serious troubles, there has been a vagina involved."

"I don't know anything about King Lear, but I think Muddy Waters had a name for you. You my man are the 'Hoochi, Coochi man.'"

"Wow Allie, these clothes fit. How did you know my sizes?"

"I called Maggie and she gave them to me. By the way, she is greatly relieved that you are okay."

My dearest *Maggie,* how am I gonna explain all this to you?

I checked out of the hotel and Allie drove me to my car at the courthouse parking lot. I drove home dreading more than a vagina. My kids must be wondering who this guy is and is he really their father. My two sons were already wondering about me and my little girl was a mama's girl. She hung on her mother like a baby cub.

When I got home, no one was there. Maggie was probably picking people up from school or some sort of practice. I went to the back of the house to my private place. I guess it was my man cave. There was a bottle of Dewar's on the shelf that looked very inviting. I was still shaking from my three-day battle with king alcohol and I thought a little nip would help me out, but first I decided that I should have some food on my stomach before taking a drink. So I went to the kitchen, made a ham sandwich and filled a glass with ice. I went back to the cave looking forward to a full glass of scotch. I ate about half the ham sandwich before I took a sip of the scotch. I then drained the glass and it felt really good going down my throat. I filled the glass again and repeated the process. I ate the rest of the ham sandwich and filled my glass yet again.

I wasn't shaking anymore and all of a sudden I had the courage to face my family.

"Jimmy Joe are you in there?" Maggie said as she opened the door.

I quickly hid the bottle of scotch and answered, "Yes I am," as she looked me square in the eye. "You had us all worried you know. That wasn't very nice of you. Sometimes you're just a selfish bastard. I know you're going through a hard time, but we all are. You have a family and you need to act like a man. You can criticize my father all you want, but he takes care of his kids and his wife. You need to start doing the same thing. It's not all about you Jim! It's time to give up Jimmy Joe, and grow up; do the right thing."

"I'm truly sorry for worrying you Maggie. You're right; it is time I grew up. I sometimes live in the past too much and I am self-centered. I'll do better Maggie. I promise."

"Where were you?"

"I was at the Hermitage hotel, drunk out of my mind and worrying about the future."

She looked me square in the eye and said, "Was there anyone with you?"

"No, there was no one with me. You can check with Allie, Cora Jane, Jerome or the hotel staff. This was the most humiliating day of my life."

"I've already checked. Dinner will be served at 6:30 PM. I assume you will be here. I hope you can be friendly and nice with the children. You'll be sleeping in the guest room. I need some time to absorb all of this without you being so close to me. You are self-centered. I've known that for a long time. I've overlooked it, but I am not going to do that anymore. I can't help but love you Jimmy Joe, I mean Jim, so that's why I don't want to split with you. It's a cliché, but I need space.

After she left the room, I put the scotch bottle back on the shelf at least for now. I loved Maggie with all my heart and I had hurt her and for that I'm truly sorry.

That night, dinner consisted of chicken salad, oven roasted potatoes, green beans and okra. I didn't really like okra, but I acted as if it was the best vegetable I had ever eaten.

I got an update on football practice, soccer practice, and a detailed rundown on the fall ballerina recital. I promised to come to the soccer match scheduled for tomorrow at 4. I read a story to my daughter about a poodle who was also a private detective. It was actually pretty interesting.

Maggie was watching television in her bedroom. I knocked and asked if I could get a few things out of the drawer and bedroom. I then walked to her and gave her a good night kiss on the cheek.

I was in the guest room when my father called.

He didn't beat around the bush. "Are you having some sort of mid-life crisis?"

"No, I'm not. My best friend is dead and the lawyers tried to paint me as the killer. I just needed time to think."

"Jerome told me you were a mess. Where are you now?"

"I'm at home. Sleeping in the guest room, but I'm home."

"Stay there for the next few days. Rest up a little. You have been through a lot."

"Thanks Dad."

There was a pause on the line. "I don't think you've ever called me that. It's about time"

"Yes, it is."

■■■

"Well, Jimmy Joe you really tied one on that time. A three day drunk is something you'll remember. At least you stayed with the good stuff."

"Yeah Rex, that was a whopper. I've never had a hangover quite so bad."

"Every 5th step has one of those stories, if not more."

"We know how to hurt ourselves."

"Yep, let's keep going!"

253

"You don't need to pee?"

"Nope, move it along, please."

- -

I spent the next few days going to a soccer game and to football practice. I was thrilled by my boys. They were really good. I talked to my Dad every day and had lunch with my mom, Mary Lynn. It wasn't all about me and I had missed a lot of the joy that a family can bring. It was my own damn fault.

Finally, I felt it was time to go back to the office, so I mustered up my courage and headed in. When I got there, I ran into Tim O'Hara. He followed me into my office and brought me up to date on the deals we had been working on. I was currently working with a software developer in Chapel Hill North Carolina. Tim had talked to the CEO of the company last week and we needed to decide when would be appropriate to time to bring them public. The CEO was going to send us their results from the latest quarter.

I reached for a package on my desk and said to Tim, "This must be the numbers. I'll get Tiffany to make some copies and we will take a look. They are probably at least six months away from being ready, but we'll see." It was just that easy to get back into the swing of things. I was very grateful to Tim for giving me an easy path back to work.

"Sorry I have been out of action for the last week. This trial was a bear and my friend's death seems to have just hit me. I hope the testimony that came out doesn't give us too much trouble. Thanks for hanging in there Tim."

"Jimmy we are good at what we do. I'm not worried about any backlash. Maybe some competitor will try to use it against us, but I doubt it will work with any of our clients. It's all been positive so far, and I expect it to continue that way. So hang tough."

It was a nice speech and I wanted to believe it, so I did.

So my life at the firm began again. I had a lot to do and I got right to it. I was on the telephone talking to clients and was crunching numbers with my two associates Beverly Armstrong and Josh Calhoun.

One evening after dinner, I mentioned to Maggie that we had not been to the beach in a while and maybe this would be a good time to take off with the kids for a few weeks. She told me that her sister had rented a large house at Ocean Isle in North Carolina and had invited us to come stay with them. It was in mid-August from the 14th to the 27th.

"That'll work out fine. We can pay for the house or our portion if they like. I'll look forward to it."

Another surprise for me was that Maggie would agree to go. I guess it was the fact that her sister and her family would be there. I actually liked her husband Dennis. He was one of the good guys and he had a great sense of humor.

It is 621 miles from Nashville to Ocean Isle in North Carolina. Most of the way, it is interstate highways or good four lane highways, but for the last 50 miles or so it is two-lane roads with lots of beach traffic and a lot of local traffic.

When we reached this point, we had stopped several times for lunch and bathroom breaks and we were into our 10th hour of driving. The children had given up on asking when we were going to be there. At the moment, they were all asleep. We left Nashville at 6 AM and we were approaching 4 PM in North Carolina.

Maggie looked over at me and said, "I hate to say this, but I have to pee. I mean I have been holding it for the last 20 miles, but this traffic is so slow that I can't hold it much longer or I'm going to pee in my pants."

"There is a little store right there up ahead. They probably have some sort of facility."

"It looks a little shabby, but it will have to do. Can you keep an eye on the children and at the same time keep an eye on me?"

"I can do it." And I did. I did it rather well. I was just thrilled that Maggie would ask me to do something for her, anything to help her, anything at all.

The Underwood's were already at the house when we got there. After all the hugging and greeting of one another, it was time to unload the vehicle. The back of our SUV was full of stuff and we had a carrier on the rack on top of the car. Maggie went into the house to sort out the sleeping arrangements with her sister. Josiah stayed around to help me. It took about 45 minutes and it was a good workout. I was sweating so much that my shirt was wet through and through and my shorts were soaked. Dennis handed me a beer and it tasted great, cold as could be as it stung the back of my throat. What a great feeling and it looks like Dennis was going to be a good friend. I hadn't had any alcohol for three days so this hit the spot.

We had burgers and chips for dinner along with the chocolate cake that Maggie baked at home and brought with us. It was absolutely delicious and I had two pieces.

This house had five bedrooms and five baths, one each for the two master bedrooms, one off the living area, and two for the other three bedrooms. A key to a good beach house was plenty of bathrooms and showers.

Maggie and I had a nice large bedroom and the bath was large with a shower stall and a tub plus two sinks. The bedroom had a very large king-size bed.

"Don't read anything into us sharing this room," Maggie said. "I didn't want to get into a long explanation with my sister and the children have their own arrangements for the other three bedrooms. So here's the blue pillow, it's the dividing line. The left is your side and the right is mine; no crossovers."

"Understood. I can always sleep on the floor if it would make you feel more comfortable."

"I think we can handle this. It will be part of your growing up process. I don't know about you, but I'm exhausted. The trip took a lot out of me so I'm going to bed."

"I'm tired as well. That drive is a bear particularly the last 50 or 60 miles."

I really wanted a drink, but this did not seem to be the right time to go for it. I was reasonably settled after the four beers I drank with dinner and I was very tired. I actually slept until 7 AM without moving.

Midmorning, I went down to the beach with Josiah and young Denny Underwood. We tossed around the football and I had a great time throwing long bombs to each of the boys. They were both good and caught the balls with ease. Dennis finally came down and joined the fun.

"You've still got a pretty good arm Jimmy Joe," Dennis said.

"Well, this arm is getting old because it sure is tired. You throw a couple Dennis because these guys don't get tired." As Dennis threw a couple of passes, I remarked, "I remember that energy, but I don't have it now. You throw a pretty good ball Dennis." I was having a good time doing something very simple and discovered something. This was far better than an investment banking deal or drinking myself into oblivion.

That afternoon, I called the Ocean Isle Fishing Charter Company and made plans for the men in the group, namely Dennis and me plus our three boys, to go deep sea fishing. We would be aboard the Carolina Cat, which was a 33 foot World Cat tournament boat with twin Yamaha 300 hp engines. All the fishing gear was furnished. We would leave at 7 AM to head for the fishing grounds about 35 miles offshore. To say our boys were excited was clearly an understatement.

I was amazed at the amount of room on the boat. The cabin was roomy and you could walk on the deck completely around the boat. We reached the fishing grounds and over a five hour period, we caught a fair amount of amberjack, snapper and grouper. Chris was exhilarated with the two fish he caught. Josiah had the best day when he landed a large barracuda. He needed some help from Capt. Brent McElroy, but for the most part, he handled it himself. I was so happy for him that tears streamed down my face. Dennis put his arm around me and gave me a big squeeze. "This is what it's all about Jimmy Joe." He was right and I had never been happier.

We still have the picture of Josiah holding up his barracuda. The picture actually showed up in the weekly newspaper in Ocean Isle.

Eight hours is a long time on a boat and we were all exhausted. For some reason, I had managed to not get drunk. While the other guys took showers, I got some ice and poured myself a big glass of Dewar's.

I was sitting on the deck, watching the waves, and enjoying the scotch, when Maggie came up and sat beside me.

"A reward after a hard day?"

"It wasn't a hard day, it was a rewarding day. I was with my sons for 8 hours straight. That is the most time I have ever spent with them at one time, if that makes sense and it was terrific."

"Josiah is ecstatic. Fact is I've never seen him so verbal and animated. The whole thing made quite an impression on him. He also told me that you cried when he caught the barracuda. That also made an impression on him; you know, that real men can cry, his words not mine."

She reached over and got my hand. We sat in silence for a long while watching the waves. Maybe there was hope for our family yet. Nonetheless, I took the moment as my own.

Chapter 18

We arrived back in Nashville in good spirits. It seemed to me that we were closer as a family. It was a really good two weeks for me; Maggie and I were getting along much better. We actually giggled and laughed together on the beach, in the house, actually wherever we were. It was a nice interlude I didn't want to go away. Interestingly, I didn't drink very much at the beach, a couple each night, and wasn't drunk at all. This was an accomplishment that I also felt good about.

We resumed our normal activities as school was about to start for the kids. Maggie was as busy as ever, but she did make it clear that I could return to our bedroom. This woman was so very forgiving and I was grateful.

I returned to work, but for some reason I wasn't happy about being back like usual. I had been associated with this firm for most of my life, directly and indirectly. I began to think it was time for me to do something different. Perhaps I could start up a regional hedge fund. There were some people who would surely invest with me, but with all the recent publicity this was probably not the best time to start some sort of venture. Most likely I should stay parked where I was and not do anything precipitous. But I was restless, not worried, just restless. Bobby's death and Katie's trial had rattled me. I was mostly over it, thanks to the wonderful interlude provided by the beach trip. I had already made the decision to spend a lot more time with my kids. How much money did we need to survive? We had enough to spare, so that I could spend more time with my wife and kids.

I went over to talk to Trip or Dad as I now called him. "Have you got time for a philosophical conversation?"

He looked at me with a quizzical expression, "The events of the last couple of months still have you by the balls? It's understandable Jim. The only other time in your life that you really experienced grief is when your grandfather died. You're facing your own mortality and that's not very much fun. Lighten up a little bit and enjoy that fine family of yours. Pay more attention to Maggie and work hard on your marriage."

"I've already made that decision. I had a great time with my boys and Abigail at the beach. Maggie and I put aside our differences and are really trying, no not trying, actually working on our marriage."

"That's great! It's about time! Mind if I tell Mary Lynn? We both have been worried about you two. We love you and want both of you to be happy."

"Dad, have you ever thought about selling this business? It's a good value and great franchise for one of the bigger firms, but with the computerization of a lot of the trading activity, I'm afraid our value may start declining. To keep up with the big boys, we're going to have to commit a lot of our capital to technology. While the guys in our technology group are good, we don't have enough of them who are suited to take us to the next level."

"I've had those same thoughts," Trip replied. "I've had some talks with folks from Morgan Stanley and UBS in the past few weeks. Both are willing and eager to have further talks with us. I'm glad to know that you're on board and I assume that you can get your sister and cousins to be on board when the time comes."

"Yes I'm sure they'll be on board."

"Would you like to be involved in the negotiations?"

"I'm flattered that you would ask, but I think I am too much of a distraction and that these guys wouldn't take me seriously. And frankly, I wouldn't blame them. But I do think you should include Tim O'Hara and Ray in the discussions. Tim has some great insight and is a tough negotiator."

"Thanks for your candor Jim. This stuff will gradually fade away and you can get back to normal activity. If we can put something attractive together, it would simplify all of our lives. I still think you are really a stupid shit for having gotten yourself involved with Katie. Even Allie has removed herself some."

"I was stupid. I hope it doesn't cost me more, but that little bitch is devious and I'm fearful that she is going to reach out from prison and grab me."

"Be positive Jim and hope that that doesn't come to pass."

I stayed out of everyone's way for the rest of the day. It was easy to do and I was grateful.

For the next month, my life was uneventful. I watched all of my children engage in their activities. Maggie and I appeared together at most of the events. Our friends were very kind and did not shun us. On the whole, it was a very pleasant time.

In early October, my criminal attorney, Patrick Bramlege, called to let me know what was going on. Somehow he had gotten wind of some conversations taking place in the women's prison involving Katie Gibbs.

"The district attorney himself, Eric Caplinger, has been at the prison along with Dale McNally, and sometimes Dianne Crozet. I've heard that Katie gets along with Dianne better than the two guys," Patrick said. "Jim I think we need to meet and plan some strategy. I don't know what they're up to, but I'm sure that it involves you."

Even though I had been expecting something like this, it still hit me hard. This was not good news. Again I had that overwhelming feeling that my life was going to change and I was never going to be the same again. I wouldn't be able to keep my cover much longer.

"I think that's a real good idea Patrick. When shall meet?"

"Tomorrow morning in my office at 10 works for me."

"I'll be there, but I won't have any bells on!"

I left the office and went home. I wanted to tell Maggie about this in person and I needed a drink something awful.

"What are you doing home so early?" Maggie said apprehensively. "It's only 2 o'clock."

"Patrick called me a little while ago. He told me that there were some interesting meetings going on with Katie Gibbs. The district attorney and some of his minions are talking with Katie on a regular basis. Patrick thinks they're talking about me. He wants to meet with me tomorrow morning."

Maggie screamed, "Won't that woman ever go away? She wants to ruin everyone's life. I never thought I could hate anyone, but I'm making an exception for her. She is a despicable excuse for a woman."

"I'm sorry Maggie, but it just won't go away. I did something stupid by getting involved with her and I'm being punished."

"Is there anything you haven't told me about your involvement with her?"

"There's nothing else. If she says there is, then she's lying. She's very capable of inventing things as we know and she can be persuasive. But Maggie, there's nothing that I haven't told you." I was getting to be too good at lying.

And so, the next period of my life began to unfold. I took some ice in a little bowl to my man cave and fixed myself a large Dewar's on the rocks. It was fitting since my life was on the rocks as well.

Patrick's office was on the 12th floor of the UBS Tower on Deadrick Street in downtown Nashville. His suite of offices was larger than I expected and there were at least four other attorneys who were part of his firm. The woman at his reception desk was pretty and very competent.

Liz Oliver came out to meet me shortly after I arrived. We sat in a conference room that had a fair view of other downtown office buildings. Lisa offered me a cup of coffee and I took it. Nice china cups indicated to me that this law firm wasn't gonna be cheap, but I was going to need excellent professional help."

Patrick came into the room and sat. After exchanging pleasantries, he looked at me and said, "Jim I think we should get our fee arrangement out in the open. Our basic fee is $400 an hour for me and $250 an hour for Liz. If we have to put on a full-blown defense, it's going to cost you at least $250,000 plus what we might have to spend on some experts. If we end up with a plea deal, it will obviously cost you less."

"It seems you believe that I'm going to be charged with something."

"Yes I do."

"Okay then, you have to pay for the best and I understand you are the best, so the fee arrangement is okay with me. Do I have to sign something?"

Liz looked at me and said, "I've taken the liberty of drawing up the contract and you can take some time to read it over."

I thought about asking Richard Newton to review the contract, but decided to do it myself. It seemed pretty standard and all the numbers were in the right place, so I signed the agreement.

Patrick took the lead, "We believe they are videotaping a deposition from Katie. Our investigator has a female friend that has a relationship with Dianne Crozet. We have learned that they are probably going to charge you with conspiracy to commit murder. We're told that they believe their case is very strong and are looking forward to putting you on trial. Eventually, they will probably offer us a deal."

"I'm not interested in any deal. I haven't committed a crime, particularly conspiracy to commit murder. So if I get charged, then prepare for trial because I'm not going to admit to any of this, since it simply isn't true." Lying again!

"Okay, that's what we will plan for then. Is your wife still supportive of you?" said Patrick.

"Yes she has been supportive. If I am charged with conspiracy, I think she'll still be in my corner, but it's going to be very difficult for her to sit through whatever Katie has to say. When that topic comes up, she gets very angry with Katie and with me."

"Will she be willing to sit through the trial?"

"Yes"

"Will she be willing to testify on your behalf?"

"I believe that she will, yes she will for sure."

"How about your parents?"

"My parents are embarrassed by the whole thing particularly my mother. Also my father is trying to do some things with the firm and my arrest would not help the cause. So I wouldn't expect either of them to be at the trial nor would I expect them to testify in any way. In fact, I don't want to involve either of them. I've done enough to embarrass them through my life."

"And then there is your sister, the lovely Allie Jeter. She was called for the defense in Katie's trial, so I expect the prosecution will call her as a witness."

"Have either of you met Cora Jane Davis, Allie's partner?"

Liz indicated that she had met Cora Jane several times, but Patrick had never met her.

"The night that Katie and I had sex in Percy Warner Park, Cora Jane came with Allie to take care of Katie and to get me home. So Cora Jane can testify about all of that. Also, while we were in high school, Cora Jane and I dated for about two years and had sex on a regular basis. She kept a diary and her mother discovered it. There was a big brouhaha about that situation with her mother telling me to never touch her daughter again. So Cora Jane doesn't really like me very much. I suppose her hatred for me turned her into a lesbian, which is really great because she and Allie are very much in love and I'm happy for them."

Patrick sat looking at me for several minutes; I suppose trying to assess my character. "Has your life always been a soap opera?"

"I think more of it in terms of a bad Lifetime movie."

Patrick sighed and then said, "You and the Gibbs family were friendly. Do you think that will remain intact?"

"I doubt it. As the trial wore on, they stopped talking to me and refused to take my calls. They probably think that I had something to do with Bobby's death. They were devastated even though they believed that Katie did kill Bobby. They were very selective about what they chose to believe and not believe."

"Is there anyone else you can think of that would have some vendetta against you?"

"There is George Watson, Jeannette Watson and Janie Watson. After the Cora Jane fiasco, my parents had a party. I was upstairs in my room and there was a knock on the door. It was Jeannette. She put her arms around my neck and gave me a big wet kiss. She then lifted her skirt, took her pantyhose off and told me to take her from behind as she leaned over the bed. She told me she had heard that I was a stud and she wanted me to prove it. I guess I did because we had an affair off and on for almost 2 years."

"You were a busy youngster," Liz laughed.

"Oh it gets worse. I saw Janie at the pool or somewhere; it's all a little fuzzy for me. I asked her out and we started dating. I told Jeannette that I wasn't gonna see her anymore. She put two and two together and knew it was because of Janie. Janie and I dated until I was a fourth year at UVA. When I came home for Thanksgiving that year, the Watson's came over to tell me that it was all over and also to inform my parents that I was a rat bastard. Poor George was furious with me and with Jeannette. He moved out of the house and started divorce proceedings immediately. It broke the family apart. I felt really bad about that, but I did love Janie and was seriously considering asking her to marry me. Luckily for me that didn't work, because I had met Maggie and I was free to pursue a relationship with her when the time was right. So over the holidays that year, I went through a grieving process; "I'd lost someone very dear to me."

"Where are they now; are they still in Nashville?"

"George is retiring from SunTrust Bank. He married a lovely woman from Memphis by the name of Claire Armentrout. They've been married for a fairly long time. Jeannette still lives here, has never remarried and has a very successful boutique in Green Hills. Janie met a guy who was graduating from medical school at Emory, and the last I heard they were living in Boston where her husband is a cardiovascular surgeon at one of the large hospitals. He has been very successful and Janie is very happy according to Allie."

"Okay Jim, that'll be enough for today. It will give us something to work with."

"Can I just say that I've been very faithful to Maggie, excepting that tragic mistake with Katie, and that my dealings both personally and professionally have been aboveboard during my career, even with Bonner."

"Take the day and do something relaxing. We'll let you know about any developments that occur."

I drove out West End Ave. to the Sportsman Grill. I had a cheeseburger with fries and five beers. I was feeling a little better, but not much.

I went home, but there was no one there. Everyone was doing some sort of activity. I went into the man cave and drank scotch whiskey until I passed out.

Maggie found me in the chair. "Must've been a rough day with the lawyers." I made it to the table, smiled at the children, and sampled the salmon. It was perfectly cooked and I was ravenous all of a sudden. I had two pieces of fish and some ratatouille as well. Over Apple pie and ice cream, I had a very good conversation with the kids about their day. After they were tucked in bed, I told Maggie about my day. I knew she was worried about me and about the situation. It was only natural to assume the worst and the damage it might do to our lovely little family.

The fall was beautiful in Nashville. The air was cooler and the colors were bright. The Vanderbilt football team won its first four games of the year, but suddenly lost to Middle Tennessee State University 17-15. In fact, they lost all of their games in October that year. Maggie and I went to the MTSU game with our friends, Bob and Sue Graham. Both of them were Vanderbilt graduates and they had great seats on the 35 yard line. I also spent a lot of time watching my kids play their games and it was wonderful. I wanted to soak as much of it up as I could, because I was fearful that all of this might come to a screeching halt.

And it did. On November 10, our front doorbell rang. It was about 7:30 p.m. and we had just finished dinner.

I looked at Maggie and said, "No one ever rings our front doorbell. This must be the cops."

Maggie shepherded the kids into their bedrooms.

I opened the front door and there stood two guys who looked very much like police detectives. "We're detectives Anderson and Edwards of the Metropolitan Police Department. Are you James J. Jeter the fourth?"

By this time, Maggie was standing beside me in the foyer.

"I am."

"Mr. Jeter you are under arrest for conspiracy to commit murder," said Detective Anderson. He proceeded to read me my Miranda rights while Edwards put handcuffs on me.

Maggie said, "I'll call Patrick."

And so it started.

Chapter 19

After my arrest, I was taken to the Criminal Justice Center which is on Second Avenue in downtown Nashville. People like me who are arrested on a felony charge are taken to this facility for booking. It's run by the Davidson County Sheriff's office.

The two detectives gave some paperwork to a Sheriff's deputy and they directed me to sit in some chairs along the wall of the room we were in. The room was fairly large and was very bright because of the florescent lighting. The two detectives sat on either side of me and waited for the Sheriff's deputy to take charge of me.

We had been waiting 30 minutes or so, when Patrick Bramlege entered the room, immediately saw me and came over, asked one of the detectives to move and sat beside me.

"You haven't said anything to anyone I hope?"

"No I haven't. What's gonna happen now?"

"You're going to be booked, held in jail tonight and you will appear for arraignment tomorrow morning. It's actually a good thing that you were arrested at night. Other than spending the night in jail, it gets you to the hearing early the next day. When you're arrested, one of the first steps towards a trial to ascertain your guilt or innocence is the arraignment hearing, in which you enter your plea. The arraignment is, in a sense, the start of the process of justice, setting it into motion. And of course, we're going to ask the judge to set bail. The DA will object, but probably won't do so very strenuously."

A Sheriff's deputy came over and said, "Are you Jeter?" I nodded my head. He then looked at Patrick and said, "Who are you?" Patrick replied, "I'm Mr. Jeter's attorney."

"Well I'm going to take him back and start the booking process. You can see him in the morning when we take him over for the arraignment hearing."

He grabbed me under my right arm and led me away. I was in really unfamiliar territory and to say I was scared was an understatement.

The deputy asked me for my personal information (i.e., name, date of birth, physical characteristics); he recorded the information about my alleged crime; and performed a computer search to see if I had a criminal background. He then took my fingerprints; he photographed me, and searched me. The Deputy confiscated my wallet and my keys and told me they would be returned upon my release; and he placed me in a holding cell.

The deputy's badge displayed his picture and name: H. Cousins. "What happens now Mr. Cousins?"

"You'll be in here until all the paperwork is approved and sent back to me. I have to take it to court in the morning. I'll take you up to the jail later."

My freedom was gone for a while. I was behind bars with no place to go. This nightmare had begun. I hope that Peter Bramlege is as good as he thinks. The deputy came back in an hour and took me upstairs to the jail. There were men in every cell; some sleeping, some talking to the guy next to him, and some staring off into space.

How nice a big bottle of scotch or anything really would be at this point. Oblivion was what I needed and could not have. The place smelled of sweat and poor hygiene. A got a whiff of the urinal every so often. I dozed off eventually and was awakened very early by someone sticking breakfast through the food entry. I looked at it and could not decide what it was. I drank the cold coffee and passed on the rest.

Under American common law, a basic tenet of due process is to make sure that the accused party in a criminal proceeding knows exactly what he or she is being charged with. The arraignment process provides this fundamental right and explanation to the accused in a court of law and also allows the accused to make a plea before the rest of the trial proceedings begin. It also specifies who is bringing the charges against the party. The process of arraignment must occur within one to two days. The short timeline of the arraignment process is intentional. It forces the government to get its details and prosecutorial case together quickly after it decides to charge someone. If the government doesn't have a case, then it shouldn't be running around charging and arresting people needlessly.

Another aspect of arraignment is the process of setting bail. The U.S. court system generally does not keep an accused person in jail until trial unless the person is an immediate threat to the public or an obvious flight risk. To make sure the accused party doesn't disappear arbitrarily when it comes time for trial, a monetary deposit (bail) is provided to the court by the accused party. Typically ranging in the thousands to as much as a million U.S. dollars in some cases, bail ensures that the party won't skip town without experiencing a huge financial loss. The judge hearing the arraignment makes the final decision on bail.

The General Sessions court, which conducts the preliminary hearings, was 2 blocks away. We were taken in cuffs and were seated in a room off the court. There were five of us to be arraigned.

Lawyers were let in the room one at a time. Patrick entered the room.

"Jimmy Joe you look pretty good. We are number three on the docket."

'You don't happen to have a spare toothbrush on you?"

"No sorry, but Maggie is in the courtroom."

About an hour later, a guard took off my handcuffs and led me into the court room. I moved over to the table where Patrick was seated and sat down. Maggie was sitting behind me in the gallery. I waved to her. I noticed that there were several photographers and reporters in the room.

Judge Hiram Reynolds assumed his position at the bench and court was called to order.

The State of Tennessee v. James Josiah Jeter IV.

"Mr. McNally are you ready to proceed."

"Yes your honor. We are charging Mr. Jeter with conspiracy to commit murder. This case involves the strangulation death of Robert Gibbs. His wife, Katie Gibbs, was convicted of murder in July of last year. We are not saying that Mr. Jeter was directly involved in the murder. It's quite clear that Mrs. Gibbs was guilty of that crime. However, we are quite certain that she had help in the planning of this murder that was provided by Mr. Jeter. In fact, Mrs. Gibbs told the Dist. Atty.'s office that she met with Mr. Jeter on more than one occasion to discuss how she might solve her problems with regard to her husband. If you would like your honor, we can show you a portion of the taped interview with Mrs. Gibbs."

"That's not necessary at this juncture Mr. McNally; just give me the gist of what she has to say."

"She and Mr. Jeter initially met at the bar of the Bluebird Café, a night spot here in Nashville. They talked about some general things and then she began to talk to him about her husband. She told Mr. Jeter that she was very unhappy and that she and her husband were having violent arguments and fights. She said that Mr. Jeter recommended that she get rid of her husband if she was so unhappy."

"A month later, they met at the Cross Corner Bar where Mrs. Gibbs was overheard talking about murdering her husband. We have a witness who will confirm this conversation. We have videotapes that Mr. Jeter visited Mrs. Gibbs in her hotel room at the Four Points Sheraton. Mrs. Gibbs said they met there several times and Mr. Jeter demanded sex. We will have supporting testimony regarding the sexual relationship between Mr. Jeter and

Mrs. Gibbs. She says he told her to not use a gun, but to wait until Robert Gibbs had passed out from drinking alcohol and strangle him with a cord. From her medical training, Mrs. Gibbs knew the correct pressure points."

"Mr. Jeter and Mrs. Gibbs have known each other since they were children. Katie Gibbs was his sister's best friend. Mrs. Gibbs will testify that he has been in love with her for years and he would be happy to see Robert Gibbs out of the way. We will have supporting evidence for this as well through individual testimony."

"Your honor, the state is certain that we have enough evidence to support our charge of conspiracy to commit murder."

"I agree and I'm going to bind this over for trial. A jury needs to sort this out. We have a pretty full slate for the next couple of months but let me look at the calendar. I would appreciate Mr. Bramlege if you would check your calendar and Mr. McNally, you should do the same. I'm going to suggest that we start jury selection on March 27 and begin the trial immediately thereafter. Is this suitable?" Both lawyers indicated that it was fine.

"Now it's time to hear from the defense. Mr. Bramlege, how does your client plead?"

I stood up next to Patrick and he turned to me and I said in a loud voice, "Not guilty Your Honor."

"The defendant enters a plea of not guilty."

"Now gentlemen, let's discuss the matter of bail," the judge said

McNally jumped out of his seat and said, "Your honor the state believes that Mr. Jeter is a flight risk. He has resources that would allow him to flee this jurisdiction."

Patrick rose from his chair and said, "Your honor, Mr. Jeter is an upstanding citizen in this community. He was born here and has lived here for most of his life. He wants to clear himself of this ridiculous charge. He has no reason to flee this jurisdiction and every reason to stay. A person should not be penalized because they have resources. This is a situation where a reasonable bail is warranted."

"What do you consider to be a reasonable bail, Mr. Bramlege?"

"I believe $100,000 cash is appropriate."

McNally jumped up, "Your Honor that is ridiculous. He will be out of here in minutes with that amount of bail."

"What's time got to do with it Mr. McNally. We need to be protecting the rights of all of our citizens rich and poor. Bail is set at $150,000 cash."

He rapped the gavel and left the bench.

I went into the clerk's office and they gave me wiring instructions for the Clerk of the Criminal Court. I called Ray at the office and asked him to wire the $150,000 to the Clerk. It took 25 minutes for the money to appear in the appropriate accounts and I was released.

I met Maggie in the hallway and she gave me a big hug. "Ugh, you smell awful."

"You should've smelled the jail. It was disgusting, but I do need a long shower to wash all the muck away from me."

I looked at Patrick and asked him what was next. "We're going to be doing a lot of work starting right now by making motions for discovery and to take our own deposition from Mrs. Gibbs. I think we can turn that around and make it work against the state. For now, you go home and relax."

I went home at least, but relaxing was not in the cards. I had my keys and wallet with me, but luckily Maggie had left my cell phone at home. We had been besieged by reporters at the courthouse and were filmed as we left. It must've been a slow news day, because there were a number of the vultures there. My standard response was "no comment." Maggie's phone began to ring as soon as we were in the car. "Don't answer it if you don't know the number," I said to her.

When we got home, there was a news van actually parked on our lawn. I was incensed that they had so little regard for us that they felt they could park anywhere and get as close as they wanted. I simply called the police and told him that we had trespassers. Again, my stock comment was no comment. Maggie bowed her head and rushed into the house.

Tears were streaming down her face. "I don't know if I can handle this Jimmy Joe. These people are just invading our lives and there is nothing we can do about it."

280

"Maybe it would be better if I stayed at the townhouse." We owned some real estate around Nashville. One of our units was vacant at the moment and I had told the rental agency to put it in my name and charge me for the rent.

"If you do that then they'll say that we have split. And that will be bad for you because it will seem like I have determined that you're guilty. I haven't done that yet."

"Yet?"

"You know what I mean Jim. I don't want it to appear that I have thrown you out. I'm not going to do that. You are my husband and I believe strongly in standing beside my man. I never thought I would say that; but there it is."

"It would be easier for you and the children. I hate the thought of them having to deal with that gaggle of vultures. It sickens me. It also sickens me that I have created this situation for my family. I can't tell you what I was thinking because I don't know what led me to do the things I did. It all started that night at the Bluebird when I began to wallow a little bit in self-pity. It just mushroomed from there. What a disaster."

Maggie looked out the window and said, "At least the police are making them back up a little and get out of our yard. It looks like more of them have arrived. Don't they have something better to do than stalk us?"

"I guess not! Let's just go on with things and pretend they're not there. I'll be out of the news in a couple of days and they'll all go away."

I was in the news that day however. All the TV channels and the newspaper featured my picture as well as some of Maggie. They had the decency to leave our children out of it. That was the only kindness we received from the news media. They continued to hound us for about a week and apparently got bored with the story since we didn't change our routine and I didn't cause any additional problems.

As I was in the news, Trip, Tim, Ray and several of our other partners were talking to potential buyers of our company. My situation was mentioned by the potential buyers, but my father told them that it had nothing to do with the sale of the firm. Our business was strong. We were not losing business to our competitors; in fact, we were gaining share in some of our markets, particularly in Georgia and North Carolina. If they wanted to make my situation an issue, Trip told them there was no reason to have further discussions. After a little backtracking, the talks got back on point.

At this juncture, I thought it necessary to have a conversation with Richard Newton, my lawyer on estate planning issues. He was still with the law firm of Caldwell, Bowles and Ritter.

Dick was a no-nonsense sort of guy and looked square at me and said, "I'm sure you have an idea of what you want to do, so let's hear your ideas."

"Here's how my assets are distributed. First there are the partnership points which I received from my grandfather and on my own as a partner of the firm. My father, mother, sister and I own about 55% of the firm. My share is about

20% which would put the value around $30 million. I want to put that in an irrevocable trust for the benefit of my three children and myself. The income can be used for their benefit, particularly health and education. When the youngest reaches age 25, the trust is to be divided equally among us. I've asked my sister Allie to be the trustee and she has agreed to do it."

Richard asked a few questions and then said, "We can do that easy enough. I assume that you want this in place as soon as possible."

"March 1 is fine. I have an investment account with our firm that is worth a little over $16 million. I want to establish two trusts, both irrevocable. The first is for the benefit of Maggie and the second is for the benefit of me. I would like for you, Richard, to serve as the trustee for both. Ten million should go to Maggie and the balance to me.'

"I assume that you want to provide for Maggie's health and welfare. That she should receive the income from the investments and that the trustee has discretion to invade principal for her benefit. Upon her death, you would like these assets to go to your children. And the same for you, I assume."

"Exactly. Plus we have some rental real estate. I have listed the one condo unit to be in my trust. The other four pieces plus our family home should be in Maggie's trust.

"It will be done in a month and then we will have time to move the assets and have the real estate titled correctly."

Chapter 20

I was sitting in a dark room inside the office suite of Patrick Bramlege. I was watching the video of Katie Gibbs' deposition which was in two parts: the first was before my arrest and the second after my arrest. It was riveting I must say. She was very articulate, firm in her response to questions, sometimes combative, and often, sweet and demure. It was an impressive performance and I had to admit that I would have to convict the perpetrator if my decision was based solely on the video.

The lights came up and I said to Patrick, "She is one really good witness."

"The DA did a masterful job of questioning and keeping the flow going. The way the whole thing is displayed and organized is terrific. They want to play this video and leave it at that. We will have to plan for the fact that they will find a reason why Mrs. Gibbs can't appear in person. However, you have the right to confront your accuser. We will argue that they either produce Mrs. Gibbs for cross-examination or they cannot use the video. The judge will probably allow them to play the video and produce Mrs. Gibbs."

"I believe it is essential that we have the opportunity to cross examine her," I said.

"Now let's talk about you Jimmy Joe. We'll wait till later to make the final decision about your testimony," Patrick said.

"I don't think there is any decision to be made. I consider it extremely important for me to testify on my own behalf. Katie and I were the only people present when all of this

284

was supposedly taking place. I don't have anything to decide. More importantly, I don't have anything to hide. I can handle both McNally and Caplinger."

Liz looked at me with compassion. "Jim, that's what everybody says, but they always get tripped up by the DA. Do not underestimate these people. They are very good at what they do and under the pressure of a trial it is easy to screw up. They have little compassion for justice; the conviction rate is what counts, particularly in a high profile case like this one.'"

"That's why I have you Liz!"

"We are better at courtroom preparation than they are and we will do everything to get you ready. That's why we're here today. We want you to see what's in store when we hit that courtroom."

Liz took over the meeting. "To that end Jim, we want to go over the list of witnesses that the opposition plans to call. There is, of course, Katie. Rick Brunis is on their list. He had an intimate relationship with Katie at the time and it's hard to predict what he might say. He likes the limelight and I got the impression that he wasn't terribly familiar with the truth. Then there is Amanda Jo Bishop, Katie's friend from Alabama, and her psychiatrist, Elise Bondurant. They also have someone by the name of Fran Williams. We are trying to dig out some information on her, but we don't have much. Do you know anything about her Jimmy Joe?"

"I haven't heard that name. So I don't know anything about her. I can't be very helpful there."

"Every day of the trial, we want you to wear a nice suit and shirt, but a fairly bright tie. You have to appear optimistic and innocent. No hanging your head when somebody says something unkind about you. Maggie has promised to be in the gallery every day. That will be helpful. How are you guys doing?"

"We're fine! You know, freaked out, insecure, neurotic and emotional. No, no were doing fine, doing okay."

Patrick asked, "Have you gotten everything straight with Dick Newton?"

"Yes, all the documents have been signed and the assets have been moved appropriately. I hope you guys have gotten your check?"

"We have. Thanks so much for taking care of that little detail. If you get convicted you probably won't be so inclined to pay us."

"I haven't even thought about that, but I guess you're right. I believe you guys are on the right track and are looking out for my interests. I'm curious about this person Fran Williams. She could be the smoking gun."

"We have two investigators on her and Liz is doing some searching, herself. We'll find her."

"What else?"

Liz looked at me and said, "Since you're so anxious to testify, I want to do some role-playing with you. Come on let's go in the other room. My associate, Herby Rosenberg, is going to join us and play the role of the DA."

We spent two hours in this role-playing activity and ii exhausted me. I couldn't imagine what the trial would be like.

I didn't think I would ever be ready for this trial. I took my usual course of action. I went home to my man cave and opened my bottle of Dewar's. The fire in my throat and that nice burn down my gullet was wonderful. I was soon in a haze and everything was alright.

Maggie stuck her head inside the door and said, "Toasting to a crisp again sweetheart?"

I responded, "Baking to a crisp my love and truly getting toasted."

She closed the door and left me alone. I suppose she was wondering if I would make it to dinner, but "frankly my dear I don't give a damn." This little drama repeated itself every day until March 27, 2006.

I awakened early on that Monday morning. I slept a little, but mostly I was awake thinking about all the parameters of this trial. I just couldn't imagine going to jail; just couldn't see how a reasonable jury could convict me; I am likable enough so I will be acquitted; but there is that possibility that one unreasonable person would be on the jury and I would go to jail. The prospect was beyond my comprehension.

I found myself sitting behind the table on the left side of the courtroom facing the judge's bench. The prosecutors table was about 6 feet away to our right. The jury box was to the right of the prosecutor's desk between the table and the bench. The witness stand was beside the bench. It was all so surreal to me. I was the Mad Hatter in Wonderland.

I greeted Liz and Patrick and we had a short conversation. They told me that I had gone out with Fran as a third-year at the University. Apparently there was only one date and the two of us had not seen each other since. Liz looked into my eyes, "Does that ring any bells? Here is a recent picture from Facebook."

"I do remember her. She was a friend of Katie's. I think Allie and Katie were down for the weekend and everyone had dates but me and Fran who had come down with Katie from GWU. So Fran and I went to the party together, but absolutely nothing happened as I recall. We had a bite to eat after the party, a few more beers and then I walked her home to the house she was staying in."

Patrick turned to me and started telling me about jury selection. He then introduced me to Brekell Lavee' our jury consultant. She had a profile on each of the jurors based on a form they had submitted along with anything she could find on Google and social media. She was 6 feet tall with long hair, large breasts, a narrow waist and haunting eyes. She was strangely attractive. She was seated between Liz and Patrick.

The jury selection process was long and arduous. Liz questioned most of the women jurors and Patrick questioned the men. Both listened to Brekell's analysis of each person and framed their questions accordingly. This would've been very interesting, if it hadn't been so personal for me. This was dealing with my life so I couldn't look at it as an educational process. It took all of the day Monday and half the day on Tuesday to finally seat the jury of 12 people; seven women, five men and two alternates, a man and a woman.

Judge Herbert Walker told the jury and the lawyers that Tuesday afternoon would be taken up with final motions and rulings on previous motions. The judge told us to be back in the courtroom at 2 PM sharp. We received a favorable ruling that Katie Gibbs must be present in the courtroom for my lawyers to cross examine her. The prosecution would be permitted to show her taped deposition or have her testify in court, but not both. Patrick and Liz considered this to be a major victory. I thought it was good that she would have to confront me in court.

The rest of the day the lawyers argued back and forth on procedural issues and the remaining motions. The judge handled things with ease and finally we were through at about 4 o'clock. I was ready to get out of there.

I drove myself home, thinking that this may be one of the last times that I would be driving this way for quite a while. My optimism was fading fast and I didn't seem to be able to pump myself up as usual. When I opened the door, Maggie was there to greet me.

"Did they finish with the jury selection?"

"Yeah, they finished. We have a jury of seven women and five men plus two alternates. Brekell, the jury consultant, seemed to be very happy with the group, so Patrick and Liz were happy. They all seemed to be pretty nice people, but I have no idea how you can tell whether they are favorable or not. I guess it's more of an art than a science."

"I'm sure they will be favorable to you. You're a nice guy and I think they will see that. Want to go in the man cave and relax for a while? I'm going to pick up the kids and dinner will be ready around 6:30."

I took off my tie and jacket, threw them on a chair in the man cave and fixed myself some scotch on ice. I flipped on the TV; the local news was on and I was the feature. I cut it off quickly before I could hear anything. I just didn't want to know what was being said about me.

I was in court by 8:30 AM, Patrick was already busily working away and Liz followed shortly thereafter. Maggie, Allie and my father appeared shortly before nine and sat in the seats directly in back of the defense table. It was good to see them, since they were likely to be the only people in the gallery in my corner. The courtroom was filled with spectators, reporters and cameramen. I had known many of the latter during my time as Bill Bonner's lieutenant.

Judge Walker called the court to order and admonished the gallery that he would not tolerate any disturbance and would gladly clear the room if any occurred. He then looked at both attorneys and said that he expected them to conduct themselves with decorum.

The DA, Eric Caplinger, gave his opening statement saying that the state would prove beyond a shadow of a doubt that I was guilty of conspiracy to commit murder. My thoughts were that was impossible. Maybe I should believe it because it is impossible. Then it was our turn. Patrick said that the state did not have any real proof that I was involved in this alleged crime. The testimony may seem somewhat factual, but, in fact, it was all hearsay and innuendo. There was no compelling evidence that I was involved. It was a good opening, Patrick was very eloquent and engaging, and the jury seemed to pay more attention to him than to Caplinger. I was heartened by his performance. Liz patted my arm in agreement and gave me the warmest smile.

"Call your first witness Mr. Caplinger."

"Your honor, the state calls Patricia Gibbs to the stand."

"Mrs. Gibbs, can you tell us what your interest is in this case?"

"I am the mother of Robert Gibbs, who was murdered by his wife in early 2005. I also know the defendant, James Jeter, who was a supposed friend of my son and our family.
"

"Mrs. Gibbs, can you tell us about your son's marriage to Katie Gibbs?"

"From the start, I didn't like Katie and she didn't like me. She wanted to control my son, his every move. She turned him against his family and most of his friends. I was often surprised that she didn't try to turn him against Jimmy Joe, I mean Mr. Jeter, but now I know why. She was really in love with Mr. Jeter and wanted a way to stay close to him. She could do that by marrying my son."

"How do you know this to be the case?"

"My son told me, that's how!"

291

Patrick jumped up. "Objection Your Honor! This is exactly what I was talking about, hearsay!"

ADA McNally jumped up. "Your honor this evidence is admissible against Mr. Jeter. Mr. Gibbs is unavailable; and the statement has been made under circumstances providing sufficient "indication of reliability". With respect to the second prong, a reliability determination may assume that hearsay is sufficiently reliable for constitutional purposes if it satisfies a "firmly rooted" hearsay exception. In practice this means that lower courts need to make reliability determinations only for hearsay that is offered under a "catchall" exception. "

"Overruled!"

Patrick leaned over to Liz and said, "The judge is going to be very lenient on this hearsay business. That's not good for us."

"What exactly did your son say to you?"

"He told me that one of the major reasons Katie married him was because he was such good friends with Mr. Jeter and new that he and my son would stay friends for life. My son thought the world of Mr. Jeter and I thought the reverse was true also."

On cross-examination, Liz asked Mrs. Gibbs, "Did you and your son believe Mr. Jeter had this affection for Katie Gibbs in return?"

"I certainly didn't, but my son never discussed that with me."

Amanda Jo Bishop was the next person called as a witness.

Liz Oliver handled the questioning for the defense. "Ms. Bishop, can you tell us how you know Katie and Mr. Jeter?"

'I have known Katie since the 80s. We worked together in Alabama at NASA and have remained friends since that time. She visited me in Huntsville from time to time and I have been to Nashville to visit her on a number of occasions. We are very good friends."

"And Mr. Jeter?"

"I was staying at the Union Station hotel on a visit to Nashville. Katie and Mr. Jeter were talking in the lobby, actually having a rather intense conversation. When I came up to them, the conversation ceased and Katie introduced me to Mr. Jeter. He seemed to be very upset about what was taking place. He left rather abruptly. I asked Katie what that was about and she told me that Mr. Jeter was helping her with a very difficult problem she was having. I asked if it had to do with Bobby and she said yes."

Liz asked Ms. Bishop if she knew the specifics of the conversation between Ms. Gibbs and Mr. Jeter, "I only know that it concerned Bobby Gibbs and the difficulty she was having with him."

"But you didn't know what the specific difficulty was that she was discussing with Mr. Jeter, isn't that true?"

"All of her friends knew what the difficulty was, in fact, everyone knew it. Bobby was seeking a divorce and wanted to take her kids away from her. That was the difficulty. It's obvious."

"Did Katie tell you that's what they were talking about?"

"No not in so many words, but I knew. I was her friend."

"Yes or no Ms. Bishop?"

"No."

It would be more of the same as Elise Bondurant took the stand.

"Dr. Bondurant, you were Katie Gibbs's psychiatrist, were you not?"

"Yes that's true."

"How would you describe Katie Gibbs' state of mind in late 2004 in early 2005?"

"She was suffering from an anxiety disorder and she was cycling very rapidly from one phase of her bipolar disorder to the other. I was increasingly fearful that she would do something harmful to herself or to someone else. Actually, she was seeking affirmation for a course of action that she wanted to take, but that she felt morally repugnant."

"Do you have any idea what she wanted to do? "

"I believe she wanted to physically harm someone. She talked about that in hypothetical terms without ever getting specific. She was hospitalized several times to deal with this problem, but was released. I tried to get her to stay until we could resolve this situation, but that never happened. In retrospect, she wanted to kill Bobby, but needed to have someone push her over the edge."

"Do you know who that someone was?"

Patrick was on the edge of his seat ready to object.

"No I don't, but isn't that what we're here to determine?"

"Objection Your Honor. Move to strike the last part of that statement."

"Sustained!"

Patrick asked the good doctor "Was my client ever identified as the person who would push her over the edge?"

"No he was not, but she talked about him a lot and in my professional opinion, he was a good candidate."

Patrick was beside himself. "Your honor please, this is outrageous. I'm objecting to that answer. Please move to strike."

"Sustained and the jury will disregard the Doctor's remarks. Dr. Bondurant, please answer the question asked and do not expand if you please."

"Then my answer is he was never identified."

Chapter 21

The next witness to be called was Katie Gibbs herself. Since it was 4 o'clock in the afternoon, the judge adjourned the preceding until 9 AM. I went home, entered the man cave, poured a drink and began to cry. I was slowly losing my life and this anorexic bitch had set all of this in motion. I hated her more than ever.

The jury filed in at promptly 9:05 AM on Thursday. The gallery was packed as everyone wanted to see Katie in person. I had a notepad and pen in front of me to list all the times she lied or embellished something. There was a large screen that was set up so that everyone in the courtroom could see. A video player and laptop was on a table a few feet away.

Patrick stood and was recognized by Judge Walker. "Your honor, for the record, we want to note our objection to Mrs. Gibbs not being in the courtroom for the entire proceeding."

"So noted and recorded," said the judge.

He turned to Dale McNally and said, "Mr. McNally you may begin."

McNally stood up and faced the jury. "Ladies and gentlemen of the jury, you are about to see a deposition by Katie Grant that was recorded on February 9 and February 23, 2015 in the Tennessee Prison for Women."

Patrick jumped out of his seat again, "The copy we received was dated February 9, 2015. Has there been a new copy or a new deposition? The state is trying to introduce a recording that the defense has not had an opportunity to review. This is a violation of the discovery rules that you yourself put in effect Your Honor."

"Your honor, we asked Mrs. Gibbs two additional questions regarding her mother-in-law, Patricia Gibbs, and we provided a transcript of those two questions to the defense along with the answers. They know the substance of these questions and they know the answers given. Mr. Bramlege is simply trying to discredit this testimony."

The judge looked at Patrick and said, "Mr. Bramlege did you receive a transcript?"

"Yes your honor, but in the spirit of your order, we should have received a new copy of the recording."

"He is right Mr. McNally! Any more shenanigans like this from the prosecution will result in a contempt of court citation. Do you understand?"

"Yes your honor."

"You may proceed."

"Mrs. Gibbs is receiving no compensation nor is she receiving any reduction in her sentence nor is she receiving any special treatment by the Tennessee Department of Prisons. I think everyone will understand why she is doing this when they hear her testimony."

The judge was getting aggravated, "Stop making speeches Mr. McNally and get on with the recording."

An assistant moved to the laptop, turned it on, reached the appropriate file and Katie Gibbs filled the screen. She was dressed in a green prison uniform and her hair was in a ponytail.

There were some introductory comments by Eric Caplinger on the video and with that dispensed, the questioning began. A lot of time was taken up talking about Katie's childhood, her college years, her employment record and her marriage to Bobby Gibbs.

Then the real questioning began. Caplinger asked her why she was willing to make a statement in the trial of James Jeter.

"I have reconciled myself to the fact that most people believe that I killed my husband. The one thing in my life that I truly treasure is my children and he was trying to take them away from me. Despite the troubles that the two of us had in our relationship, taking my children away from me just wasn't right. So I was angry and I expressed my anger to a lot of people. And yes when Rick Brunis asked me about killing my husband, I did tell him that I did not want to put him in a position that might make him lie for me. I really didn't answer the question. You may think I'm guilty and I guess the jury did, but that's not necessarily the case. But the one person that I could talk with about my husband and, who understood, was Jimmy Jeter. When I needed help I went to him and he helped me."

"What about Bobby's family or your family? Don't most people turn to their families when they need help?"

Katie rolled her eyes and said, "What kind of dream world do you live in. My family is too busy working and taking care of their own life; they didn't have time to take care of mine. My brother has a business to run, my father is a surgeon and my mother is a businesswoman. Bobby's family didn't like me very much and truly wanted him to get rid of me. I think they were in large part responsible for his decision to file for divorce and keep my children from me. The Gibbs family wanted my children for themselves. My children are so wonderful and gifted."

"Mrs. Patricia Gibbs came to visit you from time to time and you seemed to have a cordial relationship. Was that not the case?"

"She hated me the most. In fact she talked to Jim before our marriage and asked him if he could talk Bobby out of it. Jim told her that Bobby was too much in love with me to change his mind. She was the worst of the Gibbs'. She pretended to like me so she could be around my children and Bobby. She did some things with me, but it was mostly to ingratiate herself to her son. She didn't like me at all."

"What was Bobby Gibbs' relationship with Jim Jeter?"

"They were best friends, although men don't talk that way, but as a woman that's how I would describe it. They met in college, I think in their first year and have been friends ever since. Bobby went to law school at Vanderbilt and decided to stay in Nashville to be close to Jim and to marry me. I guess early on marrying me was the most important, but later on his friendship with Jim became more important. They went to sporting events, duck hunted in Maryland,

and played golf together. And they gave each other advice on business deals. Yup, they were truly best friends."

"What was your relationship with Jim Jeter?"

"That was a little more complex. I became friends with Jim's sister Allie when we were both about five years old. We became inseparable. And we went from kindergarten to the 12th grade together. We spent a lot of time with each other on sleepovers, trips to events and spare time. Accordingly, I got to know Jim or Jimmy Joe as we called him, pretty well. Like most boys, he pretended not to like girls at first, but when he got to be a teenager he really liked girls and he really liked me. I actually caught him masturbating in his room while looking at my picture. But I was a younger girl and he was too embarrassed to date me.
"

"He got into a little trouble with a girl from school and with an older woman. He was quite the lady's man. Then he went off to school and I didn't see much of him until Allie and I went to college. He actually introduced Bobby and me to one another. That was hard for him, because I could tell that he was in love with me. Even though he married Maggie and I married Bobby, he still loved me. On his 40th birthday, we started a sexual relationship. It was wonderful. He was so kind, so gentle and he was a stud. His equipment made me swoon."

There was a giggle in the courtroom. The judge banged his gavel. "Quiet in the courtroom."

"Finally, I was with the man who could help me solve my problem regarding my husband and my kids. He was the love of my life, Jimmy Joe Jeter."

"What do you mean by solving your problems with regard to your husband and your kids?"

"I mean getting my husband out of the picture and having my children be with me and eventually Jimmy Joe. I didn't want to kill Bobby. That was not my plan. I would have been happy to have a simple divorce as long as I could keep my children. But of course Bobby had all of those silly restraining orders and he was unwilling to cooperate with me. As Jimmy Joe said, I didn't have much choice."

"What did he mean by that?"

"He told me that killing Bobby would have to be opportunistic, because planning for it would be too dangerous. He said he and Bobby were a lot alike and they drank too much at times. And sometimes, they passed out. And that situation would be the opportunity. When that occurred, I could do something. I knew a little bit about medicine and I decided that strangulation was probably the best tactic. He told me to use my cell phone cable because I always had it with me; it was strong and thin. I don't like messiness and this would not be messy. Jimmy Joe agreed that it wouldn't be messy. So if I was going to do it, that's the way I would've done it. I always think clearly when I am around Jimmy Joe. I love that man and he loves me. He has loved me all my life; the only person to love me all my life."

"So you're saying that Jimmy Joe Jeter or Mr. James J. Jeter IV helped you plan the murder of your husband?"

"We just planned it, but yes Jimmy Joe helped. He has been helpful to me all of my life. I love him and he loves me."

"Where did you and Mr. Jeter do all of this planning?"

"I like staying in hotels because of the room service and sometimes I use the gym. Bobby was paying so I didn't mind the cost. We met in the hotel rooms and sometimes we met in an out-of-the-way bar. But we would run into people from time to time, and that was uncomfortable for Jimmy Joe. So I started staying in motels. It wasn't as nice because there was no room service, but it was cheaper so Bobby was happy and we ran less risk of being recognized. That was Jimmy Joe's idea and I went along with it. The rooms all had clean sheets and nice firm beds. We were happy."

"I am going to play a recording from your cell phone of a conversation between you and Mr. Jeter."

Patrick stood. "Your honor, we renew our objection to this recording. My client had no idea he was being recorded."

"Overruled."

"Can you verify that the voices are yours and Mr. Jeter?"

"Yes, that's me and Jimmy Joe."

He played the tape of our last conversation at the Hampden Inn. If you understood the context, it wouldn't be so damning, but played alone it was a hard blow.

I couldn't believe what I was hearing and seeing on that screen. She had just implicated me in this whole crime. I was taking notes like mad and really needed to talk to Patrick and Liz. They were listening intently to what she was saying. Some of it was new at least to me and most of it was a fabrication, but I could tell that she really believed it. She was in some kind of fantasy world and I was being skewered by her reconstruction of reality.

Mercifully, the video ended, the lights came up, and folks in the gallery began to whisper so much that a mumbling sound welled up from the crowd.

The judge banged his gavel. "Quite in the courtroom or I'll have the gallery cleared." The crowd quieted as the judge said, "We will take a 20 minute recess."

I stood and looked at Maggie. It was obvious that she had been crying. She stared at me with such malevolence that I shrank into my shoes. My life was changing before my very eyes and I didn't seem to have the capacity to change the momentum.

Patrick grabbed my arm and I followed him out of the courtroom, down a hallway and into a conference room. I sank into a chair and held my head in a hand.

Patrick started the conversation by saying, "I know that a large part of that testimony was fabricated, but she surely believes it."

I looked at him in disbelief. "All that testimony regarding the cheaper motels is untrue. I did talk to her in a couple of bars, including the Union Station and a couple of tourist places, but no motels, none, de nada. And I don't love her and I never have. I detested her for my whole life. Why I got involved with her in this situation I will never understand. I should've told Maggie on my birthday night exactly what happened, taken my punishment like a man and moved on. I thought I was taking the easier way, but it's been anything but that."

Liz said, "Don't worry Jim; we'll get the momentum back on cross examination."

A hush fell over the courtroom as the doors opened and two armed guards entered with a shackled Katie Gibbs behind them and two other guards followed as she clanked down the middle aisle, stopped beside the defense table and smiled at me, then allowed Dale McNally to escort her to the witness stand. It was show business at its best and Katie was reveling in the attention. Photographers were snapping pictures at warp speed and the gallery was vocal in sort of hushed tones. The guards removed the center chain and removed the shackles from her ankles.

The judge banged his gavel again and called for quite in the courtroom. Instantaneously, you could've heard a pin drop.

From the judge, "the prosecution has presented the testimony of Mrs. Gibbs via video. Therefore, we're going to move directly into cross examination. Redirect will follow the cross examination. Mr. Bramlege you may begin."

"Ms. Gibbs, my name is Patrick Bramlege and I represent Mr. James Jeter. He is charged with conspiring with you to murder your husband. And you seemed to indicate that it's true-- that is, he conspired with you. Is that what you said?"

"I said that we planned it, but I didn't say that we did it. The police investigation was flawed. They never considered anyone else, like Jimmy Joe. They landed on me and that was all they needed. The police wanted to get the case solved quickly and in these cases they always look at the wife. Maybe someone else did it. I just wanted my kids and now I'll never have them."

"Are you saying that Mr. Jeter killed your husband, not you?"

"Don't put words in my mouth Mr. – – – what did you say your name was?"

"Patrick Bramlege"

"That's an odd name. What were we talking about? Oh yeah, you are putting words in my mouth. I didn't say anything of the sort about Jimmy Joe. I simply said he helped me plan it."

"Where did he help you plan it? And please Ms. Gibbs, be as specific as you can."

"We met at the Cross Corner Bar in Brentwood, Dalts on White Bridge Road, Jimmy Kelley's, Union Station, and several other downtown bars. I can't remember the names. And then we met at the Four Points Sheraton in Brentwood, the Hermitage, Hampton Inn and in three or four other motels that had mom-and-pop names. I don't remember those except that they had clean sheets. Jimmy Joe loves clean sheets."

"It's interesting Mrs. Gibbs, when we review your credit card statements and Mr. Jeter's credit card statements, the only names that appear are the Cross Corner Bar on Mr. Gibbs' American Express and the Four Points Sheraton on your platinum Visa and Union Station on your MasterCard. None of these other items appear anywhere. And we know that you were with Amanda Jo Bishop at Union Station and just happened to run into Mr. Jeter. How do you respond to that?"

"I was with Jimmy Joe and we happened to run into Amanda Jo. That's funny, a boy and a girl named Joe. Do you think that's – – – what was your name again?"

"Patrick Bramlege."

"Do you think that's funny Patrick?"

"No I don't think so."

"Ms. Gibbs weren't you and Amanda Jo Bishop meeting each other at Union Station and in fact, you both were going to stay that night at the hotel and you ran into Mr. Jeter on your way from the bar to your room."

"That was a while ago and it's hard to remember all of the circumstances but I'm pretty sure that I was with Jimmy Joe and we ran into Amanda Jo while she was checking in."

"But you had already checked in, so Ms. Bishop wouldn't have to check in, isn't that right?"

"I'm not sure, but I think they want everybody who is going to be in the room to check in. But I'm not sure. I just know we ran into Amanda Jo. At least that's how I recall it now."

Dale McNally stood. "Your Honor, I believe a review of the transcript will indicate that Ms. Bishop corroborates Ms. Gibbs recollection."

Patrick looked at the judge. "Your Honor, I'm asking for Ms. Gibbs' recollection which seems to be a little hazy."

The judge looked at Katie and said, "Ms. Gibbs do you have a firm recollection of who you were with on the night in question."

"Yes, Jimmy Joe and Amanda Jo, just like I said."

"Who were you with at the bar that evening?"

"Jimmy Joe first and then Amanda Jo later. That's how it was. Yes, yes that's how it was?"

Judge Walker returned to Patrick. "Is that satisfactory Mr. Bramlege?"

"Yes your honor."

"Mrs. Gibbs you mentioned the Hermitage Hotel as one of the places you met Mr. Jeter, is that right?"

"Yes, I did say that I believe."

"We did a check of the Hermitage Hotel and did not find you or Mr. Jeter had checked into the hotel during the timeframe in question. And we could not find any charges on your credit cards or on Mr. Jeter's. Can you explain that?"

Ever the clever person, Katie Gibbs thought for a moment and then said, "Jimmy Joe was getting a little paranoid during that time frame and we started using cash and false names."

"Even if you're paying in cash Ms. Gibbs, the hotel requires a credit card."

"Well I didn't work out those arrangements. Jimmy Joe worked all that out and I don't know how he did it. I just know that he did it and we had a good time there. Champagne, sex, and planning. I really enjoyed all those things with Jimmy Joe. He is the love of my life."

"Mrs. Gibbs, you and Mr. Jeter were never at that hotel, isn't that correct?"

Katie got a little angry with Patrick. "No, that isn't correct. I have told you we were there and that's the truth. You'll have to talk to Jimmy Joe to figure out how we got our room."

"What about the other three or four motels you talked about, do you remember any of their names?"

"I don't really know what their names were, but maybe Hampton Inn, or Comfort Inn, or Holiday Inn, one of those Inns. They were all off the interstate and all of their customers were travelers or tourists. They wouldn't know us, so we didn't have to be so careful. Jimmy Joe was always worried about somebody seeing us."

"Again Ms. Gibbs, we didn't find any charges to your credit cards or to Mr. Jeter's credit cards and we couldn't find any information that either you or Mr. Jeter had stayed at any of the major chain motels. How do you account for that?"

"Well since I was on an allowance from my husband, I didn't think it was appropriate for him to pay for my lover as well. So Jimmy Joe took care of all that and I don't know what he did. He was so good at taking care of me."

Katie was certainly playing the helpless little girl role to perfection. I turned to look at Maggie, who was still in the courtroom supporting me; I saw the tears in her eyes and the disappointment in her face. It was heartbreaking for me. How could I put her through this any longer?

Patrick asked several more questions that were fruitless for our side and finally sat down.

The judge said, "Any redirect from the state?"

"No Your Honor."

The guards moved back to the witness stand and placed the shackles back on Katie's ankles. All eyes in the courtroom were again on Katie as she clanked her way to the doorway and left.

"The state calls Rick Brunis to the stand."

"Mr. Brunis, can you tell us your relationship to Katie Gibbs and to the defendant James Jeter?"

"I was Katie Gibbs' boyfriend after she separated from her husband. As for Mr. Jeter, I really didn't have a relationship with him, but I did meet him once when he came to meet with Katie at her hotel."

"Do you have knowledge concerning the nature of the conversation that Mr. Jeter and Ms. Gibbs were having?"

"I was kind of jealous of Mr. Jeter because I knew that Katie or Mrs. Gibbs had feelings for him. I had feelings for her and we were sleeping together. She told me that I would have to leave while they were talking, because she didn't want to get me in any trouble. She said that Mr. Jeter was helping her plan some things. Some things that would help her get her kids back. She was awfully worried about those children. She really loved them. If she had loved and trusted me, I would've advised her differently and she wouldn't have gotten into all this trouble."

"After the death of her husband, did you have occasion to talk with Mrs. Gibbs about her role in the murder?"

"Yes I talked to her. I asked her straight off did she kill her husband. She said to me that she didn't want to say because she didn't want to get me in trouble or put me in a position where I would lie. I asked her if that's what she and Jeter were planning when they met all those times and she told me the same thing that she didn't want me to have to lie. I believe he helped her."

Patrick jumped up again and shouted, "Objection, the last statement is pure conjecture on the part of the witness. We move to strike that statement."

The judge agreed.

Patrick cross-examined Mr. Brunis, but couldn't shake him from his conviction that I was involved in helping Katie to plan the murder of my friend Bobby Gibbs. What a clusterfuck!

The next witness, Fran Williams, was called.

Dale McNally was handling the questioning for the prosecution. "Ms. Williams, will you please tell us about your relationship with Katie Gibbs."

"I'm a friend of Ms. Gibbs. We met at George Washington University and were immediately drawn to one another. We have been friends for almost 20 years."

"And do you know the accused in this case, Mr. James Jeter?"

"Yes I do. We met at a party at Mr. Jeter's fraternity in 1985. Katie, Mr. Jeter's sister Allison, and I motored from Washington to the University to attend a football game and several parties. Both Allison and Katie had dates but I did not have one. And neither did Mr. Jeter, so we decided to hook up. I became his date for the weekend. We had a lovely time together."

She looked my way and smiled. I didn't have it in me to smile back. I was certain she would drive a dagger into my heart.

"Have you seen Mr. Jeter since that weekend?"

"Yes. He came to Washington to visit his sister and have a little fun in DC. The four of us went to a Georgetown bar and had some drinks. We must've visited for a couple of hours and then headed back to GW, dropping Allie at

American University along the way. Mr. Jeter ended up spending the night with me.

"Back in November of last year, Mr. Jeter was in Washington on business and we ran into each other on the Hill. Since it had been some time since we had seen each other, we decided to meet for drinks at the Old Ebbitt. We then had dinner on the rooftop at the Hotel Washington. It was a particularly warm night for November."

"What did you and Mr. Jeter talk about?"

"We talked about what had happened in the intervening period since we had last met. He talked a lot about his wife and kids. He does love those kids and he went on and on about them. I asked about his sister Allie. He told me she was managing the Big Jack Foundation. We discussed my life some and I told him about law school and my lobbying work on the Hill. It was a fascinating evening."

"Did you talk about Katie Gibbs?"

"Yes we did. He was very upset about the circumstances surrounding the death of Bobby Gibbs. When I knew them in college, they were very close friends. Many of us thought that they were way too intimate. Katie often mentioned that she thought they were lovers. She never caught them in the act, but I can see how two guys who lived together for three years or more could find love and intimacy with each other and still love women. After all isn't that what bisexuality is about?

Again Patrick jumped to his feet. "Your Honor, I don't understand the relevance of this testimony. Mr. Jeter has been married for over 15 years, has three children and is clearly heterosexual. This whole thing is irrelevant."

The judge looked at Patrick, then at McNally and said, "Move on from this subject Mr. McNally."

"Ms. Williams, can you get back to your conversations regarding Katie Gibbs?"

"We talked about the tragedy of Katie's involvement in Bobby's murder. Mr. Jeter was very upset about Katie, but he knew that the police had all the evidence to convict her and that in fact she was guilty. I asked him if he had helped her in any way. He asked me why that was important. I told him that Katie said to me that he was very much involved in helping her plan her strategy for dealing with her husband. He then told me that he had talked to Katie a lot about her problems with Bobby, but he did not help her kill him. He said Katie brought up the idea of killing Bobby, but he dismissed it as a possibility because she was so small. I guess she showed him."

"Am I correct to say that Katie Gibbs talked about Mr. Jeter's direct involvement with her on the planning of the murder and that Mr. Jeter actually discussed that strategy with her?" Dale McNally was trying to put the last nail in my coffin.

"Yes that is correct."

"Your witness!"

Patrick slowly walked to the lectern as if he were in deep thought. "Ms. Williams are you married?"

"Yes I am. I've been married about six years."

"Any children?"

"My husband and I have chosen not to have any children. It's a personal choice."

"You have suggested in an elliptical way that you and Mr. Jeter had an intimate relationship for a brief period. Were you intimate the night you had dinner in Washington?"

"We did not have sex that evening if that's what you're asking. He was anxious to get back to his hotel and talk with his children and wife. But on the previous occasions that we were together, we did."

"In fact, it bothers you that Mr. Jeter loves his wife and children, doesn't it? Aren't you in love with Mr. Jeter?"

"I'm not in love with Mr. Jeter, although I like him very much and enjoy his company. But I'm not jealous of his family in any way. I feel sorry for them because of all the hoopla surrounding this business."

"Have you had an intimate relationship with Mr. Jeter's sister, Allie?"

"Yes, when we were in college, some of us experimented with our sexuality. Allie and I dated for a while and lived together in Washington for a while. She left Washington after law school to return to Nashville to manage her grandfather's foundation."

"Did you ever go to Nashville to visit Allie?"

"Yes I came several times; she had gotten a new partner and was settling into a slower pace of life. It didn't suit me."

"In fact, you were accused of stalking Ms. Jeter, isn't that right?"

"Yes that's true, but I was never convicted of anything nor charged with anything, just accused."

"Isn't this just another way for you to get back at the Jeters's because both of them had jilted you and your romantic imagination got the best of you?"

"No, that's just ridiculous!"

"You were scorned by both of the Jeters's' and now you've come back to settle the score!"

"No further questions your honor."

"Your Honor the state rests."

Patrick rose from his chair and said, "Your Honor, the defense moves for a directed verdict. The state has failed to meet the test for finding my client guilty of anything, let alone the crime he is being accused of in this matter."

Eric Caplinger jumped up from his seat. "Your Honor please…."

Before he could get out another word, the judge looked at him. "Sit down Mr. Caplinger."

Then he paused several minutes as if he were contemplating whether to accept or reject the motion. He looked up and said, "Motion denied!"

We were at midafternoon on the second day of the actual trial. The judge looked at his watch and then said, "We will begin testimony for the defense tomorrow morning at 9 AM."

We decided to convene in Patrick's office in thirty minutes. I turned to Maggie. She looked so sad and dispirited. I leaned across the railing to tell her the plan. She looked at me and tears streamed down her face. "Who are you? I don't know you at all. You are a stranger to me." My sister put her arm around Maggie's shoulders and led her away.

Chapter 22

When I arrived, no one was in Patrick's office so I helped myself to the scotch which was in a cabinet in back of his desk. I settled into one of the nice stuffed chairs, took a sip of scotch, and called my sister. I got her voicemail and left a message for her to call me back as soon as she got Maggie settled. I had a number of thoughts running through my head, none of which seemed very palatable. That's why I needed to talk to Allie, my confidant for most of my life.

Patrick walked into his office with Liz trailing behind. "I really thought the judge was going to grant the motion Jim. I'm really disappointed that he didn't, because he had every reason to do so. It's always a risk to adopt that strategy, but tomorrow he will instruct the jury to not read anything into his decision."

"It was the right thing to do, no question about it." For some reason, I didn't want Patrick to feel bad or to think that I didn't appreciate everything he was doing to defend me. My actions have made this case really difficult to defend.

"Tomorrow we have Tim O'Hara, Maggie and Allie followed by you. Again I want to reiterate Jim that you don't have to testify and the jury will be instructed to not read anything into that decision."

I looked at Patrick. "I don't think Maggie will testify. She is very upset with me and won't be in a frame of mind to help me. This stand by your man routine has run its course."

Liz stepped into the conversation. "Surely she wants you to be rendered not guilty. If she doesn't testify, that really hurts our case because it shows that the wife doesn't believe she can defend her husband."

"Well Liz, that's exactly how she feels."

"Have you talked to her recently?"

"Right after today's court session we talked. She said she no longer knows me."

My cell phone rang and I saw that it was Allie's number. "I need to take this call," I said and left the room.

I answered the phone and asked Allie to hold on for a moment so I could get in the conference room. I closed the door. "Okay I'm settled. How was Maggie?"

"She thinks you have been lying to her throughout your marriage. She says that she could put up with most of your behavior, but not that one. She kept saying over and over that you lied to her in your home. She doesn't know whether you're guilty or innocent, but she does know you lied to her. She can't go on the stand Jimmy."

"I know and neither can you. I've come to a conclusion. This trial needs to end right now. I can't put my family and friends through this any longer. Allie, I am probably guilty of this crime. I talked to Katie on more than one occasion and I told her how to kill Bobby. I didn't think she would do it. I hate that bitch with all my soul.

"But Bobby Gibbs I hate even more."

"What are you saying Jimmy?"

"Everyone thinks that all things pertinent to this case have been revealed. I trusted that bastard. Bobby Gibbs was my longest and dearest friend or so I thought. But he was devious. He tried to seduce Maggie on four or five occasions. He tried to kiss her and fondle her more than once. He told her that he loved her. She finally told me— she waited because she didn't think I would believe her. But after the Katie incident in the park, she told me. You know Big Jack's favorite saying---don't get mad, get even. I did! I didn't kill him, but little Katie did and I nudged her to do it."

"Oh, Jimmy!"

"I'm going to plead guilty. There is something called the Alford plea that Patrick and I talked about. I can maintain my innocence, but stipulate that the state has enough evidence to convict me."

"You'll have to serve time in prison. They won't just let you walk. I don't know Jimmy, that's a huge decision. The jury just might think you're innocent. We're all tough, although Maggie's had enough that's for sure."

"You're giving me the old economist answer; this will happen if this happens, but on the other hand this might not happen if this happens. Tell me what you think."

"Jimmy you are my brother and I love you. I hate to see you fall on your sword. You got caught up in something involving a lunatic. I separated from her in college and tried to keep my distance, but she wouldn't let me. And she hasn't let you escape from her either. She put all this in motion, because she didn't get any love or respect from you. She blamed you for putting Bobby in her life because she thought she deserved better. I think it's better for you to take your lumps and get it out of the way. You'll be a young guy when you get out and you can put your life back together. You'll have a lot of money. I'll take care of that for you and of your children and Maggie. You won't have to worry about any of that. You'll just have to survive prison."

"Thanks Allie, I love you as well."

I walked out of the conference room and entered Patrick's office. Liz was still in there talking to Patrick. They were a good team and I really think they did a great job for me. But it was time to end this circus.

"I want to plead guilty."

Liz was stunned and said, "I don't think I heard that correctly. Could you say it again?"

"I want to plead guilty. I can't put Maggie and my children through this anymore. I love them too much and I want them to be able to go on with their lives. I've done everything financially to make them secure. My sister, my father, and Dick Newton will see to their safety. It only makes sense for me to plead guilty. I've talked to Allie about it and she agrees."

"But you're not guilty!" said Liz. She was almost hyperventilating and her words were not coming easy.

"I am! I am guilty. The state has put together a reasonable case that I am guilty and I don't have the ammunition to defeat them."

"We can win this Jimmy."

"Maybe Patrick, but not without hurting these people I love. And I am guilty."

"You're just saying that."

"No, Patrick, I really am guilty."

Patrick looked at me with sadness in his eyes. "Are you thinking an Alford plea?"

I nodded my head yes. "I think that's the right way for me to go."

In an Alford Plea, the criminal defendant does not admit the act, but admits that the prosecution could likely prove the charge. The court will pronounce me guilty. I will plead guilty yet not admit all the facts that comprise the crime. Upon receiving an Alford plea from me, the court will immediately pronounce me guilty and impose sentence as if I had otherwise been convicted of the crime. When a defendant indicates an intention to plead guilty by Alford plea, the judge asks two questions: "Do you now consider it to be in your best interest to plead guilty?" and "Do you understand that upon your 'Alford plea' you will be treated as being guilty whether or not you admit that you are in fact guilty?"

"I'll call Eric Caplinger," and he left the room.

Liz and I chatted about this decision and a few other things. I really liked Liz a lot and she seemed to like me.

Patrick came back into the room, "Caplinger is on his way over here with McNally. He thinks they've convicted you, but he is worried about some of the female jurors and that this jury might just return a verdict he doesn't like."

McNally and Caplinger arrived and went into the conference room to discuss things. It went on for about 45 minutes. Patrick came into his office and said to me, "Jimmy they want you to serve eight years in a medium security prison here in Nashville. There will be no prohibitions regarding parole. Probably you can get out in 5 to 6 years.

I took a deep breath and sighed, "That's good with me."

"Come with me."

"We are in agreement gentleman."

"Mr. Jeter you understand that you are pleading guilty to conspiracy to commit murder and that you will serve eight years in the state penitentiary. There will be no prohibition regarding parole nor will there be any constraints on your ability to get a reduction in your sentence for good behavior. The Tennessee Bureau of Prisons determines where prisoners are held, but we will make every effort to see that you're housed in a medium security prison in Nashville. Do you understand this?"

"Yes I do."

He handed an agreement to Patrick who reviewed it, passed it to Liz for review, and then on to me. I read it and signed. My fate was sealed.

Caplinger looked around the room and said, "I will notify the judge."

The next morning the judge entered the courtroom, the jury entered the jury box and all appeared normal. The judge banged his gavel, ordered the courtroom to be quiet and made sure everyone was in their proper place.

"Ladies and gentlemen of the jury, there has been a development in this case and we no longer need your services. Thank you for your service to this court and you are now excused." The jury filed out of the room and there was a murmur of anticipation from the crowd. "Quiet in the courtroom."

"Mr. Caplinger, you have informed me that the state and Mr. Jeter have reached an agreement wherein he will plead guilty to conspiracy to commit murder under an Alford plea agreement."

"That is correct your honor."

"Under this agreement, Mr. Jeter will serve eight years in prison with the possibility of parole at the end of six years. He will also be eligible for reduction in his sentence for good behavior."

Judge Walker turned to me and looked straight into my eyes. "Mr. Jeter do you understand this agreement and its consequences. You are pleading guilty to this crime;

although you maintain that you are innocent. You acknowledge that the state has enough evidence to convict you. Therefore you are accepting this agreement and the consequences."

Liz was standing beside me squeezing my hand. "I am your honor."

"Do you accept this plea in its entirety and you have received a written copy of this agreement?"

"Yes your honor, I accept this agreement."

"Do you have anything to say before this court sentences you?"

"Yes your honor. Under this agreement, I have pled guilty. I did not kill Bobby Gibbs, but I may have conspired with Katie Gibbs. It's all in the definition. I regret the harm that has been done to my family and my friends, but mostly to my wife Maggie Randolph Jeter. I am deeply sorry."

I stood looking at the judge as Liz continued to squeeze my hand.

"Mr. Jeter, this Court finds you guilty of conspiracy to commit murder and you are sentenced to eight years in prison. You will be eligible for parole after six years. Mr. Jeter I'm going to give you one week to put your affairs in order. On April 7, 2006 you will report to the Davidson County Sheriff's Department in Nashville at 10 AM. Do you understand all that I've said?"

"Yes I do your honor."

"This court is adjourned."

I sat back down in the chair and considered what I had just done. I am going to prison. I looked to the left and Allie was sitting beside me crying.

"Oh Jimmy Joe, I can't believe this is happening. This is the worst day of my life. "

"It'll be okay Allie. I'll survive. The humiliation will do me good. I just hope Big Jack isn't watching."

"Where are you going to spend this week? Please stay with me in the spare room. Cora Jane and I would love to have you. I don't think staying in your house is going to be a very good option."

"I think you're right. Staying with you two will keep me from getting morose and I can enjoy a little Scotch whiskey before I go to the Big House."

A Sheriff's deputy came up to me and said, "Mr. Jeter will you follow me sir?"

"The judge said I had a week before I had to report to the Sheriff's office."

"Yes sir, that's right, but we have to keep track of you. So we have to put an ankle band on you so we can keep up with your whereabouts."

I understand why Katie didn't like her ankle bracelet because the thing wasn't very comfortable, but it was better than being in jail. I headed to my now former house to get some things for the week and hopefully to see Maggie one last time before I went into the prison system.

I knocked on the door and my son Josiah answered. "Hi dad, come on in. Mom dad's here," he shouted. Maggie came into the foyer.

"I need to get a few things that I'll need this week, if that's all right. It won't take me very long."

"That's fine. Where will you be staying?"

"Allie invited me to stay with them, so I took her up on it."

"You could've stayed here," she said in a soft voice.

"I didn't think you'd want me and it would be too hard on all of us. I'll say goodbye to the kids. That'll be difficult but I have to do it."

"It seems to me that you're playing the martyr Jimmy Joe. You don't have to be the martyr. Why didn't you stand up and defend yourself against that awful woman. You just let her win and that's not like you. You seem to be defeated. I can't believe you didn't stand up and I can't believe that you lied to me so many times. That's what hurts so much. I refuse to love you anymore. It'll be hard, but I'll make myself do it."

That cut me to the quick. A dagger to the heart. A baseball bat to the head. Falling off a cliff. Any of those things would've been better than hearing those words.

The next thing Maggie said was, "I'll get the kids and will meet you in the living room."

I packed two gym bags with clothes and underwear. I then went into the living room. Maggie, Josiah, Abigail and Chris were sitting on the sofa. They looked sad. I really didn't know what to say, but I'd say something.

"I'm going away for a while. I did some things that weren't very nice, including lying to your mother. Lying is one of the worst things you can do, so make sure you tell the truth. Actually, it will be a fairly long time before I come back and you will be much older when I see you again. But the entire time I'm gone, I will love you with all my heart. Your mom, Allie and your grandparents will look after you and love you as well. I'm gonna make it because I love you. Now come give me a big hug."

One by one they came and hugged me. Josiah looked at me and said, "I won't forget you dad."

Maggie stood, so I stood and she walked over and hugged me. With tears streaming down my cheeks, I left this house for good.

Chapter 23

I reported to the Sheriff's office on April 7, 2006 at 10 AM. Liz Oliver met me there to make sure that everything went okay. She had become my watchdog for the week to make sure that I didn't do anything stupid. In fact, we had dinner on Wednesday and Thursday night. I really appreciated her efforts; she was a kind and decent woman and a pretty good lawyer.

A deputy took me into a room and searched me. I left my keys, wallet, cell phone and other important things in Allie's care. So I had nothing but the clothes on my back and my watch, which he took and placed in the bag. He took the ankle bracelet off. Then he put a chain around my waist, hand cuffs around my wrists, ankle chains, and he hooked it all together. I made a lot of noise when I moved.

He took me out of the room, picked up some paperwork and we headed for the door. Liz looked so sad. I reached over and kissed her goodbye.

"Is that your wife," the deputy asked.

"No my lawyer," I replied.

He took me down some stairs, through a side door into a courtyard and put me in a white van. He hooked my chains to a post and we were ready to go. Another deputy joined him for the ride. I was on my way to the Charles B Bass Correctional Complex for eight years. We took Interstate 40 to White Bridge Road and then headed to Cockrill Bend Road, which was a drive of about 7 miles.

Ego, balls, alcohol and a restless dick are a sure combination for glory or disaster. I had received my share of glory, but now disaster was staring me in the eyes.

We arrived at the correctional complex at noon. We drove into the complex, the gate closed behind us and I surveyed my new home or as much as I could see of it. I was taken to an administrative area and was told to sit. Finally, the two deputies returned in the company of two prison guards.

"Are you James J Jeter IV?" One of the guards asked. "Yes," I replied.

The two deputies unlocked all my chains, took them off, waited until the prison guards put new chains on me and then signed some paperwork to change custody.

"Welcome to CBBCX, Jeter," said one of the guards.

They took me into another room, began to fill out a mound of paperwork, asked me a few questions and then led me down the hall to another intake area. I was fingerprinted and had my mug shot taken from five angles. Then I was told to strip.

"That means you take everything off in case you didn't know," said a big burly guard. "Put your stuff in this box and maybe it'll be here when you get out. Anything of value?"

"No sir!"

They began to look at every inch of my body; poking and prodding in every orifice and looking as if they were gonna find something. They even held my pecker up to examine it with a flashlight. It was demeaning and degrading.

"Standstill, we gonna delouse you." They began to spray me with something that had a terrible odor to it and I thought I was gonna vomit. One of the guards laughed and said, "If you had any bugs on you, you ain't got 'em now. You got five minutes to shower that shit off."

Would you be surprised if I told you that the shower water was cold and there was little or no soap in the dispenser? Of course not, that is one thing that the movies and television have gotten right about prison life. This is probably the easiest thing to deliver in prison, so it is with certainty that they do this on purpose.

"Come on man you been in there seven minutes, get yo' towel and let's get it moving."

I dried off and attached the towel around my middle. "Some of those boys going to be really disappointed," said one of the guards. "That's just too damn bad," I said. We walked down the long hall, there was a file of inmates walking our way and my guards gave me a warning. "Keep your eyes straight forward, don't look their way." We walked into another room and there were three windows cut into one wall.

"Go to window one and stay there until I tell you to go to window two."

At window one, I received two sheets, a pillowcase, a light blanket, a towel and a washcloth. I stood there holding them because the person had handed it to me. "Move on to window two." I moved in front of window two. I received an undershirt, two pairs of underwear, two pairs of socks, two blue shirts and two pair of dungarees. At the next window, when I was told to move there, I was asked my shoe size. I told him 13 ½ E. The guy looked at me and smiled; either he thought the E part was funny or he was gay.

It was all I could do to see over the pile of stuff that I had in my hands. "Sit down on that bench over there and put on some clothes."

I put on the T-shirt, the dungarees, socks and the canvas shoes. One of the guards handed me a sweatshirt and a jacket. "You'll probably need both of these when it gets cold."

Guard Henry Jamison came into the room and said to these two guards, "Jeter ready to be moved over to unit B" He didn't wait for a reply; he put handcuffs on me which made it more difficult for me to carry my stuff, but I managed.

We walked down another hall, and headed toward two double doors that lead to the outside. Mr. Jamison said to me, "you're going to be in unit B for two weeks to a month. During that time we will decide what job you will have and where you will be permanently housed. While you're there in unit B, you are not to leave the building without a guard present. That's very important because you don't want to get into disciplinary trouble your first month. During this period of getting used to this place, you will not be allowed any visitors. There is a computer and a television in the unit which you can use, but they are in high demand. A library guy will come around every two days or so and you can read a good book to relieve your boredom. The biggest problem our guys have is that they get bored. Don't create any chaos just because you're bored."

We walked through the door of Unit B and there were 35-40 guys in the room playing cards, watching TV and working on the computer. As we walked down the center of the room everything got quiet.

"This is your bunk and that is your storage cabinet. Make sure that everything is neat and easily stored in that cabinet. Make sure your bed is made every morning before breakfast. It is now 2:10 PM; roll call will be at 4:45 PM and you will go to dinner after roll call. Any questions?" "No sir."

I stored my stuff in the cabinet, arranging it as neatly as possible so that it could be easily identified. I sat down on the side of the bed and considered all that had gone on that morning. I was in jail; no doubt about it.

A reasonably good looking fellow sat down beside me on the bed. "I've been here two weeks, first time in prison and I'll be here for a while. My name is Charlie McKnight. I am an accountant that got caught with his hand in the till and then I tried to have someone killed to keep the lid on the situation. Didn't work. How about you, what's your story?"

"I'm Jim Jeter. This is my first time in prison too. I was convicted of conspiracy to commit murder."

"Are you that guy that was involved with that woman – – the anorexic assassin?"

332

I sighed and said, "The one and the same!"

"We heard an interview with one of your jurors this morning and he said he was surprised you pleaded guilty because he didn't think the state had proved their case. But I guess somebody always says that."

"Yeah, but it doesn't matter now, because I'm in jail." There wasn't much else to say, we shook hands, and he moved on to his bunk.

Over the next three weeks, I went through the same routine. Up at 6 AM, did 50 push-ups, brushed my teeth, took a leak and got back to make my bunk and dressed for the day. I was usually standing in front of my bunk at 6:12 AM. Roll call was at 6:15 AM

The roll was called, and then we marched to the cafeteria. Breakfast consisted of cold eggs, two biscuits, one sausage patty and coffee. You could get your own water.

We left the cafeteria promptly at 6:45 AM and walked in single file back to the unit. Luckily the librarian came by early in my time there and I have three books to read. So when we got back from breakfast, I tidied up my area, watched a little TV news with the guys, talked to Charlie and went back to my bunk to read. We repeated the process at 11:45 AM and then filed out to lunch. After lunch, we always had an orientation meeting of some sort to explain how our life was to be lived. At 1:45 PM, we filed back to unit B until the same process was repeated at 4:45 PM. By 6 PM, we were back in unit B for the evening. I took a shower during this time every other day. The water was always cold, there never was enough soap and for some reason it did not matter.

One evening I found myself in a shoving match with Clovis Ramsey. He said I took his towel, I said I didn't. He tried to take my towel, but I stood my ground and was ready to fight. He took a swing; I blocked it and hit him hard in the stomach. He looked at me and decided I was pretty strong. He called me names and walked off. This was my only confrontation in prison.

At the start of my fourth week, Guard Jamison came to get me and took me back to the administration building. I was told to wait while another guard came for me and sat me in front of a desk.

A man in a white shirt and red and blue tie sat at the desk, looked at me over the top of his glasses. "Jeter you have done what you've been told to do, you haven't caused any problems and so we are ready to make your permanent assignment. You will be permanently assigned to unit G which is unusual since it houses mostly those who have committed white-collar crimes. But we don't expect any trouble from you. You get that don't you?"

"Yes sir, I get that. There'll be no trouble from me."

"You have been assigned a job in the electrical department. I know that you're not an electrician, but our electricians need help in getting work orders processed, completed and closed out correctly. You can help them with their filing and accounting. Your first day on the job will be tomorrow."

The guard and I went over to unit B, I said goodbye to the guys, gathered my stuff, and went to join unit G.

My daily routine was pretty much the same. After breakfast, I went to work in the electrical shop. Some inmates go to school instead, while others may have to go to treatment programs, including drug treatment. I had not had a drink in over three weeks. It was good that there was an interlude so that I could get over the shakes. I checked in with the guard on duty at Unit G and then went to the electrical shop without benefit of an escort. I reported back to unit G by 11:45 AM so that I would be present for roll call. When everybody was accounted for we would head for lunch.

There was another roll call in unit G at 12:45 PM and then I went back to work in the electrical shop. The pre-dinner roll call was at 4:45 PM. After that we went to dinner in the cafeteria. We wandered over around 5 PM in groups of four or five. You were not allowed to go to the cafeteria alone. After dinner we had free time until the last roll call at 9:45 PM. If the weather was good, we were allowed to spend time in the yard until 7:30 PM, and then you had to move inside for your activity. I usually spent time reading or getting a shower.

My job in the electrical shop was to get the place organized. The job orders were in a mess and the assignments were not kept in any specific place. We did have a computer and it did have Microsoft office software on it as well as a lot of dust. I put together several spreadsheets to organize the job orders and to create some sense of the workflow. It wasn't a very difficult task, but it was time consuming. Part of the problem was our Head Electrician, John Cauley. He was on the staff full-time and did a lot of work with the help of inmates who had experience as electricians. But some of the work became complicated and John would bring in subcontractors. So on a few jobs there was billing to be done and on others there was nothing to be done, but show the job completed. John had disdain for paperwork.

I created a separate system for subcontractors and a method for sending their bills to the assistant warden in charge of paying outside contractors.

At first, John wanted to see every piece of paper before I got it. I discovered that John was a great electrician who could hold a place like this together with bubblegum and paperclips, but when it came to paperwork he was a disaster. I learned very quickly that John was the problem or at least part of it. I finally convinced him to let me be the central point for all paperwork, so that I could record it on the spreadsheet and then give it to him for assignment. At least I knew it was out there and knew that every three days I had to go in search of documentation or to determine if John had assigned the work and to whom. This was a lot easier than searching through John's desk for job orders that no one knew anything about. John was making some effort to improve because he saw the benefits.

One day I was leaving the electrical shop and ran into guard Jamison. "Keep up the good work Jeter. I hear you're doing good things in there."

"Thanks Mr. Jamison."

I was flipping amazed. That complement really made me feel good. It was like I was accomplishing something in

336

here despite the circumstances. Life was crazy and I was trying desperately not to be.

Every so often, some contraband whiskey would show up during free time. My friend Charlie always seemed to be in the flow of things. When a large cup of booze would appear before me, I accepted it without question and tried not to chug it down, but I did sip it quickly. It seemed to arrive every other night and it did awaken in me the desire for alcohol. Somehow I managed to keep my craving in line with the schedule.

I didn't have a visitor for my first six weeks in the prison. The first visitor was Liz Oliver. She arrived on a Tuesday at about 3 PM. I left the electrical shop early and went to the visitation area. It was good to see her.

I smiled at her and said, "Liz it's great to see you. How have you been?"

She gave me a radiant smile back, "I'm doing great Jimmy and you look good. Tell me about how you're doing. How you're managing all of this stuff."

We talked for the full hour in an easy and open manner. She told me she was taking visitation forms to my father and my sister. They would be up shortly to visit me. She gave me a little update on the stock market. I was amazed at the small effort required to give up access to the stock market, the bond market and the currency market. That was very illuminating. When she got up to leave, it seemed natural to hug.

"No contact," shouted the guard. We both pulled our hands back as if we were shocked by electrical current. By the way, Liz was quite impressed with my job in the electrical shop. She also started coming to visit me every Tuesday at 3 PM.

My sister Allie came in the middle of July. She came on Thursday at 3 PM to give me an update on our financial circumstances which were good. No one out there was hurting for money and, in all likelihood, I would have enough when I got out. I told her that I wanted to become more conservative by the end of 2006. I had a bad feeling about the longevity of the bull market cycle and the greediness of Wall Street.

Then she brought me up to date on the activities of my children and told me that Maggie was in a bad state of depression. Allie was thinking about moving into the house for a while to help out and make sure that everything went all right. She and Cora Jane were at a tipping point and the timing would be perfect. She told me she would try to get up to see me once a month or at the very least every other month.

My dad came to visit me next. It was in mid-August and hot as blue blazes. He was really uncomfortable here and I understood it. All my visitors seem to come at 3 PM. With the exception of Liz, I think they wanted to have an obvious reason to leave. Trip was spending a lot of time with my children. He and Mary Lynn were heavily involved and I was grateful. And I told him so – – meant more to me than anything he could do. "Dad I need to say something to you that I haven't said enough during my lifetime. I love you, dad."

"I love you, Jimmy Joe," he said with tears forming in his eyes. Then with a smile on his face he said, "I still think you're a dumb shit for getting involved in all this muck."

"I couldn't agree with you more!"

He apologized for my mother not being here. I told him I understood about Mary Lynn, although I really didn't understand. She was mortified by the fact that her eldest child was a convicted felon. It was more than she could assimilate, much like Maggie in that regard. So she threw herself into the service of my children and of Maggie. And I loved her more for doing that, but she should make at least one visit.

And so my visiting schedule fell in to place. Every so often, Rick Newton came over to discuss a few things financial. Tim O'Hara dropped by to tell me a few things that were going on at the firm that he thought I would be interested in. Turns out that Tim and I were very good friends, close friends in fact and I really liked the relationship. The pattern of my life was set and time marched on.

April 2007 was a major milestone in that I had finished one full year in prison. The time had actually passed reasonably fast. But I could see time slowing down a little bit, particularly as I got more control of my job in electrical. It was no longer an adventure and was now fairly routine.

I had to fight boredom and I had to struggle with my addiction to alcohol. I really looked forward to getting some of the illegal booze that flowed through the prison yard. It was not very good stuff, but it certainly did take the edge off.

Trip came to visit me the end of April. It wasn't on Friday and it wasn't 3 o'clock. He was very happy when we sat down together.

"Sorry to change the routine," he said, "but the news I have just wouldn't wait. Yesterday, April 24, 2007, we closed the deal to sell the firm to UBS. They paid us $700 million. A nice chunk will go your way and to your kids. You're trust may keep things bound up a little bit for you, but you'll be all right."

"That's terrific, Trip, uh Dad I mean. Richard Newton will be handling things from my end and he's been aware that something was in the works. So if you would give him a heads up I would really appreciate it."

I looked at this man that I've known all my life. "What are you gonna do with yourself? You've given every day of your life to that business."

"I'm going to all open a private family office, hire a good investment professional, an accountant and run the family's money. I hope you will be a part of it eventually. Plus, your mom and I will travel some."

"You know, that sounds great. I clearly will move any money that I have over to you and of course the trust will be available for you to manage as well. It will remain a separate entity, but we can certainly appoint you as investment manager. I have somewhere between four and

340

six years in here so I don't know what I'll do when I get out, but what you're doing is really interesting dad and thanks for making it available to me. You're a better father than I've ever given you credit for and I'm really sorry about that. I could've gained a lot from you and I was too arrogant to see it at the time."

"Thanks for saying that, son. We all have a lot to learn. You sometimes seem to need a 2 X 4 between the eyes to get the lesson. Sorry I can't get your mother to appear. You know how she can be – – difficult at best."

This bit of news gave me a lot to think about. The business that I loved, Big Jack's firm, was now part of a huge international business. In fact, it didn't exist. All that our family had worked for all those years had simply been absorbed into this large entity and we had been paid a large sum of money.

I wasn't worried about my share since my part was mostly going to my kids and I didn't think my family would want to screw Maggie and those three darlings. But I had learned through the years that one could never be too careful. Richard Newton had already scheduled a two-hour block on Friday to meet in an inmate/lawyer setting. Rick was always ahead of the game and I liked that. He was also watching over me as a client much like Erskine had done in the past. Despite being a felon, my linkage to Big Jack Bradford served me well. .

For the next two years, I continued to work in the electrical shop two days a week, but now I was working in the offices of two assistant Wardens who had become terribly unorganized. I worked my magic through spreadsheets and file systems that made sense. Again this was not mind blowing work, but it was a great way to pass time and I met a large number of very interesting people. I was also part of the grapevine. A lot of information on my fellow inmates passed through my fingers, so I knew who was getting out early, who was staying full-term and who was getting add-ons. For myself, I was building up a large number of good behavior points and my job responsibilities demonstrated that I was trusted by the administration.

It was Tuesday, April 28, 2009. Liz and I were having a chat in the visiting center. She told me about her week and I told her about my increased job responsibilities in admin. I told her I was training a new guy to take over for me in the electrical shop. John was happy that I wasn't going to leave him in the lurch. He had gotten used to a smooth running shop.

"Liz, I have a question for you. You have been coming out here every week for three years. In fact, in those years, you have visited me 172 times, which is 172 times more than my mother. I have cherished every visit and I clearly don't want them to stop. Why do you keep coming out here?"

"Well I find this whole story so fascinating, that I can't give it up for some reason. And each time I come, I learn a little bit more from you. You're changing. You are no longer entitled, arrogant, and a self-centered person. You're a man that's becoming interested in being better."

"All that I hope is true. We'll have to see, but what about you?"

There was a moment of silence as if she was deciding whether to say something of great import.

"Everything okay Liz?"

"Yes, it is! You see Jim, the reason I come out here every week is that I'm in love with you." She looked me square in the eye. "I love you James Josiah Jeter with all my heart."

I smiled, tears came to my eyes. "Maggie served me with divorce papers in March and I signed them. It didn't hurt so much because on the day I received them, you visited me. Your visit was filled with the solution and the pain of losing a marriage was not so great."

"I love you Elizabeth Oliver." I reached over and gave her a quick kiss before the guard caught me.

Chapter 24

The sun was bright and the sky was blue. There was a slight breeze and the temperature was around 75°. It seemed like a perfect day and for me it was. I shook the hands of the two assistant Wardens that I had worked for over the last four years as I developed a very good paper flow system for administration. Other prisons wanted it, but my guys were reluctant to let it go into other hands. You won't believe this, but one condition of my release was for me to acknowledge that the intellectual property rights related to my work in the prison belonged to the Tennessee Department of Corrections. Then I shook the Warden's hand and we had a few pleasantries to share. On May 8, 2012 I walked out of the Charles B Bass Correctional Complex into the arms of Liz Oliver.

Liz was as beautiful as she could be. A big hug was very nice. Also there to greet me was my sister Allie along with Abigail and Chris. They ran to greet me with smiles on their face shouting the word daddy.

Allie said, "Let's all go to the Sportsman for a burger and fries or onion rings."

I laughingly said, "I haven't had a good burger in over six years, particularly with people that I love. You kids know Liz?"

Abigail spoke up. "Yeah dad, Allie just introduced us to her."

I had been released from jail based on a number of things. First of all, Liz had been working very hard on paperwork,

Rick Newton had drafted a letter for my family to send to the Department of Corrections and some of my former work partners as well, and, of course, I had lots of credits for good behavior and working hard for the prison system. Sometimes good works really pay off and this was one of them.

I would be required to stay in a halfway house approved by the Tennessee Department of Corrections. A halfway house is a place to allow convicted criminals to begin the process of reintegration with society, while still providing monitoring and support. The Aphesis House was just such a facility and I was fortunate to be accepted. It is a not-for-profit corporation. They work closely with the Tennessee Department of Corrections and the Tennessee Board of Probation and Parole. The Board of Directors and the Advisory Board govern Aphesis House, Inc.'s regular operations.

Aphesis was designed to provide transitional housing for individuals being released from incarceration, or who have a history of substance abuse, are veterans or homeless. The housing facility has a full-time staff, provides meals, and offers job search assistance, a mentoring program, community involvement, recreational activities, and a structured 90 day re-integration program. At the time it was a male only facility. The only ineligible applicants were those with medical conditions which make them unable to care for themselves.

I would be there for six months, the first 90 days of which would cover the reintegration program. I ended up taking courses in relapse prevention, critical thinking, men's health, review of personal goals before and after prison, developing good parenting skills, and developing good relationship skills. These were things that I really needed, not so much because of the prison time, but because of the way I lived my life previously. I had a lot to deal with and these courses helped.

My third day out of prison, my daughter told me something that really rocked my boat.

"Dad, I was waiting for somebody else to tell you this, but I don't think anybody has the courage to do it. I guess Josiah would, but he's not here."

"Yeah, what's it about lovely?"

"It's about mom and Allie. About three weeks ago, the family went to Richmond for four days. Mom and Allie got married. Josiah didn't come and I stayed home, but mom made Chris go. "

I was absolutely stunned. I sat there with my mouth open.

Abigail smiled and said, "It's kind of funny in a way. I mean mom divorcing you and then marrying your sister. It's so screwy that it's just funny. Grandpa says that everyone is a lunatic: my son's a convict and my daughter's a lesbian. That's what he said. You guys aren't leaving much for my generation."

I couldn't help but laugh. "Oh you guys will think of something. Just don't let it involve prison, that's no fun."

"Are you going to marry Liz? I mean she is black in case you didn't notice."

"I noticed that she was black Abigail, but somehow it doesn't make any difference to me. She came to visit me every week for six years. She fought hard to get me in this early release program. Most importantly, she loves me, warts and all."

"You better marry her fast before she gets to know you." Abigail giggled and laughed at her own joke.

"Listen lovely lady, I want you to go with your aunt or stepmom or stepdad or whatever to the storage barn and get my car. You can serve as my chauffeur until I get my license."

"That's great dad."

She really seemed to like that idea. It was great to reconnect with my children. I was looking forward to seeing Josiah on the 20th. In fact, my release was fortuitous. I was going to see my son graduate from University of Virginia and on the 28th; I would see my daughter graduate form Harpeth Hall; May of 2012 was going to be a special month.

I spent four hours each day in a classroom taking the initial courses of relapse prevention, men's health and critical thinking. The rest of the day, I spent time cleaning my room, reacquainting myself with the computer and getting reengaged in the markets. There was a lot to learn and a lot to do.

I was released into the custody of Liz for four days so that we might travel to Charlottesville to see Josiah graduate. I had to keep my ankle bracelet on, however so that my friends in the state of Tennessee could appropriately track me. We left early on the 18ᵗʰ and after several stops, arrived in Charlottesville around 5 PM. Liz had made reservations months in advance so we had a nice room at the Omni.

We were at the Sigma Chi house about 7:30 PM and met Josiah. Mary Lynn and Trip were already there as were Allie and Maggie. Abigail came over and stood with Liz and I. Chris stayed comfortably in the middle. I shook hands with my son and he embraced me. It was a warm, loving moment for both of us. I had my Sigma Chi pin on, so the people around me saw me as a Sigma Chi brother. Several of the current brothers came up and asked me about my class year.

I whispered in Josiah's ear, "I just came to see you graduate. I'm not here with any agenda or axe to grind. I'm simply your father and I'm proud of you. Plus we're brothers my man." He looked straight at me, smiled and gave me thumbs up.

I shook hands with my dad and he hugged Liz. Then I looked at my mother who I had not seen in over six years. "Hello Mary Lynn, it's been a while since I've seen you. I've missed you. I hope you have been well?"

She stuck out her hand. "I've been fine Jimmy Joe. You look good. It's good to see you." I didn't shake her hand. A hand shake from your mother, what mother doesn't hug her son? I had a resentment that I needed to work through with regard to Mary Lynn.

There was that awkward moment when her hand was waving in the wind and she didn't know what to do. She spoke, "I'm sorry that I didn't have the opportunity to visit you while you were away. I didn't have the heart to see you in that place. I do hope you understand."

"I realize that I am an embarrassment to you. It's not easy to have a felon for a son. The Charles B Bass Correctional Complex is not a great place to visit. You would've been ill at ease there and I understand that. A lot has happened during the time I've been gone. My children have grown up and my sister has gotten married."

Mary Lynn had a pained expression on her face. She knew something was coming, but she didn't know quite what to expect.

I looked at her. "I don't believe you've met my friend Liz Oliver." Liz did shake her hand bless her heart. Unlike me, Liz always puts the best foot forward.

"It is lovely to see you, my dear. Have you and Jimmy known each other long?"

"A little over seven years, I believe. I was Jimmy's attorney during his trial and for a few years after, but I have resigned that job." She looked at me with the most endearing smile, it was just terrific.

"Liz visited me once a week for six years. Sometimes she visited me more than once a week and I figure she visited me about 375 times. It was wonderful to see her smiling face."

Mary Lynn's eyelids were blinking very rapidly as if she was fighting back tears. I decided that I might ruin the party, so I called an internal truce.

We all moved closer to the bar. Liz reminded me that I was not allowed to drink during this program period. I reminded her that I was a member of AA, that I attended meetings regularly and that I did not drink. She smiled and ordered a gin and tonic.

Allie moved closer to Liz and whispered, "Well I see you have met Mary Lynn."

"Yes, she was very nice to me. I don't see what all the fuss is about. I'm sure she had heard that I was black."

"No, I don't believe so. She hasn't mentioned that fact so I don't think Trip and certainly not me has told her. But she can tell, the way Jimmy looks at you, you are his lady of interest."

"Well I certainly hope that I am more than that!"

Abigail pulled me aside. She was almost looking me straight in the eye. When did she get so tall? This is my little girl who had beautiful brunette hair and eyes with a little too much mascara and shadow.

"Did you ask her yet? I mean you have the ring with you don't you?"

"The answers to those questions would be no and yes."

"What are you waiting for? You said you're gonna ask her in Charlottesville. And we are in Charlottesville."

"Don't get excited! I'm going to ask her on the steps of the Rotunda tomorrow morning."

"Grandma is already asking questions about how serious you are about Liz. She is going to be mortified. On a lighter note dad, it's great to have you here, it's great that Liz is here, and I love you. By the way, as you know, I'll be graduating from here in four years. Don't screw up in the interim, because I expect you to be here."

I giggled and hugged my tall, beautiful daughter.

Liz was still talking to Allie and Abigail joined the conversation, so I looked around and saw that Maggie was free. I sidled over to have a chat.

"Hello Maggie. Isn't it nice to be back on Mr. Jefferson's hallowed grounds?"

"Hello Jimmy Joe. It's good to be here witnessing the second generation of Jeter's attending and graduating from the University. We're celebrating our son. That's all. No nostalgic remembrance of the past for me, just a celebration. "

"How noble of you Maggie, but that's just like you, part of the Virginia aristocracy to the end."

"Don't be mean Jimmy Joe."

"Indeed! Well you must understand that I was a bit shaken by our divorce and your subsequent marriage to my sister. I hadn't realized that you preferred women to men. But I seem to have a track record for doing that to women. I certainly hope that will be different with Liz."

"Yes, Allie and I are very happy together. It was as much a surprise to me as anyone. I never considered having a relationship with a woman, but she moved in to help me out, one thing led to another, and it only seemed right that we make a commitment to each other. Do you expect to make a commitment to Liz?"

"I do, if she'll have me. It's good to see you Maggie. We did a lot of good things together including raising a fine son. We can be proud of him as well as Abigail and Chris. So I'm here just to celebrate as well and my wish for you is nothing but happiness."

Trip advised us that it was time to go to the restaurant. He had made reservations for us all at the Boar's Head Inn. I've never eaten there, but I was looking forward to it. I cleared the air more or less with everyone that needed clearing and although there was still some baggage, I felt good about everything and was looking forward to the morrow.

Josiah and I met at the Cavalier Diner the next morning for breakfast. He asked me last night to meet him because he had something to say. He ordered an omelet with sausage and I ordered the big stack of pancakes with bacon and sausage. I was making up for time lost in prison when pancakes were not available and it was hard to tell from whence the sausage came.

"Josiah I think it's great that you've gone to UVA and are graduating near the top of your class. You have the world before you. I've learned something over last the six or seven years I've been gone. You know I'm a member of AA and I stopped drinking. It wasn't the drinking that caused me the problem so much as it was my thinking. So what I've done is learned to ask others about their opinion before I make a major decision. I talked to a half-dozen people before I decided to marry Liz."

"By the way dad, for what it's worth, I think you and Liz will make a great team. She is really well grounded and very smart. Listen to her a lot."

"I will and I hope you'll call on her as well. Your grandpa is also a great sounding board. I wish I'd listened to him more, so lean on him when you have a problem."

"Dad, I owe you a major-league apology. I should have come visited you. I didn't want to believe for the longest time that you were even there. I thought all along that you were innocent. Mom didn't want me to go and that was a good excuse for a while since I was under 18. But for the last four years that hasn't been an impediment. I apologize for my lack of courage and hope that I can make it up to you. You've paid for my education, supported me in an upscale lifestyle and I'm grateful."

"You just paid me back. Admitting that you're wrong isn't easy, but you did it. I'm proud of you." I reached across the table and we shook hands. He then stood, so I stood as well, and we had a long hug. I loved my son and he loved me.

When I got back to the Omni, Liz was sitting in the coffee shop eating a bagel and drinking coffee.

"I thought we might drive over to the campus, take a walk around and I'll show you a few things that made up my college days. You've seen the frat house, so we don't have to do that, but there are some places that are special to me."

"Let's go!"

And so we went. We had been walking around for about a half an hour when we approached the Rotunda steps. We climbed a few steps and sat down. There was a big Z painted on the steps.

"What's with the Z? I've seen it several places."

"Oh, it's a secret society, a philanthropic sort of thing. I was a member."

She gave me that raised eyebrow look. "Indeed?"

The **Z Society** is a philanthropic organization that was founded at UVA in 1892. It comprises outstanding student leaders who give time, talent, and financial contributions to groups and individuals that exemplify the spirit of the society and uphold the ideals of the university. Additionally, the Z Society encourages and recognizes excellence through a number of honorary dinners and academic awards.

The organization's membership chooses to remain anonymous because of the belief that service, when provided anonymously, provides a unique philanthropic opportunity. After graduation, members may opt to wear Z Society rings. Selection for membership is considered a high honor at the University.

"This is a strange, but beautiful place. I can understand how you would love it here."

"Oh I can't wait for you to show me around Spelman College. I've heard that the campus is beautiful as well. Emory is also great!"

"So we're both overeducated. But we can overcome it."

"I have something to ask you Liz."

"Okay sweetheart, what is it?"

I turned toward her, reached into my sport coat pocket to get the box and got down on one knee.

"Liz Oliver, will you marry me? Will you become my wife?"

"Oh yes Jimmy Joe Jeter, I thought you'd never get around to asking."

I took the ring, which Abigail had helped me pick out, and put it on her finger. It looked great. We kissed and I stood. We had a nice long hug and another passionate kiss.

"Abigail will be happy to see that ring on your finger. She has had difficulty containing herself over the last week. She is really excited for us Liz and so am I."

Chapter 25

Time moves a little faster in the real world of thunder and lightning. I finished my course at Aphesis and my 6 months of probation. The ankle bracelet had been removed and I was a free man according to the state of Tennessee. I paid my dues to society.

I was also seven months sober. I didn't start counting my sobriety days until I left prison, even though I was going to AA two nights a week. I also read the first 164 pages of the Big Book. But my thinking wasn't sober.

I met Rex at the 21st Ave. group which meets at the Belmont United Methodist Church. I was there for my first meeting on the outside and I really liked what he had to say. We met the next day at Friendship House and we've been working together since.

He told me not to marry Liz until I had been out of prison for a year, but it was okay to get engaged. We set our wedding date for May 11, 2013. We booked the date at the First Baptist Church of East Nashville.

After the Aphesis House, I moved into my condo off of Woodmont Boulevard on Windsor Park Lane. It had three bedrooms, a den, two large baths and one small bath, an office and of course the living room, dining room and a beautiful kitchen fully equipped. The lease on Liz's place was up January 1 so she will be moving in after Christmas.

The only item I bought for the place was one of those king-size memory beds. It was the only luxury item I wanted, only because I had been sleeping on a terrible mattress for six years and the mattress at the Aphesis house wasn't much better. Liz had furniture at her place and she could buy whatever she needed to fill out her decorating ideas for the new place. I was happy with the bed and a computer. I used a folding chair, two sawhorses and a piece of plywood as my office equipment. I found those items on a construction site near the Friendship House.

I was keeping very busy. Again Trip came through for me by supplying me an office and a computer tied to the firm's network. He hadn't made me a part of the firm yet. It was just too early in my return to the civilized world. It's interesting how the people in the office gave me a wide berth to start, since I was an ex-con. The first couple of days I went to the office in jeans and a nice shirt but after two days or so I started wearing a sport coat, casual shirt, nice pants and loafers. As it looked like I was trying to fit in, some of the folks began to talk to me. My dad, Trip, was terrific, although he reminded me every day what a stupid "shit" I was.

On the family front, Mary Lynn invited Liz and me to dinner at the old home place. The four of us had a very nice evening together. Mary Lynn was a little bit shaken by the choice of venue for the wedding, but Trip convinced her that it would be a new venture. My dad was evolving into a decent human being with an entirely different outlook on the world and he was slowly bringing Mary Lynn along. She had accepted my sister being a leftist lesbian, she accepted her daughter marrying my wife, and she was now accepting my fiancé, who just happened to be black. In the words of Grace Slick, it was indeed a new dawn for Mary Lynn.

I watched Rex Ryland amble across the park from the restroom. We had been sitting in that park for a fairly long time, almost 8 hours. When we started, it was pretty warm, but now the temperature was declining rapidly.

Rex grumbled, "I'm getting cold Jimmy Joe. Are you about through with this massive fifth step? My bottoms getting sore and I'm cold as hell."

"Yeah I'm through! That's enough, isn't it?"

"It is for me! I don't think I can stand it anymore. Ego, alcohol, and a swinging dick will get you in trouble every time. Humility, Jimmy Joe is what you need, plenty of it in large doses. Of course we know you can't drink and you gotta keep that pecker of yours in your pants. You got a lovely girl, a great family, and children that love you. The only thing you can do my man is to screw it up."

With those words ringing in my ears, Rex and I walked down to Rotiers on Elliston Place for a grilled cheeseburger.

"ALL YOU CAN DO MY MAN IS SCREW IT UP!"

About the Author

T. Michael Smith loves to write, tell stories, play bocce ball and be with his four grandchildren. The character in this story, Jimmy Joe Jeter, has been rattling around in his head for decades. Finally, he has emerged from the shadows to combat the anorexic assassin and relieve T Mike of his obsession with this fictional man.

T Mike has written two other books. The first is *THE ORGANIZED EFFORT* which details a selling system for investment specialists. The second is *Real Battles, Real Dragons,* a heart wrenching story of his wife's battle with breast cancer and his attempt to solve the problem.

T. Michael Smith

He currently resides in the Roanoke Valley of Virginia in an independent senior living facility named *Brandon Oaks*. He has plenty of opportunities to write and tell stories. He hangs with an active and hip crowd that provides a lot of material. A cane, iPhone and tablet go hand in hand with this bunch.

He has lived in Richmond, Nashville, Washington (DC), and Miami, but T Mike's favorite is his home in the valley.

ISBN: 978-0-692-40966-4

Brush Fork Press LLC

A Delaware Company

20672236R00206

Made in the USA
Middletown, DE
03 June 2015